HIS CURVY BOSS

A SMALL TOWN CURVY GIRL ROMANCE

BOOK BOYFRIENDS WANTED
BOOK 12

MARY E THOMPSON

His Curvy Boss

Book Boyfriends Wanted, book 12

Copyright © 2023 Mary E Thompson

Cover Copyright © 2022 Mary E Thompson

Cover Photo from depositphotos, Copyright © GeorgeRudy

Cover background from depositphotos, Copyright © tomert (lights) and Milanares (blue)

Cover watercolor stripe from depositphotos, Copyright © ronedale

Published by BluEyed Press, All Rights Reserved

Ebook ISBN: 978-1-953879-53-0

Print ISBN: 978-1-953879-54-7

Audiobook ISBN: 978-1-953879-55-4

❀ Created with Vellum

BOOK BOYFRIENDS WANTED

Come in and visit MacKellar Cove. You will get to see all the things that make this small town a truly special place to be. There's the bookstore and the local bar. There's the bakery and town square. And there's love all around. Grab a drink, a slice of cake, and get to know your next book boyfriend and book best friend! Never miss a thing when you sign up for Mary's newsletter.

Romancing the Curves comes with subscriber exclusive freebies, sneak peeks, and a first look at everything Mary has to offer. Be the first to know about new releases and sales and all the curves ahead!

SUBSCRIBE NOW AT MARYETHOMPSON.COM

Happy reading!

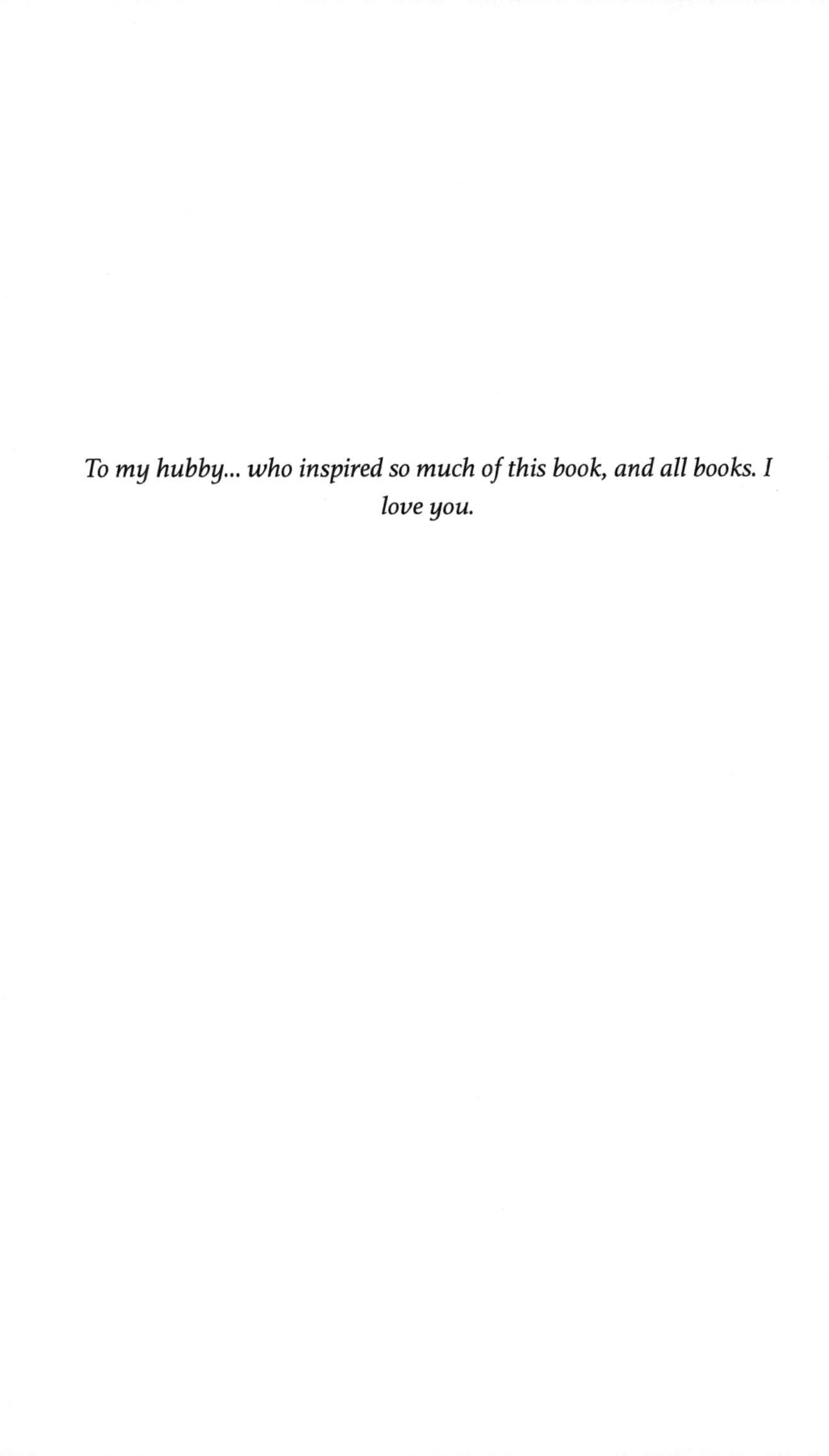

To my hubby... who inspired so much of this book, and all books. I love you.

1

GOLDIE

Deep breaths. I needed to just take deep breaths. In and out. It would all be okay.

"Who is this band? I've never heard of them. Are you sure they're any good?" Mayor Levine asked.

Deep breaths. Dear God, help me not strangle the self-righteous ass who decided I'm his enemy.

"They're very popular right now. They've grown a solid following in the area. Teenagers love them, so they'll draw in a younger demographic."

Mayor Levine held my gaze with his angry one for a beat too long. He didn't like that answer. He didn't like any of my answers.

I knew when he was appointed as the new mayor of MacKellar Cove it was going to be painful to deal with him. The previous mayor stepped down for health reasons, and Mayor Levine stepped up to finish the term. He positioned himself as an everyday kind of guy, but he was anything but. The truth was, he was ultra-conservative, to the point of still believing a woman's place was in the kitchen. He hated me for nothing more than the fact that I lacked a penis.

I had a lot of reasons for hating him.

"Well, I hope they show up. Bands like that can be unreliable. People need incentive."

"That's why this band is perfect," I said. "They want to increase their exposure and get some experience playing for live audiences. When we spoke, they were very excited about the opportunity."

Mayor Levine pursed his thin lips until they disappeared into each other. When he wasn't scowling at me, I could almost see where he was an attractive man. A few years older than me, he had a full head of dark hair and a lean build. He was married and blessed with two daughters, which made me endlessly happy because I knew there was nothing more he wanted than a son. I felt bad for his daughters, though. They would never get support from him to do anything in their lives. He was a misogynist if there ever was one.

"I guess we'll see how everything goes. This summer is very important for MacKellar Cove, and for you," Mayor Levine said. His pointed look said far more than his words.

"Could you elaborate on that?" I asked. I knew where it was going, but I needed him to say the words.

"The town budget can't support ineffective leaders. And since you're the tourism director, we need to see some value from you and the position."

"Well, the events I created for last year increased town revenue by thirteen percent, and filled local hotels to near capacity for the summer. What my team and I have planned for this year—"

"Your team is not in question, Ms. Spear. You are."

"Are you saying you're looking to fire me, Mr. Mayor?" I asked the question he was dodging.

"I'm saying your department should not be paying you

the salary you have. I've been looking at your budget and your resume and I'm unclear why you were given the position you have. Something isn't adding up."

I seethed as I struggled to keep my composure. If I yelled at the little weasel, I would seal my fate, probably immediately. I couldn't give him a reason to fire me, even though he seemed to believe he didn't need one.

"My experience matched the position, sir. Your predecessor was confident in my abilities, and my performance speaks for itself in terms of what I've been able to deliver."

"You or your team? Because it seems to me your team is the brains behind your operation."

My team was amazing, but damn. How dare he make it sound as though I was nothing more than a figurehead? "My team is talented, and no team functions well without a strong leader who can keep them on track and guide them in the right direction. My team has been on budget and ahead of projections since I took over this position. Even with the changing leadership I've worked under."

It was a low blow, and probably not a great idea, but I couldn't resist the dig. It was common knowledge he'd blown through the town budget in half the year, adding shit no one needed and doing things no one wanted. Like the new stoplight outside town hall that caused more traffic issues than it solved. Or the brand new custom furniture he had hand-crafted in Italy and sent over. Or the boats he wanted to bring into the Cove to take tourists to the local castles and on tours of the area. That was the worst one. The boats were too big for the Cove and would get stuck. But he was convinced it was a great idea no matter how many people told him it wouldn't work. I didn't know how much money he'd spent trying to find someone to tell him it was possible.

"Well, if you're so successful, then I guess you can handle a fifteen percent decrease in your operating budget for the rest of this year."

"What? I need that money. This is the busiest time of the year. We spend eighty percent of our budget in the summer months."

He shrugged and stood. "If you're unable to meet the new budget, you will be replaced with someone who can. Have a good day, Ms. Spear."

He walked out of the room like he hadn't just dropped a bomb on me. What the hell was I supposed to do?

A minute later, I finally stood. Mayor Levine's secretary, not assistant he said, was outside the door waiting for me.

"He asked me to give you this," Jane said. She was young and pretty and far too good for Mayor Levine, but she worked for Mayor Sanchez before Levine and had no choice.

"Do I want to know?"

Jane winced. "Probably not."

I took the folder from her and opened it. It was my new operating budget. One he already had prepared for me. Which meant he always intended to screw me over. Long before he asked for a meeting to discuss the Memorial Day Kick-off event happening in only two weeks.

"He's insane," I muttered.

"I know. And I'm really sorry." Jane looked up at me with sympathy in her gaze. "He was telling someone on the phone the other day that he wants to get rid of you. That you don't deserve the job. I wasn't sure if I should tell you or not."

"It's okay. He's made that clear to my face. He doesn't think a woman should be running a department."

"Or working outside the home," Jane whispered. "He

said the dress code is skirts or dresses only. That I have to look professional."

"Why do you put up with him?" I blurted.

Jane winced at the question.

"I'm sorry. That wasn't fair of me to ask. I know finding a new job isn't always easy, and leaving this job for another one could end up with you blackballed because that's the vindictive asshole he is."

Jane nodded. "Pretty much. Mike is working full time again, but it's not easy keeping things together. No one knows yet, but I'm pregnant again, so I really need to keep this job so I get maternity leave."

"Congratulations!" I whispered. "I'm so happy for you. And I promise, I won't tell anyone. But I will let you know if I hear of anyone hiring who isn't afraid to tell the new mayor to shove his opinions up his ass."

Jane smiled. "Thanks, Goldie. I really appreciate it."

Mayor Levine shouted something that had Jane jumping from her seat and waving. I sighed and watched her go, wishing I could hire her. She was smart and organized and excellent at her job. Too bad she'd never get the praise she deserved working for a man like Levine.

I left town hall and waited at the endless light for it to finally turn green. I debated running it, but with my luck, Levine would be watching me out his window and recording so he'd have a reason to fire me. A legitimate one.

I parked outside the tourism office and carried the offending budget inside. I needed a meeting with my team so we could make some changes to the plans we already made for the summer. Maybe if we could talk some of the local businesses into donating, we could make it all work.

Maybe.

"Meeting, now," I shouted as I walked in. I knew anyone

who was there would hear me and follow me to the conference room at the back of the building.

The front side was the Welcome Center for MacKellar Cove, a low traffic center that was wasted space in the worst possible way. I had no idea why it was constructed the way it was, and I'd been trying to come up with ways to change it since I took the job as tourism director. So far, I hadn't figured anything out.

The back of the building was where my team worked. Five of us were housed from those offices. Besides myself, there was my assistant Patrick, the website manager Eve, the outreach manager Theo, and the maintenance manager Howard. We were an eclectic group and worked well together.

"Hey, Boss," Theo said. He was the first into the conference room. "What did Levine say?"

"Nothing good," I told him.

Theo was the first person I hired when I took the job. Howard was there as maintenance manager already and stayed on to work with me. Theo was next because I quickly realized I needed someone to get to know the other business owners in the community and collect all the events information for the area. I hired Patrick not long after Theo when the job kept getting bigger and I realized I couldn't do it without someone to help keep my schedule and my priorities in order. Eve only came on board in the last few months, taking over managing everything online, including updating the website and making sure all online visitors had access to whatever information they needed. If something wasn't on the website, Eve went out and found it and added it.

"Did Levine push back on the band?" Eve asked. Her dark hair was spiked up in all directions, a product of her hands running through it all day. She had a piercing in her eyebrow and another in her nose to go with the five in each ear. She was no more a fan of the mayor than I was.

"No. He questioned it, but he didn't say we couldn't book them."

"Good. I'm really excited to hear them play. I think it's going to be an amazing show."

Eve was the one who brought the band to my attention. I was listening to them online one night when Paul, my fifteen-year-old, walked in and asked how I knew them. If they had his seal of approval, in addition to Eve's, they were good enough for me.

"What's going on?" Patrick asked. "Howard's up front. Said to fill him in later. A tour bus just pulled in."

My heart skipped at his voice, which I hated. I was not supposed to be attracted to my assistant, even though he was gorgeous.

"Does he need help?" I asked, hoping my voice sounded normal.

Patrick shook his head and gave me one of his grins that I couldn't help but return. "Howard's in his element. He's all good. What happened?"

Down to business. That I could handle. "Levine cut our budget by fifteen percent."

"He did what?" Theo blurted.

Eve and Patrick both gaped at me.

"He said since we were under budget last year, we should be able to operate under budget this year."

"We were under budget by three percent, not fifteen," Patrick argued.

Was it bad to be turned on that he knew that? "I know, but he doesn't care."

"He needs to pay for that stupid furniture he wanted.

And to dig out the Cove so he can get bigger boats in here," Eve snarled.

"He is not," I blurted, staring at her. She had to be joking. That would ruin the Cove and destroy the fish and animals that lived there.

Eve shrugged. "That's what I heard. He's found some group that said it would be possible if the Cove was deeper. He asked if they could make it deeper, and they said in theory yes. So, now he's holding on to that."

"He's insane," Patrick breathed.

I shook my head in disbelief. He really was. How he thought that was a good idea was beyond me, but that wasn't the biggest issue I had at the moment. "Regardless of all of that, we need to find ways to save some money. We already have most of it spent, but there are some events later in the season we might be able to pull back on."

"We need to go through everything," Theo said. "I'm not sure we can do it."

I nodded. "I know. I'll order lunch for everyone and we can get started. It's going to be a long afternoon. I'm sorry to be doing this to you guys."

"It's not you," Patrick said. "This is all Levine, and we know it."

I smiled at him in thanks and left to order food.

LUNCH WAS LONG GONE and so was our patience. We were tired, crabby, and far beyond done for the week.

"Go home, everyone. We need to put some distance between us and this. We'll pick it back up on Monday."

"You sure, boss?" Eve asked.

I nodded. "You guys have lives to get to. Things are going

to get busy for us in a few weeks. We need to get our rest when we can. Go home. I'll see you all on Monday."

"Good night," they said as one-by-one they filed out of the room. I smiled and waved, then carried everything we'd been working on to my office and dove in again.

I couldn't walk away without some sort of idea of where we could cut some major money. Fifteen percent was huge. A little here and there wouldn't do it.

"You're not leaving?" Patrick asked from the doorway.

I jumped, not realizing he stuck around. "I need to figure this out."

"You need to get some beauty rest so you look your stunning self come Monday," he said. He walked over to me, leaning against the side of my desk. His spicy scent filled the air between us. His easy smile made my lips turn up.

"I'll rest eventually," I told him.

He chuckled and shook his head. "You need to stop letting Levine get to you. You're too strong to let him twist you up like this."

"You don't know what he's like behind closed doors," I admitted.

"Did he do something?" His tone bordered on deadly.

I laughed. "No, of course not. He's not that stupid."

Patrick paused and held my gaze, his tracing my face. "You really have no idea how gorgeous you are, do you?"

I snorted and shook my head. Patrick was good for my ego, but sometimes he took it a little too far. He pushed a little too much. Like in that moment when he wanted me to believe his flirty words.

"Wow, you don't. For all your confidence in the boardroom, I thought for sure you would be the same in the bedroom."

"Patrick!" I gasped.

He shook his head and moved closer to me. My office was big enough that I didn't feel crowded, and it was Patrick. He might be the office flirt, but he was a good guy. Polite and considerate. He wasn't afraid to stand up for others and was quick to shut down anything inappropriate.

Except for the way he was looking at me. He was only turning that up.

"Goldie, you're beautiful. I know you went through hell when you got divorced, but I hope you know whatever happened, your husband was an idiot."

"He's bisexual and fell in love with someone else."

"How anyone could even notice another person when you're around amazes me. You're all I see."

"Patrick, you don't have to say these things."

He chuckled and shook his head. He removed his glasses and rubbed the bridge of his nose. It was something he did when he was frustrated. When the other person wasn't listening to him.

"I really thought you were right there with me. That you knew I was flirting with you because I'm attracted to you. But you really don't know. You don't see yourself that way. That's the biggest shame for me. Because you're the kind of woman who makes a man forget everything. Who makes me forget everything. I've been waiting for you to ask me to dinner, or to stay late one night, but I see you're not going to because you don't think I'm interested. Let me tell you, boss, I'm very interested."

I rolled my eyes. "Patrick, I know—"

"No, you don't, Goldie," he said firmly. He was close enough that I could see the truth in his gaze. The conviction. "I haven't dated anyone since I started working for you because I found myself fantasizing about you when I went out with other women. I knew you were single, and watching the way you handle things here made me sure you would make the first move. You're scared. I see that now. So, I'm going to make the first move."

He ran one fingertip down my arm as he spoke. He drew little circles on my wrist, then inched closer.

"I want you, Goldie. I want whatever you're willing to give me. But you need to know, I'm serious. And now that you know how much I want you, it's up to you to decide if you're interested in the same thing."

"Patrick," I whispered, sounding breathy even to my own ears.

He shook his head and stood, stepping away. "Don't answer me now. Because I know you'll say no. Think about it this weekend. Have a glass of wine and take a bubble bath and think about me. Think about how I would touch you if I were there with you. Think about where I'd kiss you. Think about how I'd feel inside you. Then on Monday, you can tell me what you want from me."

I sucked in a breath. My entire body felt like it was on fire and my skin was too tight. I wanted to lean into him and give in. Do all the things he said. I wanted to touch him and taste him and...

Who was I kidding? I was fourteen years older than him. I was having a baby when I was his age. There was no way he was actually serious about dating me. And I wasn't sure I could have a fling with my assistant.

He walked out without looking back, leaving me in the office with wet panties and a throbbing core.

Well, he did say to think about him. Maybe it was time for that bubble bath he mentioned.

2

————

"HE SAID TO THINK ABOUT HIM?" VALENTINA HISSED.

We were at her house for dinner. Her younger daughter, Sam, and my son, Paul, were dating, so we decided it was time to get all of us together and make sure the kids understood our rules.

Meaning we were going to tell them not to have sex.

But first I was telling Valentina about wanting to have sex with my assistant.

"I really thought he was joking all the times he said something to me," I whined. I hated feeling off-center, and Patrick kept me off-center.

"Obviously, he wasn't. What are you going to do?"

"Pretend it never happened?" I sipped my wine and hoped it would work.

"You clearly like him, though. Why not see what can happen?"

I shook my head before she even finished speaking. One and done for me. I'd tried the whole happily ever after thing and had the divorce papers to go along with it. I wasn't looking for a do-over. Especially with a man who was so much younger and would waste his life if he got wrapped up with me.

"What's holding you back?" Valentina pressed.

The three kids were all in the living room talking. They were far enough away that they couldn't hear our conversation, but I glanced at them anyway. Valentina and Dawson had a beautiful home. There was a fireplace as the focal point in the living room, which was open to the kitchen and dining room. A TV was on another wall, visible from every seat on the sectional sofa that took up residence in the living room.

"The kids aren't listening. Tell me what's going on." Valentina had become a closer friend in the last few months. Between her and Anna, I was starting to feel like myself again. But with both of them happy and not single, there was a part of me that felt invisible pressure to find a partner.

"I'm too old for Patrick."

Valentina scoffed, but I continued.

"He has opportunities for anything. He'll be twenty-seven in a few weeks. He's a baby. Why would he ever want to be tied to an old woman like me?"

"First, you're not old."

"I'm forty," I argued.

Valentina shook her head. "Forty is not old. All the equipment still works. And some men like older women."

"Yeah, until they have to carry them to the bathroom and wipe their asses. Why would anyone sign up for that life?"

"Don't we all? When I got married, I said in sickness and health. If something happened, I could be doing that for Dawson now."

She had a point. I didn't love it, but she wasn't wrong. I would have taken care of Charles if something happened when we were married. I wouldn't have thought twice about it.

"If he's saying he wants you, enjoy it. Have fun. What's the harm?"

"I don't know," I said, warming to the idea even as the voice in my head kept saying he's too young.

"You're both single. You clearly like him. Why would you not want to date him? You need some fun in your life."

I scoffed, then laughed with her because she was right. My life was pretty boring. I went to work, came home and argued with Paul, then went to bed and started all over again. I would miss it when Paul went to college and was no longer living at home, but for now, it was boring.

"I'll think about it," I said, earning a wide grin from Valentina.

Footsteps behind me had me turning to see Dawson coming from the hallway.

"Val, I need you to do some laundry. None of my stuff is clean," Dawson said, not looking up before he walked into the kitchen. He heard the kids' voices and finally lifted his head from the shirt he was buttoning. "Oh, they're here."

I plastered a smile on my face and waved. I'd met Dawson a few times. He was brusque and borderline rude, but he was Valentina's husband, so I let it go. She was amazing, and the last thing I wanted was to make her choose between me and the man she'd built a life with. I was friends with her, not him, so I didn't let it bother me. Or tried not to.

"Hi, Dawson. Good to see you again."

"Yeah," he said. "When is dinner going to be ready?"

"Soon," Valentina said. "I have a timer set. Why don't you get a drink or something?"

Dawson nodded and went to the fridge. He grabbed a

beer, then went to the living room where he sat on the opposite end of the couch from the kids and turned on the TV. He didn't acknowledge any of them, even his daughters. The looks on their faces said they were used to it but not happy about it.

"Sorry about him," Valentina said. "He's tired."

I nodded. "I understand. He's been traveling a lot for work, right?"

"Yeah. The weekend is his only downtime. He wasn't thrilled when I said we were all getting together tonight, but I told him it was the only time that really worked."

"We could have done it a different night," I said. I hated that Valentina felt the need to explain her husband. I'd done it enough for Charles to know it was a shitty feeling.

"He'll be fine." Her phone let out a jingling ring. "That's the timer. We can eat in a few minutes, and hopefully he'll be better."

"What can I do to help you?" I asked, getting off my stool and coming around the island.

Valentina pulled a large pan out of the oven and set it on top of the stove. "You don't have to do anything. You're our guest."

"Oh, please. I'm a mom, too. Put me to work. I know you'll get less of an argument from me than anyone else here. And I don't mean that in a bad way. Just that's how it is in my house, too."

Valentina flashed me a grateful smile and nodded. "Thank you. There's a salad in the fridge. Dressings are in the door. I hope this is all okay. I always feel like I don't make enough food. Baking is so much easier for me."

"It smells amazing," I told her honestly. As soon as she took dinner out of the oven, the scent filled me and made my stomach rumble.

"Thanks. It's just spinach stuffed chicken. I didn't do any rice, though. The chicken has breadcrumbs on top and I didn't want everything to be too heavy."

I set the salad on the counter and my hand on her arm. "It's going to be amazing. I promise you, we're all good."

She smiled at me and visibly relaxed. While the chicken rested, she helped me get dressings from the fridge and organized everything on the counter like a buffet.

"Is this okay?"

"Absolutely. It's how we always eat. Makes more sense than carrying everything to the table, then carrying it all back. We're casual. Do not stress on our account."

The tightness around her mouth made me wonder if Paul and I were not the reason for her stress, but I couldn't exactly ask her. We were friends, but not the kind of friends who called you on your crappy marriage. Especially when I wasn't even sure she had a crappy marriage. I'd seen her and Dawson together a handful of times. It wasn't enough to say she was unhappy and he was the cause.

"We can eat," Valentina called above the noise of the TV and the kids.

The kids jumped up and hurried into the kitchen. Paul grinned at Sam like she was a queen. They felt too young to be dating, but he turned fifteen a few months ago and Sam was going to over the summer. When I was fifteen, I was dating. A lot.

Valentina and I stood to the side while the kids filled their plates and gushed over how good the chicken smelled. The look in her eyes said she was grateful for their praise. When they carried their plates to the table, she asked Dawson if he was ready to eat.

"Yeah, yeah, I'm coming." Dawson turned off the TV and joined us in the kitchen.

I hung back with Valentina, letting Dawson go ahead of us. He didn't acknowledge the move, just added the biggest piece of chicken to his plate, then scowled at the salad.

"Is this all you made?" he asked, shooting a look at Valentina.

"Yeah. The chicken is stuffed, so it's pretty filling. I didn't think we'd need anything else."

"Well, you don't, but I don't spend all day eating dessert, so I'd like a little something extra to fill me up," Dawson said.

My blood boiled as Valentina's face fell. She rolled her lips in and twisted her hands together, crossing them over her middle. She squeezed her eyes shut for a moment, then forced a smile and glanced my way.

She immediately looked away.

I gaped at him. I had half a mind to kick his ass right there in his own home. How dare he speak to her that way?

"Valentina is gorgeous. She's kind and beautiful and talented. Why would you insult her like that?"

Dawson snorted. "Of course you'd say that." He made a point of scanning my body and rolling his eyes.

I saw red. The man was going to die. Who did he think he was?

I opened my mouth to tell him off when the doorbell rang, stopping the words before they could come out. I looked at Valentina, who looked at me, then at Dawson.

"Are you going to get that?" he asked, carrying his plate to the table and ignoring us.

I sucked in a breath and focused on my friend. She needed to get out of her marriage. She didn't deserve to be treated the way she was. The look on her face said it wasn't new, which made it even worse, but it wasn't the time to deal with it.

Valentina excused herself and went to the door. I grabbed a plate and started to get my food. Less than a minute later, Valentina called out to Dawson.

"There's someone here to see you, Dawson," Valentina said, her tense voice loud enough to carry through the house.

"Who?" he asked as he got up from the table.

"Me," a woman said, bursting into the living room.

Valentina stood behind her, having followed the stranger. Her eyes were wide, watching her husband.

"Haley? What are you... I mean, who are you?" Dawson said, moving toward the woman.

"Are you kidding me? You're married? You told me you were single. We've been dating for nine months."

The kids choked on their food. Valentina gasped. Dawson looked around the room, then focused on the woman who interrupted the night.

"I don't know what you're talking about. I don't know you."

"Give it up, Dawson," Valentina said. "I've assumed you were cheating on me for a long time. But I have to say, this is the first time a woman moved to town to be closer to you."

"You did what?" Dawson barked, focusing on Haley now.

Haley's lip quivered. "I thought if we lived in the same town, you'd have no choice but to make a commitment to me. I thought it was the distance that kept you from asking me to marry you or move in together. I didn't realize it was your family. That you even had a family."

"Jesus, Haley, what the hell is wrong with you? Things were fine. We were good. Why did you have to do this?"

"Don't blame her," I said, stepping forward. "You're the one having an affair."

"You stay out of this," Dawson growled at me.

"Don't you talk to my friend that way," Valentina hissed. "You've been fucking someone else so much that she moved here to be close to you, and you think you have any right to say anything right now?"

"Val, it's not what you think. She's crazy."

"Oh, really?" Valentina turned to Haley. "You've been dating for nine months?"

Haley nodded, looking like she was going to be sick.

"Where did you meet?"

"He helped me change a tire in a parking lot. I came out from grabbing something quick to eat, and my tire was completely flat. He walked out behind me and offered to help."

"How kind of him. Then what?"

"Then he asked if he could buy me a drink. I was meeting friends and told him where we would be. He met me there."

"And when did you start sleeping together?"

Haley's cheeks pinked, and she ducked her head. "That night."

"I see. And he never once mentioned his wife of two decades? Or his daughters?"

Haley shook her head. She glanced at the table where the kids were gawking at her. At the whole scene.

"So, Dawson, at what point did you think you had a right to say one fucking thing here? My friend is defending me. This woman was a victim of your lies, just like me. It sounds like the only one here who has no excuse is you."

"Val—" He moved toward her, reaching out to touch her.

Valentina backed up and put her hands up. "Don't you dare fucking touch me," she growled. "Get your fucking shit and get the hell out of my house."

"This is our house," Dawson argued.

"Get out!" Valentina shouted. Her eyes were wild. She was about to lose it, and if Dawson had any brain cells left, he would get away before she did.

Haley quietly backed out of the house and left. Dawson went down the hallway, coming back a few minutes later with a bag. He shoved his feet into his sneakers and cast a glare toward me.

Valentina followed him to the door. He tried to say something to her, but she just growled, and he left.

She slammed the door, then sank against it, sliding to the floor as tears started to fall.

I glanced at the kids, then at my friend. "Kids, finish eating. Clean up when you're done. And girls, I'm sorry you just saw that."

They nodded, the girls looking more than a little shell-shocked at what had just happened. Paul's face was full of sympathy for them. The three of them whispered quietly to each other, finding comfort together while I headed toward Valentina.

"What do you need?" I asked her.

"Can I kill him?"

I breathed a laugh and shook my head. "Unfortunately, no."

"Why not?"

"Because he's not worth it. He's an asshole who doesn't deserve you. And your girls need you because they clearly aren't going to have him."

"So, you're saying I should wait until they're adults to kill him?"

I laughed, relieved she could make jokes. "I'm saying he's not worth anymore of your time. What do you need right now? Wine? Liquor? A bubble bath?"

She snorted. "See? This is why you should take advantage of Patrick and his suggestions. All men cheat. All men are assholes. So, if you know going in that it isn't going to work out, your expectations will be lower. You don't have to worry about being forty-four and finding out your husband had been screwing the nineteen-year-old he met on a business trip."

"I don't think she was nineteen."

"Is that really what you're taking away from this?" Valentina growled.

I chuckled. "Okay, fine. You're right. But you can't control who you love."

"Do you love Patrick?"

I shook my head. "No, of course not. I'm just saying falling in love isn't optional. If we got involved, there's no guarantee I won't fall for him, and he'll decide he wants kids and a wife his age and it'll end."

"Or that he won't fall for someone else and have an affair for most of a year before she shows up on your doorstep because she just moved to town."

I nodded because yeah, that, too.

"I guess it's a good thing we haven't had sex in almost a year. I don't have to worry about what kind of diseases he could have given me. Last time I went to my doctor, she tested me for everything under the sun."

"You thought he was cheating before?"

Valentina shrugged. "I don't know. Yeah. I guess. But I never wanted to admit it to myself. I thought if I worked harder to be a good wife, maybe things would be okay between us."

I grabbed her hand and pulled her up. "It's not up to one person to keep a relationship working. I learned that the hard way, too. If one of the people in a relationship isn't willing to keep trying, it'll fall apart, no matter how hard the other person works."

She sighed. "I guess. But man, did it have to blow up like this? In front of my kids? And you guys? I wanted this to be a good night."

"It will be an even better night now that Dawson is gone. You can relax and enjoy the dinner you made and know that the rest of us are here for you."

Valentina smiled, her first real smile since Dawson joined us before dinner. She drew in a breath and straightened her shoulders. "You're right. I'm hungry, and I no longer have to care what my asshole husband thinks of how much weight I've gained since we got married. No one is going to see me naked for a very long time, if ever again, so bring on the wine and the chicken and the dessert. I'm going to enjoy my new freedom."

"Good for you," I said, knowing it was temporary, but even temporary was good when your world was falling apart.

3

PATRICK

I COULDN'T STOP MY LIPS FROM CURLING UP IN A SMILE AT MY dancing nephews and niece. At six, four, and two, they were still little enough to not think twice about the way they looked in front of others. I wished I could give just a tiny bit of that to Goldie.

My smiled slid to a scowl as I thought about our conversation before I left work Friday. I was sure she knew I wasn't flirting with her just for the hell of it. And I was sure she would say something. I thought it was because she was my boss, but damn. When she brushed me off and said I was too young, I was pissed.

"What has your face doing that?" Sharon asked as she sat next to me. She was used to the dancing parade in front of me and barely blinked as her kids giggled and squealed. She'd been married to my brother, Arthur, for eight years and was family. Which meant she was nosy and didn't mind her own business.

"He's annoyed because he can't get his boss to go on a date with him," Arthur answered for me. Speaking of nosy and not minding their own business.

Sharon tilted her head and looked closely at me. "How could anyone resist this face?"

"That's what I've been saying," Mom said, wiping her hands on her apron. "If she's not interested, he should move on."

My scowl deepened at that thought. Goldie might be resisting, but that didn't mean I was ready to give up on her. She was the only woman who'd ever captivated me the way she did. From the moment I walked into her office for my interview, I felt like something inside me locked into place. I couldn't explain it then and I still didn't have an answer for it, but I knew I wasn't ready to give up hope.

"He's in love with her," Arthur said.

I told him he's number one, with my middle finger, and glared hard at him. I adored my family, but damn, did they know how to get under my skin.

"He can't be in love with her. He's never been on a date with her," Mom argued.

"Doesn't matter. He's gone, Ma. He thinks she's the one," Arthur said, continuing to needle me. His gaze strayed to his children as they launched into another twisting, twirling dance to the new song that came through the TV.

"Love doesn't always make sense. And love doesn't always wait for a certain time either," Dick declared. Dick was my mom's boyfriend. They'd been together almost a year. He walked into the salon one day and Mom was the only one available. Dick flirted with her while she cut his hair and asked her out for coffee afterward. She turned him down, but he kept coming back until she gave in and agreed. He lived a few towns over, but he'd inserted himself into Mom's life after that.

"That's very true. And I think it's sweet Patrick found

someone," Sharon said. "Eventually, she'll come to her senses and realize what a catch he is."

"That's why you're my favorite," I told Sharon as I stood. I kissed her cheek and winked at her. My brother was a lucky man. She was kind and smart and kept him on his toes. She was his best friend in high school. She came into our family at a time when we were all starting to fall apart after my dad died, and she tied us back together and gave us all new life. It took Arthur too many years and too many women to see what was right in front of him, but he finally did and held on tight.

"You better mean your favorite of those two," Mom said, stepping away from Dick to grab my arm as I made a move to go past her into the kitchen, "or you're not getting dinner."

"Of course I do," I placated my mother. I kissed her cheek, too, then snuck by to get another glass of water.

I needed a minute to myself. As much as I loved my family, they were a lot. Arthur and I had four years between us, which meant when our dad died, Arthur took on the role of caretaker as well as big brother. I was only seven, and almost twenty years later, he was still trying to take care of me.

"You doing okay?" Arthur asked quietly a minute later. Right on time.

I nodded. "Yep. All good."

"Did something happen? You seem more on edge today than you usually are at Sunday dinner."

I shook my head, knowing it wouldn't fly with him. He had a sixth sense for when I was hiding something. It sucked as a teenager since he was the model child, and I was not, but as an adult, it meant admitting to shit I had no interest in admitting to.

"What did you do?"

"Why do you think I did something?"

"Because you're acting guilty."

"How does a guilty person act?"

"Avoiding eye contact," Arthur said pointedly, crossing his arms and staring me down.

I met his gaze, the same blue one I saw in my mirror every day. He said we got our dad's eyes, but I couldn't remember. Whenever I looked at my brother, I wondered if a part of my dad could be looking back at me through him.

"What's going on? You're not usually like this with women. I haven't heard you talk about dates in forever. What is it with this one?"

"She's different. Special. I can't explain it, but I can't stop thinking about her. It wasn't fair to go out with other women when I would spend the entire date wondering what Goldie would think of the meal or if she'd laugh at what I said or if she'd want me to come home with her. It was easier to just stop dating."

"Wow," Arthur said, leaning against the counter. His pose was casual, but he was anything but. Dressed in khaki pants and a blue button-down shirt, my brother was never casual. Even when he was relaxing, he looked professional.

Not that I was a slouch. My mother wouldn't allow it. The kids were the only ones allowed to be casual for Sunday dinner.

"You really are in love with her, aren't you?"

I snatched my glasses off my face and wiped at my eyes. I pinched the bridge of my nose and tried to stave off the irritation. "I'm not in love with her. I just want to know her better. She's smart and confident and amazing. She makes me want to be a better person. She takes charge and doesn't take any shit, even from our dumbass of a mayor."

"That's good. With him in charge, it sounds like she needs to be more on top of her game than normal."

"He's such an ass. He cut our budget and expects her to just deal with it."

"Really?"

I nodded. "She had a meeting with him Friday. We were under-budget last year, so he cut it for this year."

"How much?"

"Fifteen percent."

Arthur whistled. "That's a tall order. Damn."

"Yep. We spent all day Friday looking at places we could cut things. It's not going to be easy to make it through the summer. Not with all the events we have planned. Goldie was really going to make a mark on MacKellar Cove."

Arthur grinned at me. It was a mix of proud big brother and smirking know-it-all. I hated both looks.

"What?"

"You really do love her. Damn. I wasn't sure I'd ever see you fall in love."

"I'm not in love with her. I just respect her a lot. And think she's amazing."

Arthur nodded. "Understood. Just make sure we get to sit up front for the wedding."

I rolled my eyes and shoved my brother, laughing when he lost his balance and nearly fell over. He caught himself on the edge of the counter, knocking a serving spoon to the floor with a loud crash.

"What is going on in here?" Mom asked, walking into the kitchen. Her gaze bounced between us.

"He did it," we both said, pointing at the other.

Mom rolled her eyes and threw up her hands. "Clean the spoon. We're almost ready for dinner."

I muscled my way past Arthur, leaving him alone in the

kitchen to take care of the spoon he knocked to the floor. Really, I just needed out of the conversation.

DINNER WAS JUST as crazy as before dinner. Dick told stories about being a truck driver for the first few decades of his career. He stopped driving when his first wife got sick. After she died, he went back on the road because, as he put it, he had nothing to stay home for.

"Papa Dick, I want to be a truck driver like you," Henry, my oldest nephew, said. Henry was the one who looked most like Arthur. When he was born, Mom said he looked just like our father. Hearing him talk about wanting to be like Dick was unpleasant. Dick wasn't family. He wasn't my father. He wasn't anything. Just the guy who was sniffing around my mother.

"It's not an easy life, Henry. But it's important work. People always need things delivered." Dick delivered the line with a seriousness of a man passing on the wisdom of the world.

I stared at my nephew instead of looking at Dick. It wasn't that he was a bad guy, but he wasn't right for my mom. He wasn't right for our family. A little too loud, a little too opinionated, and a little too affectionate with my mother. His hand wrapped around the back of her neck and stayed there. My mother.

"I like trucks," Henry said, as if that was reason enough to want to drive trucks. At six, it probably was.

Dick barked loudly, tipping his head back and belly-laughing like Henry made the funniest joke ever. I loved my nephew, but it wasn't that funny.

I stood from my seat and carried my plate to the kitchen.

I could still hear Dick laughing and talking. My mother's house used to be quiet. Not the kind of quiet that would get into your head, but the quiet that would let you breathe for a few minutes. Since Dick started hanging around, the quiet was gone.

"Are you doing okay?" Mom asked from behind me.

"Yeah," I said, pasting on a smile. "I don't want to leave you with all the cleaning up. You fixed dinner for everyone. You shouldn't have to clean up after us, too."

"You don't have to worry about that. That's why I have a dishwasher."

"I know. And I can help you load it."

She walked over and hugged me close. She barely came up to my armpit, but she always insisted I duck down so she could wrap her arms around my neck like she did when I was little. She was my world. As much as I hated the moniker, I was a mama's boy. Maybe it was because I didn't really remember my dad, but I would do anything for my mom. Anything.

"You're a good boy. A good man," she corrected quickly. "I want to see you happy."

"Who said I'm not happy?" I asked, bristling at the suggestion.

"No one. But if that Goldie isn't interested, I think you should move on. She's a bit older than you, too, isn't she?"

"What does that have to do with anything?" I asked, my voice more harsh than I intended.

"It was just a question. I always thought you'd have kids one day. A family."

I grumbled something noncommittal, mostly because I'd never been able to convince my mother I didn't want kids. I'd mentioned it a few times, but she always insisted I'd change my mind eventually. I adored my nephews and niece, but I wasn't sure I wanted the day-to-day full-time responsibility of other people. Not just because I didn't want to be responsible for them, but because I didn't know if it was the right life for me.

"I just want you to be happy, and I'm not sure you are. You're distracted today."

I couldn't tell my mother I'd told Goldie to think about me. That I'd hoped she'd drive herself crazy all weekend imagining the things I wanted to do to her and would come into work Monday half insane. That was definitely something I was keeping to myself.

"I'm just thinking about work."

"About work, or about Goldie."

"Work, Mom."

"Are you still enjoying your job?"

"I am. It suits me."

She smiled. "I think so, too. You've always been organized and enjoyed keeping things in order. Especially me."

"Yes, well, you needed it once upon a time. You seem to be doing okay now."

She chuckled. "We've come a long way from those days when I could barely keep my appointments in order and you could barely keep yourself inside this house. Always sneaking out when you thought I didn't know."

"You knew?"

She shrugged. "Probably not always, but I knew enough."

I gaped at her. I really thought I was being sly. "Are you just saying that?"

She shook her head. "Nope. It's nice to be on a first name basis with the cops in town. They had a tendency to look out for you and let me know."

"You're kidding."

She grinned. "Nope. Thankfully, you weren't too bad. It would have been hard to explain why you shouldn't be in trouble if you actually caused trouble."

"I was a good kid. Not as good as Arthur, but good enough."

"Yes, you were. You were both good kids. I was very lucky to have you. I still am."

I hugged Mom and held her close. We were lucky to have her, too. Growing up without my father was hard, but Mom made it bearable. She became both mom and dad. She never did anything for herself.

"Group hug!" Dick called, walking in behind Mom and pressing himself to her back so she was sandwiched between us.

Mom laughed and shook her head, squealing for him to let her go. He took a minute, but when he finally did, she slapped his arm and shook her head.

"Your mother is one hell of a woman," Dick said.

I grunted and followed Mom out of the kitchen. I did not want to hear whatever it was Dick was going to say next.

I was practically vibrating in my seat when Goldie made it to work the next morning. I couldn't sleep, and I just knew she was going to give in to my proposition and ask me out. I made sure not to commit to anything with my family all week, claiming work stuff was going to keep me busy leading up to Memorial Day weekend in two weeks.

Sharon saw right through my lies, but bless her, the woman didn't call me on it. She just said they were available if Mom or Dick needed anything.

I jumped when I heard the office door open at exactly

eight. Goldie was always in right on time. Never early because she took her son, Paul, to school. But she always stayed later than she needed to.

"Morning," Goldie said on her way past my office.

"Morning," I replied. It was like any other morning, but it was going to be different. I could feel it.

She stayed in her office half the morning. It wasn't unusual for her to do so, but I really expected her to say something to me right when she came in. She was practically panting when I left Friday afternoon, and if she did what I said, she should have been ready for a date.

It was almost lunchtime before I saw her again. She called me into her office, and I knew it was go time.

I walked in and closed the door behind me. She looked up from her computer, stripping her sexy librarian glasses from the tip of her nose. "Why did you close the door?"

My confidence faltered. "Um, I thought... I'll open it."

She stared at me as I opened the door again, then took a seat across the desk from her.

"How was your weekend?" I asked.

"Fine."

"Did you do anything...fun?"

She shook her head. "I had dinner with a friend Saturday night. That was really it."

She barely looked up at me as she spoke. Did she forget about our conversation Friday? Did she not think about what I said at all?

"I've been working on this budget all morning. I have about five percent that I can cut, but I can't even begin to think about where the rest could come from."

"Can't we just go over budget?"

"No. That's not an option. We have to make this work."

"Did you think about anything else this weekend? Anything besides the budget?"

She met my gaze. "Nothing is as important as getting this right."

Well, then. I got my answer. Goldie was not interested.

That sucked.

4

GOLDIE

I GOT NOWHERE. ALL DAY, I DUG INTO THE BUDGET AND GOT nowhere. I was frustrated and defeated. I was going to lose my job. And there was nothing I could do about it.

What I hated was the budget was not the main thing on my mind. What was on my mind was Patrick.

After our meeting, he was cold. Distant. Separated. I knew he was hoping I would say something about thinking about him in my bath Friday night, but I just couldn't. Not after dinner with Valentina and watching her life implode.

I finally left the office way too late, hating that I was putting my job ahead of my kid. It wasn't fair to Paul, and I wanted to change it. Guess I'd have plenty of time to spend time with him when I lost my job.

Paul had already eaten dinner when I got home. He was at the table doing homework and talking to Sam.

"Hi, Sam," I said, hugging my son and waving at Sam.

"Hi, Ms. Spear. How are you?" Sam asked, smiling at me through the screen.

"I'm good. How are things at home?"

She winced. "Not great. My dad hasn't been back since Mom told him to leave."

"How's your mom doing?"

Sam shrugged. "I think okay. She's acting pretty normal."

"Good. I'll check in with her in a little while. Did you guys eat yet?"

"Yeah," Sam said as she nodded.

"Mom," Paul groaned softly.

"Good to see you, Sam," I said, waving to her before I left to change out of my work clothes.

I heard Paul apologizing to her for me. I rolled my eyes. Because I was so embarrassing. Teenagers.

I closed my bedroom door and stripped off my clothes from the day. I was tempted to take a shower, or a bath, but I had already missed enough of Paul's day. I changed into my pajamas and used the bathroom, then went back to the kitchen.

Paul was saying goodnight to Sam when I walked in. They were cute, even though they were too young to be cute.

"How is Sam doing?" I asked once they hung up. I knew Paul had a hard time when his father and I divorced and he would be there for Sam, but I still hated that she was going to be facing it.

"She's okay. Her dad was always kind of a jerk anyway. She wasn't really close to him."

"He's still her dad."

Paul rolled his eyes at me. It was something I told him all the time about his own father. No matter how frustrated he would get, Charles was still his father.

"Donating genetics doesn't make someone a parent," Paul argued.

I sighed. "I'm not in the mood to argue with you. Your dad never wanted to hurt you. I can't speak for Sam's dad, but most people don't want to hurt their children. You know it's not easy for any of them. It's going to be a tough few months."

Paul nodded. "Yeah. She's acting like she's okay, but I know it's going to suck."

"Yes, it is." I hated that he understood just how much it would suck. "You already ate?"

"Yeah. I was hungry, and I didn't know how late you were going to be."

"It's okay. I understand. How's homework going?"

"Good."

He didn't tell me much about school but *good* was a good answer. It meant he wasn't having trouble with anything. When school was giving him trouble, he wasn't as positive. But Paul was smart. Almost prodigy level smart. So it was rare he had any issues.

I fixed my plate and sat next to him at the table. I looked at his computer. "Chemistry?"

He nodded. "Yeah. We're mostly doing review for finals."

"You think you're going to do okay?"

"Yeah."

He went back to his work while I ate my dinner. It was the best I could expect. It wouldn't be long before he was closing his computer and going to his room to talk to Sam again.

"Want to watch something with me tonight?" I asked.

He shrugged. "What do you want to watch?"

"I don't know. Is there anything you've been wanting to watch?"

"No. Well, there's this movie..."

"What movie?"

He hemmed for a minute before saying, "It's about this

monster that's hunting people and if they make noise, it finds them and kills them."

"Seriously? That's what you want to watch?"

"We don't have to."

"Let me think about it. You know I'm not a fan of horror movies."

"It's fine. We don't have to."

I hated the way his shoulders slumped. Charles was the horror fan. He was the one who got Paul into those movies. It was a bonding thing for the two of them. And since Charles and I divorced, Paul hadn't had anyone to watch scary movies with.

"I'll watch it with you," I said.

"You don't have to, Mom."

"No, I want to. I know you miss watching those with your dad."

He shrugged. "I know you don't like them."

"But I love you. And I will suffer through it for you."

He grinned. "Yeah?"

I nodded. "Yeah. Let me clean up and you can get the movie going. As long as your homework is done."

"Yeah, it's all done. I was just doing some review stuff. Thanks, Mom."

I smiled at him. His excitement was palpable. It was good to see. I'd missed his grin.

He turned on the TV and found the movie while I cleaned up. When I joined him on the couch, he pressed play and I grabbed a pillow to hug and a blanket to cover my eyes if I needed it.

I was definitely going to need it.

I jumped at every sound in the movie. I hid behind the blanket. Paul laughed at me, but he didn't say anything about how much of a wimp I was. He just enjoyed being able to watch a movie.

When it was finally over, thank God, he turned to me. "Thanks for watching with me, Mom. I know you don't like these movies."

"You're welcome. And I don't, but you do. I want to do things you enjoy, too."

His lips turned up in a small smile. His eyes glazed over. It was the look he got when he was thinking about his father.

"Are you okay?"

He shrugged. "Just realizing a few things."

"Like?"

"Like I always felt like I was closer to Dad. When he left, I was angry he didn't take me with him. Not because I didn't want to be here, but because I..."

"You and your dad had a different connection," I provided for him.

He nodded.

"And now?"

He shrugged slightly. "Now I see that we only had that connection because you encouraged it."

"What do you mean?"

"Just that things are different, and it feels like Dad doesn't know anything about me anymore."

"It's hard when he's not living with us," I hedged. I would never speak poorly of Paul's dad to Paul, even if I wasn't always thrilled with him.

"Mom, you can cut the crap. Dad chose his new husband over us. When he left you, he left me, too. He didn't want me in his life, and he's proven that since he's been gone."

"Honey—"

"You don't have to defend him to me. I wish he cared

more about me, but he's made it clear I'm not as important to him as I once thought I was."

"A child is supposed to believe they're the center of their parents' world. In my opinion, a child should be the center of their parents' world, not just think they are. But your father... His world has changed a lot in the last few years."

"Maybe, but maybe not. Dad came to stuff when you didn't. He showed up when he had to. We would watch these movies because he liked them. A lot of the things that happened were because it was what he wanted."

"Paul, don't start to paint your father as someone who doesn't care. He loves you very much."

"I know. But there's a difference between loving someone because you have no choice and loving someone because you can't imagine your life without them in it. He's not the second one."

"Paul—"

"I think I'm going to get some sleep. It's late." He stood and hurried to his room, leaving me to stare after him.

I drew a breath and debated calling my ex-husband. It wouldn't fix anything if I did. For the last few years, I'd been trying to bridge the gap between the two of them, and I was failing. But it wasn't my job to keep them connected. If Charles wasn't interested in knowing the amazing man our son was becoming, I couldn't force him to. Even though it killed me to stand back and watch Paul get hurt over and over again.

I turned off the TV and cleaned up our snacks. I folded the blanket I'd used and shut off the lights, then headed toward my room. I knocked on Paul's door and waited for him to reply.

"Yeah?"

"I just wanted to say goodnight," I told him as I walked in.

He was sitting on his bed with a photo of him and Charles on his lap. It was one I took of the two of them when Paul was only five. They were smiling at the camera, laughing at something one of them said to me.

Paul set the picture back on his nightstand, facedown. "Goodnight," he said, climbing off his bed to hug me. He was almost as tall as I was, and still growing. His voice was deep, and he shaved almost every day. He was no longer my little boy, but a man who was learning about disappointment in the worst possible way. From his father.

"I love you."

He smiled. "I know. I love you, too."

I hugged him again. When I finally let go, he avoided my gaze. I didn't push, knowing he was struggling with his dad. It all came back when he saw Valentina and Dawson arguing.

I left his room and headed into mine. I closed the door and sat on my bed, grabbing my phone and tapping Valentina's name on the screen.

"Hey, Goldie," she answered.

"How was today?"

A door closed on her end. "Well, the girls seem to be okay."

"And you?"

She sniffed. "How can I be okay? Even though I had a feeling he was screwing around, how am I supposed to just be okay with this?"

"Are you hurt or mad?"

"What?"

"Hurt or mad? There's a difference. When Charles told me he was bi-sexual, I was hurt. He kept something from me. Something major. We were friends before we were lovers, and we'd built a life together. I thought he was my best friend. Our marriage wasn't perfect, and we were drifting apart, but we were still close. I thought one day things would get better. After Paul went to college, after work settled down, whatever. But when he told me he'd fallen for someone else and wanted a divorce, I was angry. I couldn't believe he'd done that."

"Okay?"

"What I'm saying is the man I thought of as my friend hurt me by keeping a secret. The man I married, who I was supposed to love with my entire heart and soul, pissed me off. My pride was wounded, not my heart. I almost didn't care that he wanted a divorce. The hardest part was Paul. Which made the whole process easier for me emotionally, even though it sucked."

Valentina took a deep breath and let it out slowly. "You know, most people would just buy me wine and ice cream and let me wallow."

I laughed with her. "You know I'm not most people. You need truth and love right now, and you're not going to get either by lying to yourself."

"You're right. And the truth is, I don't want to be married to Dawson anymore. God, I hate saying that."

"Why?"

"Because he's the father of my girls. He's the person I've spent my entire adult life with. Shouldn't I want to be with him?"

"No. Hell no. Do not should yourself into staying with him just because you have history. Take the cheating out of this. It was the reason you had the courage to tell him to fuck off, but it's separate. If you're unhappy, you do not need to stay in your marriage."

"But—"

"Your daughters will be fine. You need to teach them what a healthy relationship looks like. Not teach them to sit down and shut up and take whatever a man delivers."

"Dammit. That..." She blew out a slow breath. "I hate you."

"I love you, too."

She chuckled, a husky, raspy sound that told me she was full of emotion and losing her grip on it.

"What are you doing this weekend?"

"Working. And trying to stay busy so I forget my husband was screwing someone else for long enough that she picked up her entire life and moved here to be close to him."

"So, not much?"

Valentina laughed again. "Yeah. Why?"

"You're coming to Book Club with me on Sunday."

"What? No. I can't. Not when they're all happy and in love. I'll be the depressed separated woman going through a divorce and I'll bring everyone down."

"I'm not taking no for an answer. You're coming. You need to be around other women and laugh and remember that you are fucking awesome."

Valentina groaned, but said, "I'll think about it."

"You can say that, but I'll be at your house to pick you up at six-thirty."

"Fine," she grumbled.

"Are you really doing okay?" I asked, my voice softer.

"I don't know," she said. "There are times it hurts, and times I just feel stupid. I'm trying to hold it together for the girls."

"You need to find a way to let it all out."

"I need to live vicariously through you. What happened with Patrick today? Did you tell him you'll go on a date?"

"We do not need to talk about him."

"Why not? I need some joy in my life. When you were talking about him, you were glowing. You deserve to be happy."

"He's just not the right one for me."

"What? Why not? What happened?"

"Nothing happened. He works for me. I'm his boss. And I'm a lifetime older than he is. It just wouldn't make sense."

"So, you chickened out? You told me all about how he's cute and he's charming and he wanted you to think about him while you took a bath, which is so damn sexy. And instead of grabbing on to some fun, you got scared."

"I just—"

"Listen to me, Goldie. Don't let fear hold you back. I have for years. I wondered for a long time if Dawson was cheating on me. I figured he was on all the business trips, especially since we stopped having sex. But I was afraid to ask him. If I said something, I would have saved my girls from having another woman show up at our home."

"I'm sorry, Valentina."

"I know. I am, too. But don't let it hold you back. Brantley came over today after school and was telling me he was sorry. I guess Dawson stayed with him Saturday night after I threw him out, but he didn't admit what happened until Sunday. Brantley refused to let him stay any longer and apologized to me. I can't have the people I care most about tiptoeing around me. That means you can't say no to Patrick because you deserve happiness."

"So do you."

"I know. And maybe one day I'll be willing to look for it again. Right now, I'm a little bruised. It's only been a few days. But my marriage has been over for a while. I won't settle again."

"What do you mean?"

"Nothing. I didn't mean anything by that. I'm just saying we should go for what we want. And if you want Patrick, go for it."

I drew a breath and thought about it. All my reasons for not wanting to get involved with Patrick were flimsy. The age difference was a concern, but only because I was putting my own beliefs on him. I didn't know him, not that well. Maybe it was time to let him in and get to know him a little more.

"I'll think about it."

Valentina laughed. "Good. And when you agree to a date with Patrick, I'll go to Book Club."

"You first," I told her.

She laughed again. "We'll see."

We said goodnight, and I hung up thinking about Patrick. Valentina was right. I owed it to myself to find some happiness. Just like hers, my marriage was over long before Charles told me he wanted a divorce. And it had been years since our divorce was final. I had dated some, but no one I'd felt a connection with.

But Patrick... there was something there. Even if I wanted to tell myself there wasn't, I knew there was. And I owed it to myself, and to him, to find out what it was and see if it could be more than flirty banter and a good working relationship.

One could only hope.

5

———————

Valentina grumbled at me when I picked her up for book club. I grinned, and she just rolled her eyes.

"Did you agree to a date yet?" she asked as I backed out of her driveway.

All week, Patrick had given me the cold shoulder. It wasn't like he was rude or insubordinate, but he wasn't his usual flirty self. He would talk to Theo and Howard and flirt with Eve, but when I'd walk into the room, he'd stop talking.

Everyone noticed, but they either knew what was going on or weren't willing to ask in front of me.

"We'd have to be speaking in order for me to agree to a date," I admitted.

"You're not speaking? I thought he worked for you."

"He does, but apparently the only time he's willing to speak to me now is when we're talking about work and he has no choice."

"Wow, you really hurt him."

I scoffed. "Patrick was not hurt. He likes to flirt. He talks to everyone that way."

"You really think he tells all the women he knows to think about him in the bathtub?"

My cheeks warmed at the memory of his silky voice when he said that to me.

"You know he doesn't," Valentina argued. "You're scared. I get that. But he put himself out there. He told you how he felt. And you ignored him. He's hurt."

"I don't know. He might be mad, but hurt is a stretch." I parked in front of Book Boyfriends Unlimited and got out.

Valentina drew a deep breath and looked up at the building. "We had a deal, you know. You said you'd agree to a date if I came here."

"And you're here. I can't go on a date with someone who has no interest in me."

She breathed a laugh. "I might be the idiot who didn't want to admit my husband was cheating on me, but you're the idiot who's not willing to admit your assistant is interested in you."

I looped my arm through hers. "Well, let's be idiots together. I think life would be easier if I stopped thinking about dating and just spent time with friends."

"You might be right."

I knocked on the door and waited for Finley to let us in. She smiled widely and welcomed Valentina. "It's so good to see you. I'm glad you joined us."

"Yeah, well, Goldie talked me into it. Since I'm single and lonely and pathetic, she decided I needed friends."

Finley chuckled. "I wouldn't ever say you're pathetic, and single I can't help you with, but we'll take care of the lonely part. And we have cake."

"I'll take it," Valentina said.

We walked toward the back, pausing when someone else knocked on the door. Finley told us to go ahead while she returned to the front door. Valentina and I hugged Karissa, Blake, and Elise. Elise asked how Valentina was doing.

"I've had better weeks. But I guess I—" She stopped mid-sentence and stared.

I turned to look at who she was looking at and saw the woman who'd shown up at her house standing next to Sofia.

"Oh, shit," the woman said.

"Oh, shit is right," I replied. "You shouldn't be here."

The others gawked at us. Sofia stood behind the woman, blocking her.

"I... You're right. I'll go. I'm sorry. I didn't realize you'd be here."

"No. Wait," Valentina said, stepping around me. "Haley, right?"

Haley nodded and took a step back.

"You have every right to be here. You were manipulated and lied to, just like I was. Dawson doesn't get to take anything else away from either of us." Valentina reached out for Haley's hand.

Haley hesitated, but she put her hand in Valentina's. The two of them squeezed hands, then smiled at each other. After a minute, Haley collapsed into tears.

"Whoa," Elise said. "What's going on?"

"Haley showed up at my house last Saturday. She'd been involved with my husband and didn't know he was married. She moved up here to be closer to him," Valentina provided.

"She moved into my building," Sofia said, helping Haley into a chair. "When she told me she moved to be closer to her boyfriend, I was excited for her. I hadn't seen her since the first day, but we ran into each other today and she said their relationship ended. I'm so sorry. To both of you. I had no idea."

Valentina shook her head. "Dawson doesn't deserve

either of us. I threw him out last weekend. I haven't seen him since. He stayed with Brantley for a night, but once Brantley made him confess what happened, Brantley threw him out. I don't know where my husband is, and quite honestly, I don't care."

"I'm so sorry," Haley gasped from her seat. "I really didn't know he was married. I feel so stupid. And I ruined your family. I don't know how you don't hate me."

"Because you didn't ruin my family," Valentina said. "My husband was the one who had an affair. You're not the one who promised to love, honor, and cherish me for the rest of your life. He is. And he broke that vow and every other one he made to me. It hurts, but none of it is your fault. If it wasn't you, it would have been someone else."

The room was silent for a long moment. Valentina proved, again, what an amazing woman she was. When my marriage ended, I was angry and hurt and blamed everyone. Even years later, I didn't like to hear about Charles's new husband and the life they built together. I blamed him for stealing my husband, even though it wasn't as simple as that. But he knew we were married. He went into the relationship with Charles with his eyes wide open. Haley didn't have that same clarity.

"I think this calls for cake," Elise said, breaking the silence in the room. "Too bad we can't get drunk, too."

"We can go to O'Kelley's," Finley offered.

Haley and Valentina shared a look and shook their heads.

"I already get stared at all day at the bakery. I'd rather not spend my evening off doing the same," Valentina declared.

"How in the hell does anyone know what happened? I mean, this is the first I'm hearing these details," Blake said.

"I don't think anyone knows the details, but you know how this town is. Everyone knows Dawson is gone," Karissa said. "Which means they all think either he fucked up or Valentina did. They're waiting for her to fall apart and tell everyone."

"Which I just did." Valentina sighed.

"No one here is going to tell anyone anything. Except maybe their husbands and boyfriends. But your life isn't gossip. It's painful. Trust me, I know," Finley said, her voice full of emotion.

Another knock on the door sent Finley to the front of the store. The rest of us were silent as we waited for her to return. Melody, Willow, Zoey, and Piper walked in with Finley, laughing at something when they reached us.

"Hi!" Willow said. She spotted Haley and walked over to her. "I'm Willow. I don't think we've met."

"I'm Haley, the home wrecker," Haley said.

Willow paused and looked around the room. "Um, that's a weird last name."

Elise stepped forward and gave the short version. "Haley moved here to be closer to her boyfriend, but her boyfriend was Valentina's husband. We're all catching up and assuring them this information will not leave this room."

"Holy shit. Are you okay?" Melody walked over to Valentina and hugged her. "I'm so sorry."

Valentina hugged her back and shrugged. "You know what? I don't want to talk about this anymore. I'm not sure about Haley, but it's too raw right now. Too close to the surface. Goldie needs some advice on dating her assistant now that she's made him think she's not interested, even though she is."

I glared at her.

"Sorry. I figured if they had something else to distract them, I'd be off the hook. You can't deny me. I'm hurt."

I still glared, but she was right.

"Tell me about this assistant," Elise said, wagging her eyebrows at me. "And why you made him think you weren't interested."

I groaned. Might as well get it over with. "Patrick flirts with me all the time. It's just how he talks. I always dismissed it, but Friday before last he told me he's serious and he's interested in me. Said to think about him over the weekend—"

"In the bath," Valentina interjected. "Don't leave that part out."

I shook my head. "Yes, in the bath. Anyway, he said to think about him and let him know on Monday how I felt."

"I like him," Elise said with a smirk.

"And? What did you tell him?" Willow asked.

"Nothing. I didn't tell him anything. And he hasn't acted the same around me since. He's cold and distant and shuts down when I walk into a room."

They all looked around the room at each other.

"You didn't say anything?" Elise clarified.

"No. I mean..." I glanced at Valentina. "I'm divorced, and I was there when Haley showed up at Valentina's house, and I don't want to go through anything like that. Not again. Been there, done that, got the tee shirt."

"Please don't tell me you're giving up your chance at happiness because of my cheating asshole of a husband," Valentina said. Her brown eyes were fierce and fiery.

"I know, but—"

"She's right," Haley said. "Dawson was a liar and a fool, but you can't let him ruin your life."

"How can you two say that? How can you say I should

keep trying?" I asked. Whined, really. I was entitled to a little whining.

"Because the kind of love that matters, the kind that changes your world and makes you believe in everything again, is out there. You haven't found it yet, but it's out there," Finley said. Her lips lifted at the edges in a secret smile. "I never thought I'd find love after a one-night stand, especially when he refused to accept the baby was his."

"Yeah, but—"

"I never thought I'd find it with the man who was right in front of me most of my life," Blake said.

"Or with a stranger who was more patient with me than anyone I've ever known before," Elise said.

"You guys are making it harder to stay away from him," I grumbled.

"Good. Because you shouldn't," Valentina said. "There's no reason not to go out with him. It might not work out, but what if it does? What if he's the best thing that ever happened to you? What if he shows you that everything you've been through in life has been leading you to him?"

"You sound like you're talking about your own someone new," Melody said with a freakish clarity.

Valentina's eyes went wide for half a second, long enough to tell me Melody hit a mark Valentina wasn't ready to talk about yet.

"My marriage imploded eight days ago. Trust me when I say I'm not interested in anyone right now. At all." Valentina shook her head, avoiding the gazes of the women in the room.

Soft smiles graced their faces, but none of them pushed her. She'd been through enough.

"Goldie, you need to tell Patrick you like him," Willow said, leaning forward.

"That you want to jump him," Elise added.

"Or maybe just that you miss talking to him during the day," Blake suggested.

"If he changed how he speaks to you, I'm guessing he's hurt and is trying to distance himself from you," Melody said.

"That's what I said," Valentina agreed.

"Is that really what you want? For him to distance himself and for you to not have a relationship?" Blake asked.

I thought about it for a second and shook my head. "No. I don't. But I'm not sure I'm ready for... I don't know what."

"So start with getting back to where you were. With flirting and talking and being human to each other. Then tell him why you panicked," Elise said.

"Why would I tell him that?"

"Because men are just as insecure as we are," Elise said. "With my past, Colin thought he messed up constantly with me, but it was my past biting me in the ass and telling me not to trust him. But he's amazing. Once I opened up to him and he knew everything, he understood better how to not only treat me, but how to help me not freak out again."

"I don't know if Patrick is like that," I admitted.

"And you'll never know if you don't give him the chance to be," Valentina said. "You're not marrying the guy next weekend. You're flirting with him and confessing your friend's marriage blew up in front of you and you got anxious and panicky and want to take things with him slow. If he's not okay with that, you've lost nothing."

I sucked in a shaky breath and let it out slowly. I was still scared, but they were right. I couldn't complain about things if I wasn't willing to try to fix them. And I wanted to fix things with Patrick.

"Okay. I'll talk to him tomorrow," I promised them.

Then I ate my cake.

I CHICKENED OUT ON MONDAY. I tried to talk to him, but Eve walked in and I made up an excuse and left.

Tuesday wasn't much better.

By Wednesday, I felt like an even bigger ass. I was hiding. It wasn't fair to Patrick, and it wasn't fair to me. We both deserved better than me acting like I wasn't upset because I hurt him.

I was done trying to tell myself that wasn't the case, too. I knew it was reality. I hurt Patrick. The carefree man who never let anything get to him was bothered by my implied rejection. I needed to talk to him.

I set up a meeting on our calendars to review things for the weekend. We had our Memorial Day Kick-off to Summer Event and there were a ton of moving pieces. I knew everything was in order, but it was an excuse to schedule a meeting with him.

Five minutes before the meeting, I ran to the restroom to splash some cold water on my face. I drew a deep breath and tried to encourage myself. It didn't really work, but I had to go. He was going to be waiting.

My office was empty when I walked back in. I sat down and waited. At the exact moment the meeting was scheduled to begin, he walked into my office.

"Shut the door, please," I told him.

He hesitated but did as I asked. He took the chair across from me and folded his hands over his tablet. "What can I do for you, boss?"

"I messed up, Patrick. I know that, and I'm slow, but I wanted to apologize."

He sat silently, not giving an inch. I didn't blame him.

"I miss the way things were between us. Before... before I made it seem like I was rejecting you."

He snorted. "Made it seem. If that's all you wanted, I have work to do." He started to get up.

"Please, don't go yet," I half-shouted. "I'm sorry. For yelling just now and for not saying anything to you. I did think about you, but then something happened."

"What happened?" he asked, his blond brows tugging together.

I chewed my lip, debating telling him the whole story. It wasn't mine to tell, but I knew he wouldn't understand unless he knew. "I was having dinner with a friend and her family. There was a knock on the door when we were just sitting down. Her husband's girlfriend had moved to town to be closer to him. Because she didn't know he was married."

"What?" Patrick gasped. "You're joking."

I shook my head. "I'm not. It won't be long before everyone knows, but for now, it's one of the few secrets in MacKellar Cove. But it rattled me. It reminded me of my own divorce and how easy it was for Charles to toss me aside. I—"

"I would never do that to a person," Patrick said vehemently. He leaned forward, his forearm on the edge of my desk. "That's not me."

"Maybe not, but I didn't think it would be Charles either. Our marriage wasn't perfect, but I never thought it would be like that. I never thought he would tell me something so crucial to who he was, something that would mean we couldn't be together."

"I'm not bisexual," Patrick said.

"It's more than that," I confessed. "He was my partner. My friend. The person I was sharing my life with. The person I created a son with. And he lied to me about who he was, then he went out and found someone else to be with. Someone who suited him better."

"And that's shitty."

I nodded. "It is. It definitely is. And I'm not going to make excuses for him because there are none. But for me, it means I've lost my trust in myself. In my ability to make smart choices when it comes to relationships. I've dated a little since my divorce, but nothing more than a date or two. Because I get in my head. I second guess. I worry that he's got some big secret he's going to drop on me one day. And I just back away. But with you..."

"With me what?" he whispered.

"With you, you dropped a secret on me. One that scared me more than others. You gave me a few minutes of hope. That maybe there's a chance I could find romance again. Maybe I didn't have to buy a bunch of cats and train them to dial nine-one-one after I died. Maybe there was someone else out there."

"And?"

"And hope is the most dangerous emotion. It makes us believe in things. And when those things aren't what they seem, or aren't even real, and hope pops like a balloon, it takes more with it than just hope. It takes faith and confidence and the ability to try again."

"I'm not going to hurt you, Goldie."

I smiled at him. "You can't promise me that, but I appreciate you saying it."

"Does that mean you're going to give us a chance?"

I drew a breath and nodded. "It means I'm willing to have hope."

6

PATRICK

Damn. Hope. It was big. I could tell. If I messed everything up with her, she'd never trust another man. But when that thought went through my head, the one that followed was I didn't want her to ever have to think about another man. I wanted her to be mine. For good.

I resisted the urge to devour her. It burned through me, but she was scared, so I had to take things slow. I had to be careful. If I wasn't, I'd scare her off and never get another chance.

"Having hope is a good thing," I finally said, the words barely making it out past the tightness in my throat.

She smiled faintly, the corners of her mouth lifting just enough to tell me she was happy but still terrified. "Is everything set for the event this weekend?"

Getting personal wasn't something she did often, so I understood the subject change. I nodded and unlocked my tablet to pull up the full schedule.

"We're good. We have the food trucks ready for Friday night in the park with DJ Jericho. That'll wrap up at ten and we'll turn over the park for the craft fair on Saturday. I confirmed with Marco that Unhinged is ready to play a two hour set Saturday night. They sound really excited for the exposure."

"Good," Goldie said. "Paul is really excited about that. I think it's the only part of the weekend the teenagers are going to attend."

I laughed. "Probably. But that's to be expected. Once the show is done, we have a crew set for the fireworks show from MacKellar Cove Inn with support from the fire department on shore and on the water. Sunday we have day two of the craft fair and the Cove Performing Arts Center production that evening. Krystal said they're ready for their taste of the summer show. She loves that guests will see a little piece of all the shows they're doing this summer and will be able to buy tickets right then for the full performance. That was a great idea you had."

Goldie's cheeks darkened. "Thank you."

I winked at her, then looked back at my notes. "And Monday we have Yoga in the Park and the Garden Walk with maps already printed and in Eve's office."

She nodded as I spoke and stayed silent when I was done. She was running through the list she kept in her head, making sure there wasn't anything missing.

There wasn't. I made sure of it. Even though it hurt when she didn't say anything, I was not going to let it affect my job, or the town. I loved MacKellar Cove as much as anyone did, and making sure our Memorial Day Kick-off to Summer Event was flawless was important to me. It was the way we showed residents and visitors that MacKellar Cove was an amazing place to visit and live.

"Thank you. All of that sounds perfect. Have you set your schedule for the weekend?"

"I have. I'm working Friday night, then off Saturday and

Sunday, but I'll be available if needed. I'm back at it on Monday. Then I'll take off next Wednesday and Thursday and work through that weekend."

She nodded again, that far-off look still in her eyes. "That sounds good. I appreciate your help. More than you know."

I narrowed my eyes at her. There was something in her tone that made me wonder what else was going on. "Are you okay?"

She forced a smile and nodded, fake cheer ringing out from all around her. "I'm good. Thank you. I am really impressed with all the work you've done. I know I haven't always made things easy, but I'm very proud of this department."

"Are you leaving?" I asked. Those sounded like the words of a woman who was about to walk away.

"I don't have any plans to leave."

That was cryptic. I knew Goldie well enough by now to understand it was also intentional. Something was going on, but she didn't want to tell me about it, so I let it go.

"You should take some time off when you can get it through the summer. Things are going to be busy with events almost every weekend. You have everything on track now, so if you want to take the rest of the day, you're welcome to."

"I don't need to do that," I told her.

"How about a long lunch then? Something? I hate making all of you work the hours you put in through the summer. Eve's off tomorrow and Friday, but working this weekend. Howard hired more people to get through the summer and is home today and tomorrow. Theo is working through the weekend but taking next week off. You need a break, too."

"What about you?"

She shook her head and avoided my gaze. "I'll be fine. I enjoy working."

"But everyone needs downtime, Goldie. We all need to be able to take a break once in a while."

"I will. You should go have lunch with Arthur. See how things are going there. And just take the rest of the day off."

"Are you trying to get rid of me because you told me you want to go out?"

"I didn't say that!"

I shrugged. "You kinda did. You said you have hope about a future. That means you want to date me."

"I... Go to lunch, Patrick."

I grinned and stood. "Want me to bring you something back?"

She shook her head. "I'll see you tomorrow."

"I'll be back this afternoon."

She rolled her eyes. "Enjoy your lunch."

"I'd enjoy it more if it was with you, but I guess my brother will be a decent substitute."

She laughed softly, her lips lifting in a smile that finally reached her hazel eyes. They were a little more green when she was happy, which made me smile even bigger.

"See you soon," I said, waving as I opened her door and walked out.

I locked up my office and sent Arthur a text that I was coming to have lunch with him. He gave me a thumbs up as I was getting in my SUV.

O'Kelley's was busy, but not so busy I couldn't find a seat. A server came over with a water and told me Arthur already ordered for us and it would be out soon. And that my brother would be, too.

I played a game on my phone while I waited for Arthur

to join me. When someone slid onto the seat across from me, I turned my phone off and looked up. But it wasn't my brother. It was a woman I didn't recognize.

"Hi," she said, smiling widely while looking me up and down. "How are you?"

"Good. How are you?" I was giving her the benefit of the doubt while also keeping my guard up.

"I'm single."

"Good for you."

"Want to go hook up in the bathroom?"

I drew back. "Seriously?"

She nodded and twirled the straw in her glass with her tongue. "Yeah. I'm in town for the weekend and you're hot. You can meet me later if you'd rather do that."

"I'm not available," I told her. It wasn't a complete lie.

"I won't tell if you won't."

I shook my head and tried to push down the revolting feeling. Was this how Goldie felt when her friend's husband's girlfriend showed up? Like it was all wrong and twisted and sickening.

"I'll know. And that's enough."

"Ooh, I love men who are loyal," she said, running her nails up and down my arm in a way I thought was supposed to be sexy but made me feel like I was being clawed to death by a kitten.

"If that's true, why would you be willing to sleep with me knowing I'm not available?"

She pouted in a way that was supposed to be was tempting but wasn't. She tilted her head to the side and stuck out her boobs. I didn't look at them. I didn't care what they looked like. I just wanted her to leave.

"You're not being very nice."

"I'm not the one who approached you. I was minding my

own business and waiting for my brother to join me for lunch."

"You have a brother? Ooh! Two for one."

"Time to go," Hudson said, catching the woman as she fell sideways out of her seat and almost hit the floor. "Your friends need to get you back to your hotel."

"But I don't wanna," she pouted, running her hand down Hudson's cheek and continuing to his throat, then lower.

He dropped her, throwing his hands up and backing away as two other women collected the drunk, single one and scowled at him.

"Your friend needs to learn to keep her hands to herself," Hudson growled at the women.

One of them had the decency to look ashamed. The other still shot daggers at us.

Hudson nodded toward the bar. "It's safer."

I grabbed my water and followed him to the bar, taking a seat in the center where there was another stool open. "Thanks."

He shook his head. "She's been a pain in my ass all week. She comes in here when I open and drinks until she can't stand, then tries to get someone to screw her in the bathroom and pouts when they say no."

"Wow, you have her pegged. That's exactly what she said to me."

"I was her first attempt," he admitted with a grimace.

I snorted.

"Anna was not as amused as you."

I grimaced. "Yeah, I can understand that. I can't see how any woman would find it appealing to have someone hanging all over her man."

"I would feel the same if someone was all over Anna."

The thought of a man doing that to Goldie nearly sent me out of my seat.

"You, too, huh?" Hudson chuckled.

I shrugged.

"Goldie giving you a shot yet?"

"Nope," Arthur answered for me. "She's barely speaking to him right now."

"Damn. Sorry," Hudson said.

"Actually, that's not true. We talked earlier," I countered smugly.

"Really?" my brother asked with a raised brow. "About something other than work?"

"Yes. About having hope," I said.

"Hope?" Hudson asked.

I nodded.

Hudson whistled. "That's not a small thing for her. I get it, though. Goldie's been through shit with her ex. It took me a long time to be willing to try with someone. She's the same."

"You two talk?" I asked, feeling irrationally jealous of that new knowledge. Goldie had friends, and she was allowed to share things with other men. Not to mention, Hudson was marrying Anna in a few months. I had no reason to be jealous. Except I was.

Hudson met my gaze and nodded. "We do. Because we're friends. And being a bartender, people tend to tell me shit they wouldn't normally admit. Like Goldie is afraid of getting hurt again. And having hope is something she's worried about for years. If she has hope, and if it's because of you, don't fuck it up."

I wasn't sure whether to laugh or nod, so I kind of did both.

"He's in love with her," my brother provided. "The only way he's going to fuck it up is by telling her how he feels."

"Yeah, definitely don't do that," Hudson said. "How long have you two been together? I didn't realize you were dating."

"They're not," Arthur said. "He just wishes they were. He's been pining over her forever. He might be getting closer to her agreeing to a date, though."

"She did agree," I said. "Work is just busy right now, so I'm not sure when we'll be able to make it happen."

"Don't wait. Not with a woman like Goldie. She's incredible, but she's going to be hard to pin down because she's going to use any excuse she can to get out of putting herself at risk. If she's agreed to a date, make a plan."

"You think?" I asked.

Hudson nodded. "Yeah. Hey, you two should come to guys' night tomorrow."

"Me and Goldie?" I asked.

Hudson chuckled. "No. You and Arthur. Why haven't you come before?"

Arthur and I exchanged a glance. "We weren't invited," Arthur said for us.

"Well, you are now. It started out as Ian and Ramsey, James when he could, coming here to hang out. It's grown. Seems half the men in town show up now. Talk about their women and offer each other shitty advice."

"Sounds like exactly where I need to be," I grumbled.

Hudson laughed. "It's only shitty because it's usually exactly what you need to hear but don't want to hear. And all those guys adore Goldie. They'll help you figure her out."

I wasn't sure I wanted to hang around with a bunch of men who knew and liked Goldie, but maybe it was worth a shot.

"We'll be there," Arthur answered for us, clapping me on the back.

Hudson tapped the counter and walked away to help someone else.

"We'll be there?" I questioned my brother.

"You need help, and those guys know Goldie. It'll be good."

"Really?" I was more than a little skeptical.

"If nothing else, it's new friends."

I rolled my eyes and shook my head. I never won an argument against my brother. I wasn't going to start now.

MY STOMACH HURT from laughing so hard. I swiped my glasses off and wiped the tears from my face. Damn, those guys were funny.

James, a local cop, was picking on his partner, Rowan, about something that happened at work, but Rowan turned it around on James. Then Ramsey, who grew up with James, and Xavier, whose wife was close to James's wife, joined in on James, and James was just left the butt of every joke.

"You know you started it," Rowan said to James.

James answered him with his middle finger. "Why don't we talk about someone else? I think I've had enough fun for one night."

"I feel bad for your wife," Ian said. Ian also grew up with James and knew him better than the others.

James just shook his head and chuckled. "My wife is well taken care of. You don't have to feel bad for her at all."

"Hey, speaking of wives," Rowan said. He turned to Brantley. "I heard a rumor about Valentina."

Brantley was a high school physics teacher and coached

varsity cross-country and baseball. I had seen him around town but never met him until tonight. But I thought he was single.

"What about Valentina?" Brantley asked. His jaw was tight, and his knuckles turned white.

"Dawson was cheating on her and moved the girlfriend to town. Any truth to that?"

Oh, shit. I knew that story. And I knew the name Valentina. She was friends with Goldie and worked at Cove Bakery. Which meant the story Goldie told me was about her. Maybe.

"Where did you hear that?" Brantley asked, giving nothing away. He relaxed his posture and his hand, but he was facing off against two cops and answering a question with a question was almost a sure sign he was hiding something.

"A stop we had today. One of their neighbors said she saw Valentina throwing Dawson out shortly after the girlfriend showed up at the house," Rowan said.

"Fuck," Brantley breathed, all his bravado sagging his shoulders.

"So, it's true?"

Brantley shook his head. "Not entirely."

"You want to enlighten us?" James asked.

"Why? So you can pile on?" Brantley snapped.

"I like Valentina," Ian said. "She deserves better than a piece of shit like him. If he cheated on her, good riddance to him."

Brantley's shoulders sagged just a touch. "I agree."

"I'm not interested in piling on," James said. "I just feel for her."

Brantley held his gaze for a long minute, then nodded. "They were having dinner. Goldie and Paul were there, too.

Haley, the other woman, wanted to surprise Dawson by moving to be closer to him. Neither of them knew about the other woman, and Dawson did not invite her to move here. He was living his peaceful fucking life and ruining the lives of two women. Not to mention his daughters."

"Damn," Rowan said. "That's fucked up. I've known a lot of people who were stepping out and it's just ugly. It's not worth it, and it's not okay."

"Agreed," the other men all said.

"How's Valentina?" Hudson asked Brantley.

Brantley shrugged. "As good as she can be. Once she hears that the story is out there, she'll be upset again."

"She's lucky to have you for a friend," Ian said.

Brantley nodded, but the look in his eyes said he wanted to be friends with Valentina as much as I wanted to be friends with Goldie.

"How old are her daughters?" I asked Brantley.

"Fourteen and fifteen. Both have birthdays coming up," Brantley said.

"Where's Dawson living? Did he move in with the girl-friend?" Rowan asked.

Brantley shook his head. "He stayed with me the first night. Asshole wouldn't tell me why Val kicked him out. Once I dragged it out of him, I threw him out, too."

"I thought you two were good friends. Didn't you intro-duce them?" Ian asked.

Brantley nodded. "Yep. Worst mistake of my life."

"You can't blame yourself. You had no way of knowing this would happen decades later," James said.

Brantley nodded, but it was jerky and uncomfortable.

"It's more than that, isn't it?" I asked Brantley.

He met my gaze with a knowing one. "Yep." He was in love with Valentina.

I tipped my glass to his, somewhat relieved to know I wasn't the only one sitting at a bar on a Thursday night and wishing I had the woman I loved waiting at home for me. Nope. I'd be going home alone. Just like Brantley. And it sucked. Big time.

7

GOLDIE

Wʜᴀᴛ ᴛʜᴇ ʜᴇʟʟ? I ѕᴛᴀʀᴇᴅ ᴀᴛ ᴛʜᴇ ʙᴏᴏᴛʜ ᴡʜᴇʀᴇ ᴏᴜʀ breakfast provider was supposed to be. *Supposed to be* being the problem. I checked my phone, then opened my email.

Where the hell were they? Crowds were forming, and instead of having three options for food, there were two. Cove Bakery was amazing and had agreed to extra signage to encourage diners to wander through town a little farther. Cracked was right next to the park and prepared to participate. But the booth we had brought in for our visiting chef was empty.

I tapped my screen to call the contact I had for them. Patrick arranged everything and didn't mention there was an issue, but something obviously went wrong.

"The person you have called is not available. Please leave your message at the tone," the automated recording said.

I hung up. I scrolled through more emails, hoping to find another number or way to contact them. Were they in an accident? Did something happen? They signed a contract to provide grab and go savory breakfast for three hundred people. Breakfast sandwiches, quiche cups, and egg bites were a good alternative to Cove Bakery's sweet treats and Cracked's sit-down meals. But only if someone showed up.

My finger hovered over Patrick's name. I was tempted to call him and find out what was going on, but it was supposed to be his day off. I could handle it. I had no choice.

I sent an email to the chef's assistant, the person we'd been communicating with. Patrick copied me on almost everything, but I hadn't seen any emails that week.

"How's everything going?" Theo asked, handing me a cup of coffee with Cove Bakery on the side.

"Not good. Did Patrick say anything to you about Chef Julian canceling on us this morning?"

Theo shook his head slowly. "No. It's not like Patrick to not keep you in the loop on something like that."

"That's how I feel, too. But Chef Julian isn't here, the booth is empty, and I can't get in touch with anyone there."

"Let me try. What's the number?" Theo read it off my phone screen and typed it into his phone. "It's ringing."

I stared at him, willing him to get some answers. His eyes went wide, and he grinned.

"Good morning. I'm calling from the MacKellar Cove Tourism Department. We're wondering if everything is okay with your staff since no one has shown up yet."

Theo's grin faded as the person on the other end spoke.

"Wait, who changed the agreement?"

My heart stopped. Why would Patrick change something? Or anyone? No one outside my team had contact with any of the vendors. How was that even possible?

"She said someone called Friday afternoon and said Saturday morning was double booked and needed them to move to Sunday," Theo explained.

I reached for the phone, thankful when Theo handed it

over. "Good morning, this is Goldie Spear. I'm sorry, but who did you speak to?"

"I don't know," the woman said. "He called late yesterday and was in a bit of a panic."

"He didn't tell you who he was? And you just changed everything?"

"I'm believed him. He said he worked in the tourism department and that he was really sorry, but things had gotten all mixed up. We were ready for today, but when we got the call, we had to shift a few things. I told him we could do it, but the change would cost an extra five percent. He agreed to it."

"Five percent?" I took a deep breath. It was pennies compared to what it could be for a change like that, but the money was the least of it. "I don't know who called you, but they were wrong. We didn't double book today. There's no one here right now, and we have another chef coming in tomorrow. Is there anyway you guys can come here now?"

"Now?" she blurted.

I sighed. "Yeah. We're opening soon, and we have an empty booth. It's not available tomorrow."

"Crap. Um, okay. Let me make some calls and find out. I'll call this phone back in a few minutes." She hung up without waiting for me to say anything else.

I handed the phone back to Theo, who stared at me with raised brows, waiting for me to tell him what was going on. "She's going to see if she can get them here. She's calling you back."

His shoulders sagged with relief. "Good. Hopefully she can make it happen."

"Yeah, but what I want to know is why. Who in the hell called and changed them to Sunday?"

"Don't know, boss. It definitely wasn't me. You know

Howard and Patrick wouldn't do it. Neither would Eve, but the woman said *he* so that took Eve out anyway. Weird, though."

"What's weird?" Eve asked, joining us from behind Theo.

"Breakfast got moved to tomorrow," Theo said.

"Um, what?" Eve asked.

Theo nodded to the breakfast booth. "The chef for today got a call late yesterday saying we double booked today and needed to move them to Sunday."

"Who would have told them that?"

"That's what we're trying to figure out," Theo said.

My mind went to one person who had an interest in making sure I looked bad, but I had a hard time imagining Mayor Levine would go to those lengths.

Theo's phone rang. He answered it before the second ring. Eve and I stared at him, our breath held, until he sighed and smiled.

"Thank you so much. That's perfect. Whatever you can do. Thank you. We'll see you soon." He hung up and met my gaze triumphantly. "They're on the way. It'll be a little while, and it might be an hour before they have food ready to sell, but they're coming."

"Thank you, Theo," I said, grabbing his arm. "I really appreciate the help."

"Happy I was here, boss. Just wish I knew who she spoke to. I'd love to give that person a piece of my mind."

"Me, too," I agreed.

"What else needs to be done?" Eve asked.

I shook my head. "I haven't even checked. I saw they weren't here and started calling. I want to walk around the setup and make sure people have everything they need."

"I'll start on this end, you start on the other end," Eve said. "We'll meet in the middle."

"I'll wait for the chef and help them get setup," Theo said.

"Perfect. Thank you both." I headed toward the water, where Eve pointed. I walked through the lanes, checking in with every single vendor getting set up for the craft fair. We had open applications, but we reserved the right to decline any that didn't fit. We had a limited number of booths, but thankfully, we only ended up with three more applications than booths. Patrick found a way to squeeze in three extra spots for the last few vendors so all of them could participate.

A few vendors had minor requests, but most of them were ready for the day. It was supposed to be beautiful, and we were expecting a full crowd. Some visitors were already starting to wander through the booths, even though the craft fair wasn't supposed to open for another forty minutes.

I met back up with Eve at the center of the park. "All good on my side," she said.

"Good. At least nothing with the craft fair was messed up."

Eve nodded. "Who would cancel a vendor? I just don't get it."

"I don't either," I said, keeping my guess to myself.

We went back to the breakfast booth and found Theo carrying trays into the booth and Chef Julian inside trying to get food going.

"Chef, thank you for coming," I said.

"You're welcome. I am so sorry about the mix-up." He barely looked up as he whisked eggs together and poured the mixture into a sheet pan and slid it into the oven.

"It is not your fault. I'm going to find out who called you, but right now, we're just grateful you were still available for today."

He nodded, turning his focus to the next item on his list. I understood the creative mind and knew he needed his space to work. Chefs were like any other artist and had their process. His was messed up from the delayed morning, which meant he was frazzled more than what would be normal. I didn't take offense to his distraction.

"Ms. Spear," a short, Black woman outside the booth said. "I'm Justine. We spoke earlier. I apologize for the mix-up."

"Call me Goldie, Justine. And please, don't apologize. Clearly, someone reached out who shouldn't have. It isn't your error. Thank you for getting over here so quickly."

"You're welcome. Theo has been a huge help getting everything carried inside for my husband. Julian is a bit of a perfectionist when it comes to his food. Having Theo to help me while Julian got started was very kind."

"He volunteered. I have an amazing team."

"You do. Patrick has always been very kind and accommodating. I should have known something was off when it wasn't him who was in touch with me. Because I didn't question, we will honor our original pricing. You should not be charged for a change that neither of us was responsible for."

"Thank you for that. But if this cost you extra, please make sure that goes on the invoice."

She shook her head. "It won't. We were set and prepared. Julian always has things ready the day before. The increased charge was to purchase new ingredients for the things he wouldn't have used after today. He's particular about his greens."

"And that is one of the reasons his food is so delicious."

"Thank you. I will tell him you said so."

"Justine!" Chef Julian called from inside.

"I should go. I'm his runner when he's cooking. Please stop by and get something to eat soon. If it's okay, I'd like to shop today, too."

"Of course. You're welcome to leave the vehicle where it is or we can move it for you and make sure you have access to whatever you need."

"Thank you. You're so kind. I should know this after the wonderful things Patrick says about you, but it's good to see."

"Justine!" Julian called again.

"You go," I told her. "You have our numbers. Call Theo or myself and we'll take care of whatever you need."

She squeezed my hands. "Thank you."

Justine jumped up into the booth and shouted back at her husband. He laughed and shook his head at her. She tied her hair up and added a hairnet, then jumped in and worked side-by-side with him in a way that only people who knew each other well could do.

I smiled as I turned away, relieved to have one crisis averted. Theo and Eve were speaking to an older couple who were looking at the booth longingly. They smiled and nodded, then Theo and Eve joined me.

"They'll have the first things done in thirty minutes. It'll be a little later than planned, but it'll work out," Theo said.

I nodded. "It'll be fine. We got it set, and we're good to go. The rest of the day will be smooth sailing."

THE REST of the day was not smooth sailing. Not even close. The power went out to a section of the booths after lunch.

Wind kicked up off the water and blew over two tents. And the worst one? The band was missing.

"What is going on?" I hissed to Theo. He stuck by my side all day, helping me figure out the issues we were having.

"I can't reach them," he replied.

We were off-stage, trying to figure out how to appease a very unhappy crowd of teenagers and families. Unhinged was an interesting name for a band, but the music was all ages appropriate and the band was talented. For them to not appear had me wondering if they got a call from the mystery person who rescheduled our morning guest chef.

"What's going on with the band?" Patrick asked, appearing behind me.

"Did you cancel them?" I barked at him.

Patrick threw up his hands and took a step back. "Whoa. Why would I cancel? I spoke to Marco yesterday morning. They were excited to be here."

"Well, apparently that excitement waned because they aren't reachable."

"Let me try. They're staying closer to Syracuse because all the hotels here were booked when we reached out to them." Patrick put the phone to his ear and listened. After a minute, he shook his head and hung up. "That's weird."

"Par for the course today," Theo said.

"What does that mean?" Patrick asked.

Theo shrugged. "It's been a shitshow. Chef Julian didn't show up, said someone called yesterday and told him we were double booked for this morning and he needed to come Sunday. We got ahold of him and it all worked out, but we're not sure who called him. Then we lost power and the wind, and now the band is MIA."

"Someone called Chef Julian?" Patrick asked, looking between Theo and me.

"Yep. All Justine knew was it was a man who said he worked with us. He never told her a name. She said he sounded flustered about it, so she never questioned it." Theo had as much frustration in his voice as I felt.

"What the hell? Is someone trying to sabotage the weekend?" Patrick's question was more rhetorical than not, but that didn't mean he was wrong.

"That's what I'm wondering. Especially with this. The show was supposed to start thirty minutes ago, and Unhinged isn't here. They're not coming. Do we have a backup plan?" Theo asked.

I gawked at Patrick. A backup plan never occurred to me. Not when the band was so excited to play. If they'd canceled at the last minute, we still would have been screwed, but we didn't think that would happen. I didn't think that would happen.

Patrick shook his head. "No. No backup plan."

"Okay, well, we need to come up with one. Now," Theo said.

Patrick and Theo jumped into action, talking about people they knew who could play. It was supposed to be a two-hour show, but we would be lucky if we ended up with entertainment for an hour. People were already leaving, hopefully getting a good spot to watch the fireworks.

"Good evening everyone," Patrick's voice boomed through the speakers. I hadn't noticed him walking on stage. "We've had a pretty eventful day today. I hope you've all enjoyed the Memorial Day Kick-off to Summer Event!"

The crowd cheered at Patrick's excitement. Some of my anxiety eased.

"Unfortunately, we've had a hiccup with the band that was supposed to be here tonight. Unhinged is apparently not going to make it."

A chorus of boos followed that announcement.

"I know. I'm disappointed, too. We're going to find out if we can reschedule with them for another time later this summer because everyone was really looking forward to their show. But for tonight, we have a few local performers who've agreed to help us out. You guys might recognize some of these kids. They're all seniors at MacKellar Cove High School. Let's give a big round of applause to The Elements!"

Again, the crowd cheered when Patrick's voice went up. The kids took the stage, looking like children pretending to be adults. I didn't recognize any of them, but as soon as they started to play, I breathed a sigh. They were good. Really good. Better than I expected them to be.

They started with a few covers to get the crowd into it. Their lead singer, a Black boy who introduced himself as Johnnie Junior, talked to the crowd after the first two songs. He introduced the other four members of the band, then counted them down to play one of the band's songs.

Patrick wandered over to me as the band captivated the crowd. "Are you okay?"

I laughed mirthlessly and shook my head. "Not even a little. But these guys are amazing. Thank you for getting them up there."

"That was all Theo. The drummer is his friend's kid. Said he heard them play a few times and was impressed. He was talking to the dad and getting the kids to agree while I was on stage stalling."

"Well, thank you. I don't know what we would have done if we didn't have any entertainment."

Patrick nodded and was quiet for a minute. "Why didn't you call me earlier?"

I searched my mind for a reason I would have. "Was I supposed to?"

Patrick turned to me. "The chef didn't show up. Power went out. Tents blew over. It sounds like you could have used the help."

"It's your day off. I wasn't going to make you work when you needed the break. Theo and Eve were here to help me."

"Still, you could have reached out. I'm always here for you if you need something."

I nodded, trying not to let those words sink in. If they did, I might have a hard time letting go of that when he wasn't there for me any longer. When someone else captured his attention and he moved on from the old, divorced mom.

"It sounds like you were a rock star, though. As always."

I chuckled. "Hardly. I was barely holding it together. At this point, I'm just crossing my fingers the fireworks actually work."

Patrick grinned. "Everything will be fine. And I'll make sure I'm here tomorrow for the day in case there are more issues."

"You don't have to do that."

"I know, but I want to. I want to help, Goldie. Whatever you need, I want you to know I'm willing and available to help you."

"Thank you," I whispered, letting those words and that promise in a little deeper. I just hoped I didn't regret it.

8

<hr>

THE REST OF THE NIGHT WAS EASY. THE BAND WAS ENERGETIC and talented. They definitely impressed the crowd. I told Theo to make sure we had contact information for them so we could figure out some sort of compensation.

The fireworks went off without an issue. The show was almost as good as the band. And when people wandered home and the park was empty, my team had everything cleaned up in record time.

Sunday, I was up early and holding my breath that we had an easy day. Our guest breakfast chef was there and cooking when I arrived. The vendors were setting up and ready when we welcomed guests.

Patrick arrived shortly before the day started, and it seemed he was the good luck charm because the day went by without any major, or minor, disasters.

When the craft fair wrapped up, all the vendors said they had a wonderful time. Many of them sold out of the products they brought with them. And all of them I spoke to said they hoped to come back in future years if we did the event again.

My mind ran with possibilities as the Cove Performing Arts Center team took the stage. They were funny and talented. Krystal, their narrator for the night, starred in many of their shows. She talked a little about each performance before the actors took the stage. They wore costumes, but not their show costumes since each show would have a different look and changing so many times would have been a nightmare for the performers.

When they were finished with their show, and tickets for future performances were sold, the crowd lingered in the late evening. It was nice out, and early compared to the night before. The crew we'd hired to take down the tents from the craft fair was hard at work, and the locals noticed and pitched in, breaking down everything in record time, then setting up the park for games.

Cornhole boards appeared, and teams started playing. Music played from phones all around the park. Food and drinks were carried over from the restaurants and bars not far from the park.

It was what I loved about MacKellar Cove. People stepped up to help each other and went above and beyond to do things. Families walked with kids, and when a kid tried to get into a cornhole game, the people playing showed them how it was done and cheered when they made good throws.

I loved it.

"Today was amazing," Valentina said, joining me on the edge of the park.

"Hi!" I hugged her. "It really was. It's been stressful, but today was so much better."

"Bianca told me about the band yesterday. What happened?"

I rolled my eyes. "We're not entirely sure, but it seems someone is trying to ruin things for me."

"What do you mean?"

"Little things yesterday, the biggest being the band not showing up. We haven't been able to get in touch with them, so there's still a chance something is wrong."

"Really?"

"I hope not, but yeah. Patrick said they've been posting on social media, so he thinks they're okay, but they aren't answering his calls."

"That's so weird."

I nodded, feeling more and more confused about the whole thing.

"You don't think it was a coincidence, do you?"

I hesitated, then shook my head. "I don't."

"And you have a guess as to who's behind all this, don't you?"

I nodded slowly.

"Someone from your team?"

"No," I said quickly. "Not a chance."

"Okay, but then who?"

"Our mayor."

"What? Why would he do that?"

"He threatened to fire me if this season isn't a success," I whispered.

"It already is. You plan a ton of events. How could he think you're not doing amazing?"

"Well, he cut my budget fifteen percent, then told me if I don't hit it, I'm gone."

Valentina whistled.

"Yeah. I can't prove it, but I think he's the one who called the chef, and he probably had something to do with the band."

"Wow. I knew he was an ass, but this is a whole other level."

"Yep. But there's nothing I can do. If I can't prove he's the one who did it, I just have to roll with it. Even if I can prove it, I'm not sure what I can do."

"You tell people. Shout it to the whole town. He won't get elected if you show people who he really is."

"Maybe, but it's not like it would get him tossed out."

"It might, actually," Valentina said. "If he's actively trying to harm the town, it could be grounds for impeachment."

I drew a sharp breath. "Wow. That's... good to know."

"Yeah, just watch your back. If he's coming at you from both sides, it's going to be a fight."

I nodded. "It definitely is going to be a fight. And please don't tell anyone about this. I don't want it to get around town. I don't want Paul to worry. Or my team."

"You know I'll keep a secret."

I smiled at her. "So, how are things going with you?"

She shook her head and glanced out at the crowd. "The rumor mill is having fun."

"Shit. Really?"

She nodded. "Yep. Brantley said one of my neighbors told James and Rowan that Dawson moved Haley up here."

I scoffed. "And why would he do that?"

"Who knows? But it's only going to get worse now that people know who Haley is. I feel bad for her."

"Why?"

"She's going to be seen as the home wrecker. The woman who came in and ruined my marriage. You know how people are here. It isn't Dawson's fault that he screwed around."

"Yes, it is. And I'll tell anyone who asks me that."

Valentina smiled, but it was a sad smile. "Thanks. I just

hate that he's messed up so many lives. And I feel guilty that there's a part of me that's relieved my marriage is over."

"Relieved?"

She nodded, not looking at me. "I didn't have the guts to leave him or kick him out, but I haven't been happy. I've been killing myself to make him happy, and it's made me miserable. He wasn't supportive of me or anything I've wanted to do. He's dismissive with the girls a lot of the time. He's just not the man I thought he was when we got together. He's changed."

"So have you, I'm sure. And I'm not saying that's a bad thing. When things with Charles were at that point, when he said he wanted a divorce, he told me I'd changed, too. I resented it at the time because it felt like he was saying it was my fault, but I realized he was right. Everyone changes, and if you don't change together, you grow apart."

"True. I'm not the same person I was twenty years ago. And I don't want to be."

"And that's okay. That was the hardest thing for me with my divorce. Accepting that it was okay to be happy with who I'd become and content with my marriage ending."

"Not everyone is meant to have a happily ever after," Valentina said softly.

"I don't think you should give up yet." I smiled as Brantley approached us with eyes only for Valentina.

She turned to see him coming and grinned. "Don't even start."

"I didn't say a word." I smiled at her, and she shook her head.

"Hey, ladies. How are we doing tonight?" Brantley asked.

"Good. How are you?" I asked him.

"I'm doing great. This has been a fun event. Great weekend."

"Thank you. Valentina was just telling me she wants to play cornhole. I have to get back to work, so maybe you can be her partner." I smiled up at Brantley, knowing he didn't need any encouragement.

"That would be great. Sounds fun," Brantley said, his gaze sliding over Valentina before he locked onto her eyes.

"Let's go," she said.

The two of them turned to walk toward the games. I smiled at their backs, Valentina catching me when she turned to glare at me. I waved.

She needed some fun and happiness. And I had a feeling Brantley could help with both.

"Is this what you think a successful event looks like, Ms. Spear?" Mayor Levine asked me early Tuesday morning.

I'd been summoned to his office as soon as it was open. Jane sounded apologetic when she called, but I didn't blame her for his attitude.

His face was red, and he looked like he was going to pop. If his frustration wasn't directed at me, and if I didn't believe he was to blame for the issues over the weekend, I would have found it funny.

"We're looking into the problems we encountered. Friday night went to plan, so did Sunday and Monday. The only errors happened on Saturday."

"Well, one out of four days with problems is one too many, Ms. Spear. This is not the kind of thing that brings me a lot of confidence in your supposed talents."

I seethed and resisted the urge to lash out at the miserable little man. "I agree, Mr. Mayor. That's why my team is contacting all future vendors and notifying them to only accept changes from someone they have been in touch with previously and to make sure they get contact information from anyone who tries to reschedule or cancel anything."

That tidbit had him a bit flustered, which only served to confirm what I already suspected.

"And beyond that, we will find out what happened to the band and find out what happened to Chef Julian. Chef Julian's wife has been very helpful in terms of providing us with information about the person who called her to reschedule. We will get to the bottom of the events that occurred to mess with Saturday's schedule."

"Are you sure that's the best spend of your time, Ms. Spear?" His mouth twisted as he spat my name.

"Yes, it is. Because if someone is trying to ruin town events, it's important we find out who and put an end to it. No one is beyond reach. I would think you, as mayor, would want to know who is behind these incidents. If people believe they aren't going to get what's promised to them when they come here, it'll look bad on everyone in the town. It'll slow tourism and it'll mean people don't move here. How would that go during the next election?"

He opened and closed his lips, rolling them in and scowling at me while he worked out a response. "I agree," he finally pushed out.

"Good. I'm happy to know I have your support, Mr. Mayor. I will be in touch when I have more information about what happened to the band and why they didn't show up or call us to cancel the performance. I'll see you soon." I stood and smiled sweetly at him.

The rat bastard scowled again and waved his hand for me to leave his office. I was more than happy to.

"I didn't hear a crash," Jane whispered when I walked out.

"He knows he has no room to argue with this one. He's the one who messed up."

"Wait, do you think...?"

I nodded. "I do, but don't tell anyone."

"Why not?"

"Because until I have evidence of that, it's a guess."

She nodded and glanced toward his office. "If I find out anything, I'll let you know."

"Thanks, Jane. I appreciate it. Good luck. I have a feeling he's going to be in a bad mood all day."

She rolled her eyes. "Nothing new."

I wished there was something I could do to help her, but until he was out of office, there wasn't. But if I could prove he was interfering with town events and causing MacKellar Cove to lose money, I would have grounds to make sure he was removed.

I checked my email when I got back to my office and found one from Marco with Unhinged. It was their invoice for the performance they didn't show up to. An invoice that stated we violated the cancellation policy in their contract by giving less than forty-eight hours notice, which meant we were obligated to pay the full fee.

It was legitimate. And I didn't blame them for wanting their full payment. They were owed their fee, but I was owed some answers.

This time, Marco picked up the phone.

"Yeah?"

"Hi Marco, this is Goldie Spear with the MacKellar Cove Tourism Department."

"Yep."

"I saw your invoice and we will get it paid this week, but I'd like to ask you a few things first."

"What?"

I couldn't blame him for being short with his answers. He was pissed. He wasn't the only one.

"I'm assuming you received a phone call telling you we needed to cancel your performance. Is that true?"

"Seriously? Why are you asking me this?"

"Because my team never contacted you."

"What? Yes, they did. A dude called late Friday and said you didn't have room for us, that someone bigger agreed to play and we weren't needed."

"Did you catch his name by any chance?"

"No. I didn't really care. I was pissed. We were already in the hotel. We'd planned to spend the day at the event so we could mingle with the people in town. The band was mad. I didn't care which of your people was telling us we weren't good enough."

"My team didn't call you, Marco. We were trying to reach you on Saturday night when you didn't show up because we all expected you to be there."

"That's not possible."

"You weren't the only vendor this happened to. The other one we were able to get in touch with and correct it, but we couldn't reach you guys."

"We went out. Left our phones in the hotel. We didn't want to deal with anymore crap."

"I apologize for that, Marco. We're trying to find out who was reaching out and changing things on us. My team is very small. You spoke to myself or Patrick, right?"

"Yeah. That's it. Until this other guy called. Shit. I should have known. I just thought you two were chickening out from telling us and had some intern or something do it."

I shook my head. "No, but I understand why you would think that. I know you don't owe us anything, Marco, but we'd really like to have you guys play in MacKellar Cove. We had a lot of disappointed fans."

"I don't know. I'll have to check with the guys."

"I understand that. We will pay the invoice for this weekend. If you have an opening in your schedule and are willing to try again, we will sign a new contract and I will make sure you have contact information for everyone on my team. No changes or cancellations will be made without confirmation from at least two of us for the rest of the summer. We're reaching out to all our vendors to make sure they're aware of the issues we're having, and we're looking into who could have called you."

"Do you want the number? It came up on my phone."

"Yeah, that would be great."

Marco read off the number, and I wrote it down. Then sighed. It was a generic number for the town. One a bunch of the offices went through. It wouldn't help me narrow down who called, but it was a step in the right direction.

"You don't know who that is, do you?" Marco asked.

"No, but I'll find out. Please let me know if you guys want to come here. I'll reach out to some local hotels and see if I can get you guys lodging, too. It'll be easier to confirm things if you're right here in town."

"Yeah, that would have been better. I apologize for not double checking the person who called."

"Not on you, Marco. Thanks for taking my call today. I hope to hear from you soon."

"Thanks, Goldie."

We hung up, and I sighed.

"That sounded like it went well," Patrick said. He was leaning against my doorframe.

I nodded. "He thought we didn't want to call him ourselves. Thought we were chicken. Whoever called him said Unhinged wasn't good enough, and we found someone better."

"Wow. That's a shitty thing to say."

"Yeah. I can't say I blame him for not answering our calls."

Patrick laughed. "True. And you still don't know who's behind this?"

I shook my head, avoiding his gaze as I straightened up the papers on my desk.

"I don't believe you, but you obviously don't want to tell me."

"Not until I have more than a gut feeling."

"Just tell me one thing. Is it someone in this office?"

I shook my head instantly. "No. No one in this office has ever been on my list of potentials, and I pretty much have proof no one here did it."

"What kind of proof?"

"Marco gave me the number the call came from. It's one of the old, generic numbers at Town Hall. They haven't switched all their phones to the new system yet, and this number is the default those phones call out as."

"So, someone in Town Hall used a phone they knew couldn't be tracked in order to cancel the band and reschedule a caterer?"

I nodded.

"And you're not sure who?"

I tried not to smile, but I failed. Still, I wasn't going to admit it.

"That's what I thought. Let me know what I can do to help you bring him down."

I nodded. It was good to have people I trusted on my side. Damn good.

9

PATRICK

"This man needs a drink!" Arthur said as we sat down at O'Kelley's two nights later.

I was off Wednesday and Thursday since I was working the weekend, and Arthur talked me into attending guys' night again. My cheeks warmed at the attention he was drawing to me. I didn't like to do much of anything that made people focus on me. But my brother did not feel the same.

"He's twenty-seven today," Arthur told Hudson as Hudson set a beer in front of me.

"Shit, dude, really?" Ian said from my right. "I feel like an old man. I turned forty in January."

"You are an old man," Rowan told him.

Ian flipped Rowan off with a grin. "Yeah, well, I'm not the oldest one here."

Ian pointed to Nico as he took a seat next to James.

"What am I?" Nico asked.

"The old man of the group. Patrick turned twenty-seven today," Ian told him.

"Jesus," Nico gasped. "I need a drink just hearing that."

"How old are you?" I asked Nico.

"Forty-five." I didn't know Nico well. We'd only spoken a few times. Goldie's sister worked for him. She wasn't close to her sister, but Goldie always spoke highly of Dr. Allison.

"Forty-five doesn't make you an old man," I said. "Unless you're forty-five in dog-years or something."

The other guys laughed. Nico shook his head and grinned at me. "I feel like it sometimes, but nope. Just regular old human years. Hell, I never would have guessed you were so young."

I nodded and sipped my beer. It was something I'd been told most of my life. Whether it was a product of having to grow up fast after my dad died or just part of who I was, it didn't matter. Some people told me I had an old soul. I just thought I was more suited to be in my forties instead of my twenties. Staying out all night and drinking myself into a stupor were never appealing for me. I didn't judge those who enjoyed those things, but I felt like I fit in better with the guys I was sitting with. Men who were settled in their lives and content with their place in the world instead of searching for it.

Not that I was content, but I knew what I wanted my life to look like, and it bore a striking resemblance to the lives of the men around me.

"So, what are you wishing for this year?" Rowan asked me.

"A date with his boss," Arthur answered for me.

Again, my face warmed. The men we were sitting with were friends with Goldie. They knew her. Hudson was aware I had a thing for Goldie, but I was pretty sure the rest of them didn't know until my brother opened his big mouth.

"I can understand that one," Gavin said. He owned MacKellar Cove Inn with his wife, Piper. We'd worked with them one more than a few events. They were both great people. "Goldie is kind and thoughtful."

I nodded, not trusting myself to speak without spilling my guts about all the other things she was to me.

"Patrick's always had a thing for older women," Arthur provided.

"Dude!" I shouted.

Arthur shrugged. "Please. You need friends in your life. And they all know Goldie. No one here is going to do anything to hurt her, and I know you wouldn't do anything either. But maybe they can help you figure out how to get her to give you a shot."

I scowled at my brother, but the other guys went with it.

"She might have an issue with you working for her," Rowan said.

"I think it's the age difference," Nico added.

"Or maybe she's just not sure about dating," Ian told the group. "When Blake and Willie broke up, she didn't want to date anyone else for a while, even though they weren't right for each other. After being in a relationship that long, it's hard to move on. Even when it's the right decision."

"It's all the above," Arthur said.

"Why do you want to date her?" Gavin asked.

"Because he's in love with her," Arthur answered.

"What the hell?" I asked him.

Arthur shrugged and nodded to Hudson for another drink. He was driving me home, so Hudson refilled his glass with tonic water and a twist of lime. "You like her. A lot. I know it, but I don't know her, so I can't help you. But you're going to downplay it with these guys. They need to know you're not looking to hurt her. You care more than all of them combined."

I closed my eyes and counted to ten. I loved my brother,

but when he thought he knew what was right for me, he was a huge pain in my ass. I blew out a breath slowly and opened my eyes again, finding the others watching me.

"I've been there," Ian said. "It sucks to be in love with a woman who isn't willing to see it."

"You have to proceed with caution with Goldie," Rowan said. "She needs to know you're not going to run the moment shit gets real."

"And she needs to know you're serious," Gavin said. "But I know you need those things, too."

I nodded slowly, surprised at their insight and advice. "I've told her I want her, but she didn't believe me."

"Then tell her again. Ask her on a date. Plan something and tell her what you have planned so she knows you're serious." Nico met my gaze and held it. "There's more to her than just her divorce. Or being a mom. Goldie had to deal with her parents getting divorced and her dad starting a new family. She and Ally aren't close. That's not on Goldie, but it seems to me as though she takes it on sometimes. You need to understand all the moving parts to Goldie and be willing to see the entire person."

I understood exactly what Nico was saying, and what he wasn't saying. Goldie wasn't a toy, and she wasn't one-dimensional. She was complicated. And I needed to be serious if I was going to get involved with her. "I see all of her. And I want to be the person she turns to outside work as well as at work."

"Damn," Ian said. "Tell her that and you might be good to go."

I chuckled as the others nodded. One could only hope.

FRIDAY WAS NOT a normal day at work. We were getting ready for the events scheduled for the weekend, and after the disaster that was created for us the previous weekend, we were busy contacting every vendor and reconfirming their attendance. Again. Goldie wasn't letting anything go to chance this time.

By lunch, we were all exhausted and a little cranky. Eve was off, which left Theo, Goldie, and me to make the calls. Howard was handling the welcome center, choosing to avoid contact with vendors in favor of families arriving for the weekend instead.

"This sucks," Theo said after he hung up his latest call. "We need a break."

"I'm ordering in lunch. What do you guys want?" Goldie said.

Theo and I exchanged a glance and grinned. "Tacos," we said together. It had become a running joke for us that tacos were our chosen food. We always requested them when we were asked.

Goldie laughed. "I should have known. I'll put in an order. Will one of you check with Howard?"

"I'll check with Howard, then place the order. That's part of my job, not yours," I told her gently. She was the boss. I was the assistant.

"Thank you," she said, sighing heavily. "I think I'm going to get some fresh air for a few minutes."

Theo followed her out the door and disappeared into his office. I wanted to see if she needed anything else, but I wanted to give her a few minutes first.

Howard smiled when I told him we were ordering tacos and gave me his order. Knowing what Theo and Goldie liked, I called in our food. It was busy at lunchtime, but they said our order would be ready in twenty minutes, so I headed outside, hoping to catch Goldie before I left.

She was sitting on a bench under a large tree, staring at her phone. Her shoulders were slumped forward, and she'd kicked off her sandals. She looked defeated and worn out. I was fairly sure she hadn't taken a day off since the summer events started, even though she was adamant everyone else did so no one got burned out with the extra hours. She needed a break.

"You doing okay?" I asked as I approached her.

She straightened immediately and forced a smile to her tightly drawn lips. Lines around her eyes were deeper than normal, showing her exhaustion. I knew better than to tell a woman she looked tired, but she really did.

"I'm good. Just hoping we didn't overlook anything for this weekend. Are you going to get lunch?"

"Yep. They said it'll be ready soon."

"I can go. You don't have to."

I shook my head. "Take a break. Just enjoy the fresh air for a little while. You've been working every day, haven't you?"

She avoided my gaze. "I need to make sure everything is done right."

"And it is. But you can take time off to sleep."

Her spine stiffened. Her lips thinned to a single line. She did not like me telling her what to do. "I can take care of myself."

I sat next to her and took her hand. She tried to pull away, but I held on. Not tight enough that she couldn't get away from me if she really tried, but enough to make it clear I didn't want her to.

"You are amazing. You're strong and smart and endlessly capable. I've never doubted for a second that you couldn't take care of yourself. But I worry about you. I see the hours you're putting in. You weren't like this last summer. Is something going on that I should know about?"

She avoided my gaze and shook her head. "I'm just trying to make this the best summer yet."

"And what about next summer? Will you do the same?"

"I don't know. Probably. Why is that a bad thing? This is a beautiful town. It's an amazing place to live. I want others to see that, to feel it and know it. I want this summer to be amazing so I can continue—"

"Continue what?" I whispered. There was definitely something going on.

"Nothing. Just continue bringing visitors here and showing them how great MacKellar Cove is."

"I don't believe you. There's more to it. I wish you felt like you could be honest with me. That you knew I'm here for you. Whatever you need."

"Are you?"

I sighed and moved closer to her, close enough that my thigh rested against hers. I wrapped my fingers through hers and rested our hands on my leg. "Always, Goldie. I meant what I said a few weeks ago. I want you. But it's not just me wanting you. It's me wanting to know you. To be here for you. To show you that I'm interested in you as a person and as a woman."

"There's a difference?" She laughed.

"Yes." I moved my hand to her wrist and skimmed my fingertips over her pulse. "I want to know you as a woman in every possible way I can. I want to know what your lips taste like and how you like to be touched and what it feels like to wake up next to you in the morning. But I want to know you as a person, too. To know what makes you tick. What makes you smile. What you need when you've been working too many days straight and feel like you're facing the world alone."

She swallowed roughly and held my gaze. Her lips parted as she drew in a tentative breath. "Mayor Levine wants to fire me."

"What?" I gasped. "Fuck. He's the one who called Unhinged and Chef Julian, isn't he?"

She nodded. "I think he is. I can't prove it, but he called me into his office first thing Tuesday. He's the only one who would have anything to gain by messing up the events this weekend. He has the power to fire me, and he's already told me he plans to if I don't reduce budget by fifteen percent and make everything perfect this summer."

"That's ridiculous."

She shrugged. "It's the rules of his game. I have no recourse."

"You can get him fired."

"For what?" she asked with a mirthless laugh. "It's not against the law for him to be an ass or for him to want to spend less of the town's money. He thinks I'm under-qualified for my job. He'll bring in a man who can do it ten times better than me and he'll be the hero."

"He's an asshole who let the little bit of power he has go to his head. Why does he think anyone is going to let this go?"

"Because no one knows. Because it all happens behind closed doors. Because he's been getting away with his behavior for years." She sounded more defeated than I'd ever heard her.

"I want to take you out," I blurted.

"Excuse me?"

"A date. I want us to go out on a date. Nothing crazy, but

we both need a night off from thinking about work. What do you say?"

"We have too many things going on this weekend. I can't be away from it all. Not when I know Mayor Levine will try to do something."

"Then Tuesday. Or Wednesday. Next week. You pick the date and I'll set everything up."

"Set everything up? What do you have to set up?"

"I just meant I'll make reservations. Please, Goldie. I want to take you out. One night."

She smiled softly, her lips barely curling up in a grin that I knew would have been bigger if she wasn't so exhausted. "Okay."

I wanted to jump up and pump my fist in the air, but I held it in and just smiled. "Okay."

She chuckled as though she knew I was holding back my excitement, then stood. "I should head back in. And you need to go get food. Theo's going to chew off his arm if you don't hurry."

"Theo will survive. You're more important."

"Thank you, Patrick," she whispered.

I squeezed her hand, then let go and walked to my SUV. When I looked back, she was watching me. I couldn't do anything about my grin when I saw that.

She shook her head and turned toward the building. I watched her until she was inside, then gave myself a minute to celebrate that Goldie finally agreed to a date.

FRIDAY NIGHT WAS A SUCCESS. Saturday started out that way. I was cautiously optimistic about the day. I didn't know why, but it felt like it was going to be a good weekend.

After the big events the weekend before, this weekend was more subdued. Friday night started with a movie in the square. MacKellar Theater closed down for the night and donated the equipment and the movie so the whole town could watch together. Vendors came in from neighboring towns to provide additional food options for the people who were spending their evening in the park.

Saturday was the MacKellar Cove amateur burger contest. The only people allowed to enter were people who cooked at home. No chefs or restaurants allowed. It was another of Goldie's amazing ideas to get the town involved. She said some of the best food was made by people with no training. She wanted to showcase the unsung heroes of the town. Parents who worked hard to provide for their families. Home cooks who enjoyed cooking but never considered it as a profession. Anyone who wanted to join in.

There was no entry fee, and the food was all provided for the chefs. There were no limitations to what they could make, as long as it could be called a burger.

"Have you tried this?" Theo asked, joining me toward the edge of the park. Catherine Park was stuffed with people eating burgers and enjoying the beautiful spring day.

"What is it?" I asked him.

"Mac and cheese stuffed burger. I thought they were joking, but it's so damn good." Theo took another bite and groaned. "You gotta try this."

"I will. How many burgers have you had?"

"Too many to count. I'm just glad they're all sliders so I can eat more of them. The flaming burger was good, but it lived up to its name. I needed about a gallon of milk after that one. The Mexican burger was different, but it had a ton of flavor and the tortilla shell as a bun was genius. The Italian burger was tasty. But this one is my favorite."

"I'm glad you're enjoying everything." I laughed at him as he took another bite, smearing gooey cheese across the side of his face.

"Where's the boss?" he asked.

"Last I saw, she was making the rounds. Why?"

"Just making sure there aren't any issues today."

"There better not be. She needs a break."

"Agreed. She's working too many hours. She'll be burned out by July Fourth at this rate."

"That's what I said, too. Hopefully, she'll slow down a little. But she's worried about Mayor Levine and... the budget stuff." I didn't think Goldie wanted Theo to know the mayor threatened her job. Hell, she didn't seem like she wanted me to know either.

"We'll make it right. She's done more for this town than anyone ever has. Including Mayor Levine. She deserves a bigger budget, not a smaller one."

"Yeah, well, as long as she gets a budget, we'll make it work."

Theo popped the last bite into his mouth and clapped me on the back. "Yep. Gotta grab another burger. You want one?"

I glanced around for Goldie and didn't spot her, so I nodded and followed Theo into the crowd toward the burgers.

10

GOLDIE

I HELD MY BREATH AS THE LAST FIREWORKS FADED INTO THE night air and the crowd cheered. Everything went off as planned. Every single thing. It felt like it wasn't real. Like some disaster was coming. But none happened yet. And the night was over. Was it possible we were going to make it through the weekend unscathed?

People filtered out of Catherine Park toward their vehicles and homes and hotels. I smiled and said good night to people when they thanked me for the event. I still held my breath. There was nothing else to do, but I was tense.

"Hey," Patrick said, coming from out of the crowd. He looked good. He wore a pair of dress pants with a golf shirt that brought out the bright blue of his eyes. His smile was tentative but kind. His glasses caught the light of a passing car and hid his gaze from me for a second.

I wanted to sink into him and rest for a minute. I'd never admit that, but it was all I wanted at the moment.

"Hey," I replied when he got closer.

"I didn't notice any issues today."

I shook my head. "None. I'm still not sure it's real."

"It's real. You did amazing. People raved about the burgers and the variety and how good everything was. That was a great idea."

I smiled. When I first thought of it, I kept it to myself. I never thought it would be a success. I was so happy to be wrong. The vendors smiled all day, and the money they each brought in was great for their families. A few of them donated the funds back to the Tourism Department to help pay for future events, which I appreciated more than they knew.

"People seemed to have a lot of fun. And having fireworks again was a good way to end the evening."

"I thought so, too." Patrick stepped a little closer. His scent tickled my nose and drew me toward him. "Are you ready to go home?"

I shook my head. Paul got a ride home earlier with a friend, and I was exhausted, but standing in the evening light with Patrick, no one else around, cast a spell on me and made me want to stay right there.

"What else do you need to do?" he asked.

"Nothing," I admitted. "I'm just not ready to go home yet."

His gaze snapped to mine and awareness filtered in. He drew a breath and let it out slowly, closing the distance between us with the same painstaking patience.

"Where do you want to go?" His voice was barely above a whisper with a rough, jagged edge to it that touched all my nerves and lit me up.

"I don't want to go anywhere. I want to stay right here." The confession came without a thought, without hesitation. I told him I wanted to have hope, but I was still scared. Getting involved with him was not a good idea. He was too young and too attractive, but I couldn't find it in me to continue resisting him.

"Goldie, I'm going to kiss you. Is that okay?" His hand found mine in the darkness, his fingers threading through mine and pulling me ever so slightly closer.

I nodded, knowing it was all the encouragement he needed to finally cross that line I'd drawn between us.

He jumped over the line, our joined hands going behind my back to pull me into his body. His other hand went straight to my hair, tilting my head as his lips met mine.

Sparks lit inside me, brighter and better than the fireworks that dazzled the town. His lips parted and opened mine with them, giving him access to press his tongue into my mouth. He swiped through once, then tangled his tongue with mine and groaned as he pressed his body impossibly closer to mine.

Jesus, the man could kiss. It was like an orgasm for my mouth. It had been an embarrassingly long time since I'd been kissed, but never in my life had I been kissed like Patrick was kissing me. Like I was the one and only thing that consumed him. Like he couldn't get enough of me as he was devouring me.

A kiss was always just a kiss before, but this kiss was the kind that told me I'd been missing out on so many things.

His fingers tightened in my hair, then released and trailed down my throat. He eased them over my shoulder and down my arm before snaking that hand around my body and clasping a hold of my oversized butt.

He pressed his hips to mine, letting me feel the erection throbbing between us. Dear God. He was just as lost as I was. Just as ready to continue the kiss, and everything else, right then and there.

Then he eased back, withdrawing from me with the

same painful slowness he used when approaching me, this time feeling like he couldn't bear to part from me as he was doing it.

"Fucking hell," he breathed. "I always knew kissing you would be amazing, but that was..."

"Yeah," I agreed.

He looked at me with a smile that could only be described as boyish. "I can't wait for our date."

I'd almost forgotten he talked me into that. I put it in a box and set it aside because if I let myself think about it, I knew I'd get anxious. But after that kiss, I was more excited than anything else.

"You haven't changed your mind about our date, have you?" he asked when I was silent.

"No," I blurted. Fast enough that he chuckled.

"Good. I'm looking forward to it, too."

"Why do you want to go on a date with me?" I asked. It had been bouncing around in my head, but I didn't have the nerve to ask him before. After that kiss, I had a hard time thinking his intentions were anything but honest, but men like him didn't date women like me. Not when I was his age, and definitely not now that I'm... not.

"I am amazed by you every day. I took the job working for you because I've always thought women made better bosses, more fair, and I love MacKellar Cove. But when I first applied, I wasn't really sure where I wanted to go with my career. Now, I know exactly where I want to go. I want to stay in the tourism department, working for you, as long as you'll have me. And I want the same for dating you. As long as you'll have me."

I snorted. "I'm not going to be the one who changes my mind."

He grinned. "Good. Then I get to keep you in my life for good."

I rolled my eyes. He was good. He was a flirt, and he made me feel good, but he also made it seem like he was serious. Like he really wanted to date me for... well, forever. It would end, but until then, I was going to try to enjoy it.

"Are you ready to go home now?" he asked.

"Not really."

"Then can I kiss you again?"

I smiled. "I'm willing to agree to that."

Patrick took my hand and led me to the covered area of the park. On the top of the hill and overlooking the water. It was where the performers set up and where picnic tables and chairs stayed through the summer.

As soon as we were under the cover, he spun and pressed my back to one of the support beams, pressing his body to my front. He held nothing back as he thrust his tongue into my mouth and cupped my butt, pulling me to him as he pushed himself against me.

It was a full body assault, one that left my head spinning and my heart sighing. I could fall for him. In another lifetime and another decade. He was the kind of man I'd always wanted to end up with. Pressed and polished, but also kind and passionate and empathetic. He got me in a way no one else in my life ever had.

When Charles and I met, we were friends. Over time, we became more and built a life on friendship, and lies. But with Patrick, everything felt different. Everything felt like it was just simple. It was there and nothing was going to change.

But that wasn't ever going to be the case. He would get bored with me when I didn't want to go out or he would decide dating an old lady wasn't fun. He would move on to someone his age, someone who could give him kids and a future that included all the things someone his age should and would want.

Until that happened, I was going to enjoy all the kisses I could get from the man who made me feel like I was still in my twenties and stunning. Being with him was new and exciting and fun. And when it was over, I'd have memories of our time together to carry me through. Because if he kissed like an orgasm, I could only imagine what it was like to have sex with him.

And I had every intention of finding out.

THE REST of the weekend was easy. I hated to use that word, but it was. Nothing went wrong, and we went into Monday with a new level of confidence in the events we had set up.

For all my confidence at work, inside I felt like I'd swallowed an entire butterfly farm. My stomach fluttered every time I looked at Patrick and he gave me that sexy smirk that said he knew what my body felt like under his fingertips. It sent tingles from my head to my toes and everywhere in between.

He made me so crazy I thought about sneaking home for lunch on Tuesday so I could have some private time to get myself under control. But I didn't get a chance to sneak away because he caught me.

"Where are you going?" Patrick asked, walking out right behind me at lunch.

"I was going to run home."

"Oh. I was going to ask if you wanted to join me for lunch."

"Oh, um, I guess I can do that."

"You don't have to if you need to take care of something."

My cheeks warmed at the innocent comment that struck too close to home.

"Why are you turning red?" he asked. His gaze scanned my body before settling on my face again. "Goldie?"

"I'm fine. I'm all good. Lunch is good."

"You sure? Because you're all flushed like…" He trailed off and ran his gaze down my body again, pausing on my nipples and licking his lips when I pressed my thighs together. "You're turned on."

"Fine," I snapped. "I am. After you kissed me the other night, I haven't been able to stop thinking about our date tonight."

"And sex?"

"Yes," I hissed.

"Are you hoping we'll have sex?" he asked.

I narrowed my eyes. "I assumed." I took a step away from him. "Unless you're not interested."

"No," he blurted, moving into my personal space. "I'm very interested. More than you know. But I don't want you to think this is just about sex for me. You mean more to me than a quick fuck at the end of a date. I figured you'd want to wait a few dates before we…"

"And I figured you'd want to have sex and move on."

"Seriously? Is that really what you think of me?"

"I don't know, Patrick. I don't know what to think. I haven't dated much, ever. I married the first man I slept with. We were together for almost twenty years. I've slept with men since him, but not many and not any that meant anything."

"You're saying I don't mean anything?"

I sighed heavily. "I'm saying I don't know what this is,

but I really like you. I'm not trying to mess this all up before we even go out."

"Are you sure? Because it kind of seems like you might be."

"I'm not," I said, stepping forward again and putting my hand on his arm. "Kissing you the other night was amazing. It made me want more, but that's dangerous for me. I told you I'm trying to have hope. For me, that means being willing to be open to possibilities. I want to be open, but I also want to make sure I'm not setting myself up for heartbreak."

"I'm not going to break your heart, Goldie."

I nodded. "I know you believe that. And I hope you're right."

"I am right. But I know I need to do a little more work to convince you that I'm in this for the right reasons and that I'm not going anywhere." He kissed my cheek and took a step back. "You should go home. Take care of yourself. Think about me and our date tonight. I'll see you later."

He didn't give me a chance to reply before he turned and walked away, leaving me feeling even more turned on, and a little bit pissed off.

I drew a breath and headed to my car. He pulled out of the lot ahead of me and turned toward town. I sighed and turned the other way, toward my house.

The house was quiet, as expected. Coming home in the middle of the day always felt wrong to me. Like I was violating some rule about being there. I stood in the middle of my living room and looked around, debating. Should I just get something to eat and go back to work?

I looked at the kitchen and knew I was going to be unsettled all day if I did that. I wasn't doing anything wrong. I had vibrators for this exact reason. Because I enjoyed orgasms, and I didn't always have someone to help me have one.

I opened my drawer and let the anticipation build inside me. My body tightened with it. I chose the vibrator I wanted to use and stripped out of my clothes, folding them and setting them on the end of the bed before crawling in.

The first buzz had moisture pooling between my legs. I spread them wide and closed my eyes, imagining Patrick there with me. I circled my nipple with the vibrator, moaning loudly at the touch. It had been a long time since I did this when I was home alone and I needed to let it out.

Knowing it wouldn't take long for me to go flying, I brought the vibrator to my clit. I kept the pressure light, the vibration gentle enough to tease me and inch me higher. I pressed a bit harder, my body jerking with the tremor that rolled through me.

"Patrick," I whispered in the silent house. "Oh, fuck."

I eased my vibrator to my entrance and pressed it inside until it hit my g-spot and made me cry out. I retreated, fucking myself with it until I was coming apart and needed the release.

"Yes," I grunted. I slammed the toy inside me, letting my body hold it in place while the external vibration stimulated my clit and sent me soaring and screaming and coming.

I panted on my bed, the vibrator sending after-shocks through me, and knew I wasn't done yet. I wanted Patrick, but until I could have him, I wanted to feel hands on me. I slid my fingers through my wet folds and back to my clit, rubbing fast and hard until it all sent me flying once more. Yelling his name and screaming loudly enough to make my throat sore, I came over and over again until my body was wrung out and ached.

I laid there a few more minutes, knowing if I had a

partner there with me, I wouldn't be done. My muscles were sore, but my body was still tense with the need to come. I couldn't do it again. But if I was lucky, those wouldn't be the last orgasms I had that day.

A thin layer of sweat coated my body, so I jumped in the shower to wash it away. I changed into clean panties and put on my clothes from earlier in the day, then went back to work, not caring that I never ate lunch. I wasn't all that hungry for food anyway.

Patrick was outside when I got back. He was sitting on the bench and looked like he was waiting for someone.

"How was your lunch?" he asked, standing as I approached.

"Good. How was yours?"

He held up his hand and shrugged. "Not nearly as good as if I hadn't been alone, but I have a very active imagination. Thinking you were doing the same thing I was made it very easy for me to lose my fucking mind. Which meant I still had time to pick up food. Are you hungry?"

My head spun with his admission, then spun again when he changed the subject to food.

"What?"

"Lunch? Are you hungry? Usually orgasms make me hungry. I thought you might be the same."

My stomach rumbled in answer for me, and he grinned.

He handed over a bag. "Enjoy."

I took the bag from him and gawked as he walked away, smiling like he hadn't just made me want to go home again.

And take him with me this time.

11

———

PATRICK

WALKING AWAY FROM GOLDIE WAS NEARLY IMPOSSIBLE. BOTH before lunch and after. But I knew waiting would only make things better. I wanted to do things right with her. That didn't mean pretending I didn't know exactly what she was doing or teasing her a little. But it did mean taking care of her in other ways, too.

The rest of the day was painfully slow. I expected it, but when I looked at my phone and it was finally time to leave, I nearly cried with relief. It was less than two hours until our date.

I stopped by Goldie's office on my way out. She was staring at the computer like it held all the answers to the world.

"You heading out soon?"

She jumped at my voice and straightened up. She forced a smile. I hated when she forced anything with me. I wanted her to be herself.

"Yeah. Just finishing a few things. I need to check in with Paul."

I nodded. "I understand. I'll pick you up at six-thirty?"

She nodded and turned back to the computer.

I wanted to ask what she was so interested in, but if she wasn't volunteering the information, it wasn't my business.

When I got home, I was restless again. The anticipation was getting to me. So was the thought of Goldie sneaking off at lunch to alleviate her anticipation.

I laced up my sneakers and put earbuds in, cranking up the music on my favorite running playlist. It wasn't the same as having Goldie to sink into, but a good run would help.

Before I took off, I did some stretches to loosen my muscles. I hadn't been running much. My muscles were tight, and I knew after my run I'd be sore. But I needed the distraction.

I took off down my street and turned down another, sticking to sidewalks and residential areas. Running on the road wasn't something I enjoyed, but running on sidewalks could cause just as many issues.

I dodged a family pulling their kid in a wagon and a few people walking dogs. I made the loop, reaching the back half of my run as my muscles started to ache. It was a good ache. The kind that reminded me I was alive and ready for anything.

By the time I got home, I was worn out and exhausted but feeling good. I stripped as I headed through my apartment, tossing my sweaty clothes in the hamper before I stepped under the cool shower spray.

I sucked in a breath, the shock of the cool water making me feel alive again. I leaned my head under the stream and let it run down my back until it didn't feel quite so cold.

With my eyes closed, I thought about the look on Goldie's face when she returned from lunch. Satisfied but anxious that I knew what she'd been doing. Surprised but happy that I brought her food. She continued to amaze me and make me want to do things for her. I'd never been so wrapped up in a woman, especially one who barely gave me the time of day. I couldn't explain it if I tried, but Goldie was different. I saw a different side of her by working together. She was beautiful, but there was just so much more to her that made me want her in my life.

I wrapped my hand around my cock as I thought about her. The way she laughed and how she looked when she was serious. Her love for MacKellar Cove and her care for all of us who worked for her. She protected the people in her circle.

I stroked myself as I imagined her touching herself. The images flooded my mind and swelled my cock to a painful limit. I wanted to see her, to touch and taste her, to know the sounds she made and the way she liked to be fucked. I wouldn't find out on our first date, but I hoped we'd have many more and I would learn everything about her.

My balls pulled up tight, and I grunted my release, moaning her name as I let go and came all over the wall of my shower. I slapped a hand to the wall, barely catching myself before my knees weakened.

"Jesus," I hissed. The woman was potent, and she wasn't even there.

I finished my shower and padded to my bedroom as I dried my hair. The restaurant I chose for our date was nice, but not too nice. It was the kind of place where you could wear jeans or a tie and fit in. I chose a pair of khaki pants and a pool blue golf shirt. I pulled a comb through my hair and made sure it wasn't going to get wild on me, then I checked the time.

My apartment was neat and clean. There were a few dishes in the sink from the morning, and the dishwasher needed to be emptied. I had no intention of bringing Goldie home with me after our date, but there was a part of me that hoped she'd ask. She wouldn't, and I knew she wouldn't, but my cock rose at the thought of getting inside her.

I told myself I was cleaning up because it had to be done anyway and I had time. I also told myself there was no way I was inviting her back to my place. Both were lies. I was thinking about it. I was aching for it. But if I was going to prove to her I was serious about something more than just sex, I needed to show her that.

The drive to her house was quick, like the drive anywhere in MacKellar Cove. Before I could get all the way out of the SUV, she was walking out the front door.

"I was going to come to the door."

She waved her hand. "There was no reason for that. I can walk out to a car by myself."

I nodded and hurried around to her side to open the door for her. She looked at me like I was crazy, but I saw the way her lips lifted as she sat down.

I rushed around and started my SUV, then pulled out of her driveway. Then it got awkward.

I didn't know what to say to her. At work, we talked about work. We flirted, but there was a subtle understanding that it was still work. Even after kissing her a few days ago, we still had that haze over us that said I worked for her.

Going on a date was different. We didn't have to do the whole getting-to-know-you thing. I knew her. She knew me. We weren't strangers.

But we were.

The restaurant was busy when we got there after a short and nearly silent drive. She met me in front of the SUV and smiled up at me.

It was all going to be okay. We would get through it. We were going to have fun.

"Why is this so weird?" she asked as we studied menus.

I laughed. "I've been trying to figure that out, too."

"I don't date much, but I feel like I don't know what to say. And I never feel that way at work."

"But there we're talking about work. Here it's different. Tell me about Paul. How's school going? Is he ready for exams?"

She nodded. "He's always ready. I never have to worry about his grades. He's thinking about taking some college classes in the summer."

"He can do that?" To my knowledge, he was only a freshman in high school. I knew older kids took college classes, but not kids that young."

"He's already taking sophomore and junior level classes. He's talking about graduating a year early."

"Wow. That's amazing. Right?"

She breathed a laugh and shrugged. "There are times I think so, and there are times I don't. He can have trouble connecting with the other kids his age. That's why I was so happy when he started dating Sam, Valentina's daughter. Sam's a good kid, but she's also more outgoing and has helped Paul to be a little more social."

"I never would have imagined your son wasn't social. You always seem like you're surrounded by people."

She smiled. One of those real smiles that made me feel like I won something.

A server approached and took our drink orders. He told us the specials and said he'd be back to get our dinner orders when he brought our drinks.

"Have you ever been here before?" Goldie asked as she looked at her menu again.

"No. Arthur and Sharon have, though. They both said everything is good."

"How's Arthur liking working for Hudson?"

"Good. Once he got past the interview stuff and Hudson and Anna. He was not going to take the job until he found out about all of that."

Goldie chuckled. "I don't blame him. Hudson was a bit of an ass when he thought he lost her. I'm relieved they worked it out."

"Yeah."

Silence fell between us again. I didn't know what to say. The server came back with our drinks and took our orders, then we stared at each other once more.

"So, are you close to your family?" she asked.

I sipped my drink and nodded. "I am. My dad died when I was seven, so it's always just been Mom, Arthur, and me. Of course, now Sharon and the kids are in the picture, and I love them, and there's Dick."

She choked on her drink. "Excuse me?"

I grimaced. "My mom's boyfriend."

"His name is Dick, or that's what you call him?"

I snorted. "Both, I guess."

"Why don't you like him?"

"He's just not a part of the family, you know? They've been dating about a year and he acts like he's one of us."

"And he's not?"

I grunted. "No. He's not. But I don't want to talk about Dick tonight. What did you do when you got home from work? You changed your clothes, I see."

"So did you." She raised a brow and smiled at me.

My blood heated at the visions that continued to race through my mind. "I did. I went for a run and then I got rid of some stress the old-fashioned way."

Her eyes widened. She licked her lips. She sucked in a breath that lifted her chest. The red top she wore pressed against her breasts and outlined her nipples just enough for me to see how hard they were before she exhaled heavily and they were hidden from me again.

"Patrick," she breathed.

"We don't have to pretend we're not attracted to each other, Goldie. I've been very clear about how much I want you. Even though you don't want to hear it, it's the truth. And before our date, I jerked off while thinking about you because if I hadn't, I might have taken you back to my place instead of bringing you here for dinner."

She inhaled sharply at my confession. "So, dinner is a precursor?"

I shook my head. "Dinner is because I want to spend time with you. Get to know you outside of work. Find out what makes you tick."

"No sex tonight?"

"God, you're killing me." I reached across the table and captured her hand in mine. I slid my thumb over the racing pulse in her wrist. Her eyes dilated. Her breathing sped up. She leaned closer to me. "I want nothing more than to drag you out of here and spend the night learning every inch of your body. To strip you down to nothing and lay you out on my bed and watch you touch yourself like you did on your lunch break today. To fuck you until neither of us can breathe or see straight, then have you again. I've been dreaming of the day you'd agree to a date with me, and fantasizing about the day I'd be able to touch you. But I know you think this isn't real for me. So, no. No sex tonight. But that doesn't mean I'm not open to sliding my hand up that skirt you're wearing and finding out how wet you are."

She gasped and shifted in her seat. "You're dangerous."

I smiled. "Only because I know what I want."

She bit her lip and looked up at me through her lashes. I was going to regret my choice to not have sex with her, but when the day finally came that I did, it was going to be worth the wait.

THE REST of dinner went well. We definitely shattered the ice once I made it clear we were not going to have sex. We talked and laughed and teased each other. I shared my dinner with her, feeding her from my fork and following each bite with a kiss.

It was sensual and sexy and frustrating as fuck. But it was everything I hoped a first date would be with her.

She tried to pay for dinner, but I flat out refused and handed over my card.

"Thank you," she said softly. "You know I'm not one of those women who expects the man to pay. Especially since I know how much money you make."

"Well, I'm not one of those men who thinks the person who was asked out should be responsible for the check. If I wasn't able to pay for dinner, I wouldn't have asked or I would have chosen a different place for us to go."

"Thank you."

I got the feeling there was more to her gratitude than she was saying, but I wasn't going to push it.

When we walked outside, the cool evening air was far too tempting to pass up enjoying it a little longer. "Want to take a walk?" I asked.

She nodded. "That sounds nice."

Most of the towns up and down the Saint Lawrence River had sidewalks and were easy to wander through. Even though we weren't in MacKellar Cove, I knew we would be able to walk for a while, maybe even end up near the water.

I took her hand in mine and set off down the sidewalk that ran in front of the restaurant. We were quiet for a few minutes, letting the night be our background noise as our food settled.

"I haven't been fair to you," she said after a little while.

"What do you mean?"

"I've put a lot of my own issues on you, and that wasn't right."

"What kind of issues?"

"My divorce and my own life plan. I had a lot of fun tonight."

"Tonight isn't over quite yet. And I hope you'll let me take you out again."

"Maybe I should take you out next time," she said, squeezing my hand.

"Yeah? Does that mean you're in this?"

"It means I like you, Patrick. I kept you at a distance because I didn't want to get hurt, but I like you."

"I don't intend to hurt you."

"I know. But I know most people don't go into a relationship with that intention."

"Oh, so we're in a relationship now?"

She chuckled and bumped me with her shoulder.

I stopped us on the sidewalk and turned to face her. The smile slid from her face as I reached up and cupped her jaw. I ran my thumb over the sensitive skin on her throat. She shivered.

"You're so beautiful," I whispered.

"You're always complimenting me."

"Because I know you don't see yourself the way I see you."

"How do you see me?" Her voice was barely above a whisper, as though she was afraid of my answer.

"I see you as a strong, independent woman. Someone capable of doing anything she wants. Someone who cares deeply for those in her circle and will do anything to protect them. But someone who rarely lets anyone care for her. You're full of passion, whether it's for MacKellar Cove or your son or life itself, it radiates from you. And when you unleash that passion on someone or something, it stretches far beyond where you think and is intoxicating to everyone around you."

She breathed a laugh. "Not everyone would see all those as good things."

"No, but you know who you are. You aren't willing to pretend to be someone else in order to make others happy. You're your own perfectly imperfect self."

"Thank you. I think."

"It's definitely a compliment. Watching you get worked up about something is such a turn-on for me."

"Most people think I'm bossy."

"You're the boss, but that doesn't mean you're bossy. Most people say someone is bossy when they aren't willing to listen to what they have to say. You're respectful and considerate of others. You're an amazing boss. And you're an amazing woman."

"Thank you."

"I'm going to kiss you again, Goldie. Are you okay with that?"

"Yes," she breathed.

She met me in the middle, just as eager for another kiss as I was. Her body trembled against mine. My hand rested on her hip. I was trying to be mindful of where we were, but after a few seconds with my lips on that woman and I was lost all over again.

I pulled back and heaved for breath as I stared at her. "Let's get out of here."

"Yes, please," she said with a smile that went straight to my dick. And my heart.

12

WE COULDN'T GET BACK TO MY SUV FAST ENOUGH. I FELT like a teenager again, stealing kisses from the girl I liked. Trying to hide before anyone caught us. Back then, even though I was young, I understood on some level that people wouldn't understand. She'd been my babysitter, the girl who stayed with me after school when my mom worked and Arthur had other activities. Allie was a neighbor, and after two years of her staying with me after school, she became a crush.

Two years later, she became my first girlfriend. She was a senior, and I was a freshman in high school. We snuck around because we knew people would think it was weird that she was once my babysitter, but we didn't care.

Our relationship ended when she graduated high school and went to college, but it taught me a valuable lesson. Don't let anyone outside the relationship define the relationship.

As I hurried back to my SUV with Goldie's hand in mine, desperate to get her alone, I remembered that lesson.

Whatever happened with Goldie and me was between us. No one else got a say.

"I haven't run that fast in a very long time," she gasped as we settled into the vehicle.

I grinned and cranked up the engine. All my rules about not sleeping with her on the first date were flying out the window. I wanted her. More than I'd ever wanted another woman in my life. I couldn't stop myself, even though we had a twenty-minute drive back to MacKellar Cove.

"I'll drive fast," I promised her, backing out of the parking space and taking off down the street. I put my hand on her thigh, pulsing when she shifted toward me so my hand slid between her thighs. "You're playing a dangerous game."

"Who said I'm playing?"

"I need you to know this isn't how I planned tonight to go," I told her. My hand eased higher, her thighs parting for my wandering fingers.

"It's how I planned tonight to go."

"It is?"

She nodded. "I know how crazy my life is, Patrick. I know I'm not the most desirable woman on the planet. I understand what this is. It's not going to last forever. Because of all that, I'm not holding back. I like you. There are times it's too much, but I enjoy spending time with you. Mayor Levine is looking for a reason to fire me, and I'm hoping this isn't it, but—"

"No. Hell no. This is consensual. This is a mutual thing. I do not feel pressured or forced. I know I can say no to you at any moment. Really, I feel like the opposite is almost true. Like I'm forcing you."

"You're not," she declared. "Not at all. I trust you. And I am going into this with my eyes wide open."

"And your legs?" I teased.

She spread them a little farther. "That, too."

My hand slid all the way up, finding her warm center and damp panties. I groaned and pressed a finger against her body.

"Patrick," she whimpered.

"It's killing me to not be inside you already," I admitted. I pulled her panties to the side and slid my fingertip along her entrance.

She moaned and shifted forward to give me better access. "Please."

I pressed a finger into her, gritting my teeth at the feel of being inside her body. It was hard to focus on the road with the woman I'd been fantasizing about for a year wet and willing in my car. "You're so damn wet."

"I've been thinking about you all day. It wasn't enough when I went home."

"It'll never be enough." The admission slipped out. One night, one month, forever, it would never be enough for me with Goldie. I wanted a lifetime with her. Many lifetimes.

"You feel so good." She shifted her hips to match the slow pace I was setting between her thighs. "I think I might come like this."

"I fucking hope so." I added a second finger and pumped in a little harder, making her gasp. "I wish I could watch you."

"Next time."

"I'm going to hold you to that." I pushed her panties to the side more and rasped my thumb over her clit. She moaned and leaned her seat back, giving me even more access. "Fucking hell."

My cock throbbed behind my zipper. I'd never finger-fucked a woman while I was driving before. It was erotic in every way. I had to keep my focus on the road, even though all I wanted to do was push her over the edge and see her fall apart. I slowed down to make a turn, and she whimpered with frustration.

"I might need to pull over," I admitted.

"No. Keep driving. I don't want it to take longer to get to your place."

I pressed the gas and her clit at the same moment, racing us closer. She panted, her hips lifting each time I thrust my fingers into her. She was getting closer to her orgasm, and I was praying I didn't come in my pants.

"God, you're beautiful," I whispered, stealing a glance at her. Her skirt was up around her waist, her white panties shoved to the side. My hand was buried between her legs. Her red shirt was shifted to the side, pulled tight across her breasts. Her eyes were closed, her mouth parted in an O. She gripped the sides of the seat, bracing herself as she climbed the mountain toward bliss.

"Oh, God," she moaned.

"Let go for me, Goldie," I begged. I ignored her earlier plea and pulled over so I could watch her come apart.

She tensed, then threw herself forward, her orgasm pulling everything tight. She screamed, moaned, and begged me to never stop making her feel like that.

If she only knew.

My dick pulsed, desperate to get in on the action. I'd never seen anything more beautiful than Goldie letting go and falling apart. She was stunning. And I wanted to see that over and over again.

"I don't think I've ever come that hard," she admitted when she calmed down enough to take a full breath. "Wow."

"Wow, yourself. That was beautiful."

I eased my hand from between her thighs and licked my

fingers clean. She watched me, her pupils dilating with each finger I sucked on.

"I never thought that could be so sexy," she whispered.

"You're sexy."

She smiled. "And you pulled over."

"I had to watch. I'm not going to apologize. If I'd missed that, I never would have forgiven myself."

"Then you better drive fast or I'll be returning the favor right here. And I'm not skinny enough for that to be easy."

"Fucking hell," I groaned. The thought of Goldie sucking my dick was enough to nearly end my hopes of being able to hold back. I hit the gas, sending us flying back against the seats.

I kept both hands on the wheel and drove like a crazy man. Goldie fixed her clothes so we could get out of the vehicle without drawing attention.

We made it to my apartment in record time. I slammed the vehicle into park and reached for the handle to get out just as her phone vibrated.

She looked at me, then dug out her phone. "It's Paul."

Just like that, I knew our night was over. Her son would always come first. I knew that was the way it had to be, and I was not upset by it. But the kid's timing was less than favorable for me.

"Crap," Goldie whispered. "I need to go home."

"Okay," I said without hesitation. I started the car and reached to put it in reverse.

She stopped me with a hand on my arm. "I'm sorry. I really wanted to come in."

I turned to her and cupped her cheek. "Paul comes first. He's your kid. It doesn't matter what's going on, you always need to be available for him. I would never ask you to change that. That's part of what makes you an amazing person."

"You're not mad," she said. Her voice registered her shock.

"No. Not even a little. Disappointed, sure. But not mad. Never mad when you're putting your son ahead of anything else. It's what I'd expect from any parent."

"You'll make a good dad one day."

I forced a smile for her and nodded. It was what I always did. I used to tell people the truth, but no one ever believed me when I said I didn't want kids. Admitting that to people made them look at me differently, so I quit saying it. Now, I just smile and nod when someone says something about my future never-to-exist children.

I backed out of the parking space and headed toward Goldie's house. She texted Paul on the way, keeping her phone in her hand and her focus on that until I parked in her driveway.

"I'm sorry our night ended like it did," she said.

"I'm not. I got to watch you come apart, and I'll be reliving that moment for the rest of the night. Maybe for the rest of my life."

She chuckled. "You're really good for my ego."

"You're really good for my spank-bank."

She breathed a shocked laugh and leaned across the console. "Thank you. And next time, I'm paying and you're coming."

"I might have to hold you to that," I whispered. I cupped her jaw and closed the distance between us. I wanted to make her crazy with a kiss, but she had to check on Paul so I kept it gentle, although no less potent.

When she finally leaned back, we were panting, and the

windows were fogged. She chuckled. "You make me feel half my age."

"Age is just a number," I told her.

"That's something only young people say."

"You're not heading for the grave yet, Goldie. You still have a lot of years left."

"I think you might have taken a few with that orgasm earlier."

I laughed. "Nah. Orgasms make you younger, not older. I think you gained a few years with that one. Next time you need two."

She groaned. "You might kill me."

"Death by orgasms. How did you know that's my ultimate fantasy?"

She laughed and leaned forward to kiss me once more. She pulled back far too soon and smiled. "Thank you for tonight."

"Thank you. I hope everything is okay with Paul."

She nodded, her face sobering at the mention. "It will be. Just drama with his father."

I kept my face and body neutral. Getting upset because of her ex-husband wouldn't do any good. I would love the chance to tell the man exactly what I thought of him and the way he treated his family, but it wasn't my place. Not when I was barely in the picture.

So, I kissed her goodbye and waited until she got in, then I went home and relived every moment of our date until I couldn't hold back and shouted her name as I came. By myself.

I didn't hear from Goldie the next day, which was a day off for both of us. I wanted to reach out, but I wasn't sure giving her an orgasm meant I was allowed to text and ask how her kid was.

Thursday, we were both back in the office. She wasn't there when I got in, as always. I went through emails and checked voicemail, making sure I knew what needed to be confirmed for the day and laid out the plans we were working on for August events. The entire summer was planned out, but some guests hadn't been confirmed yet.

When I heard Goldie arrive, my pulse spiked. A smile crept onto my face. I couldn't wait to see her, which made me feel like a lovesick puppy, but I had been for a year. Now, I got to kiss the woman who made me feel like that.

"How was your day off, boss?" Eve asked Goldie as I walked out of my office.

"It was fine. Not as relaxing as I'd hoped."

Eve chuckled. "And here I thought you were going to tell me you had a hot date Tuesday night and spent all day yesterday tied to a bedpost. That was the only reason I could imagine you didn't call to check in."

Goldie huffed a laugh. "No to all the above. My ex wants Paul to visit him for the summer, and Paul is not interested in spending time with his dad and step-dad. It was a bit of a mess Tuesday night, and Charles accused me of trying to keep Paul from him, so yesterday I spent the day talking to my lawyer and making sure I wasn't violating our agreements by not forcing Paul to go see his dad."

"Ouch," Eve said.

"Yeah. But it'll be okay. Paul is the one who matters."

Eve caught Goldie up on the workday she missed while I stood there frozen. Her ex causing trouble was not good, but my brain was stuck on Goldie saying she didn't have a date.

Why wouldn't she admit that we went out? We agreed it was consensual. Was she embarrassed to be dating me?

I was spiraling, and before I could get the hell away, Goldie turned and saw me standing there.

"Patrick. I didn't see you."

"I noticed."

"How long were you standing there?"

"Long enough to have caught up on your day off." I forced a smile and went back to my office.

Goldie followed me.

I tried to close the door, but she pushed it open before it closed all the way. "Patrick," she hissed.

"Yes, boss?"

She tilted her head and closed her eyes. "Don't do that again."

"Do what?"

"Act like we are strangers."

"Aren't we? I mean, you just told Eve you didn't have a date and all about Charles causing issues for you."

"Was I supposed to tell her everything that happened between us?"

"No, but damn. I mean, you could have admitted we had dinner."

"I don't think that's a good idea."

"You don't think what's a good idea?" My neck tingled in anticipation of her next words. I knew they were coming.

She sighed. "I think it's better if we keep what's happening between us quiet."

"You don't want people to know we're dating?"

"I don't want...the office to know."

"We see these people every day."

"I know, but I don't socialize with them. Not saying I

don't like them, but they're not people I'm sharing the details of our date with. Are you?"

"I want to tell everyone I meet that you finally let me take you out."

"Patrick." Her voice was the mom voice. The one that said she thought I was being ridiculous.

"Don't act like I'm a child, Goldie," I spat.

"I'm not."

"You are, actually. You're making it sound like I'm being unreasonable by not wanting to hide who I'm dating. Why is it wrong to tell people?"

"Because if Mayor Levine finds out about us, he can use it to fire me."

"I asked you out. I pursued you. How could he use it to fire you?"

"If there's a way, he'll find it."

"Not if I don't file a complaint against you. And I'd never do that."

"He's my superior, and he has the power to fire me. He doesn't need a reason, not a good one. But he doesn't like women. He doesn't think a woman should be in charge. If he finds out about us, I have no doubt he'll use it as some kind of evidence that I'm unable to handle this job."

"So, you want to keep us a secret because of your job?"

"I'm a single mom, Patrick. I have a mortgage and a son who's going to college. I can't lose my job."

I sighed. "I get it. I understand. I'll keep it between us until you tell me you're comfortable with everyone knowing."

"That doesn't mean you can't tell your friends. Or your family. Paul doesn't know, but Valentina does. And my other friends. I just don't want us to become office gossip."

"I guess that means I can't kiss you then." I moved closer to her.

She took a step back. "Definitely not."

"And I can't sit next to you in meetings and find out if you're as wet as you were after our date the other night."

"You're going to make me question all my rules."

I laughed softly. "Good. Because I plan to break all your rules."

She sighed. "I need to go to my office now."

"You sure you don't need to go home?"

She glared at me and walked away, leaving me chuckling, and just as turned on as she was.

I DIDN'T SEE Goldie the rest of the morning. Arthur asked me to meet him for lunch, and Goldie was head down at her desk when I walked by her office.

"I'm going to O'Kelley's. Want me to bring anything back for you?"

"Yes, please. That would be great. Burger and fries."

"Got it."

"Are you having lunch with your brother?"

"Yeah. I try to get over there about once a week. We have dinner every Sunday, but that's with our Mom and Dick and Arthur's family, so we try to have lunch during the week."

"That's nice you do that. My sister and I barely speak, let alone get lunch together."

"I always forget you have a sister until you mention her. Nico talked about her, too."

"You know Nico?" Goldie asked.

I nodded. "Hudson invited me to guys' night. Is that okay?"

She looked a little panicked but nodded. "Of course. Yeah. Enjoy your lunch."

I wasn't sure what that was all about, but I left her office anyway. Her attitude was on my mind until I got to O'Kelley's. I was so focused on her that I didn't notice Dick was sitting with Arthur until I was almost at the table.

"There's my other boy. Thanks for coming!" Dick bellowed.

I shot a glare at my brother and took the seat between the two of them. "I didn't realize you were joining us, Dick."

"When you two mentioned that you get together every week, I figured it would be a good time for me to talk to the two of you without your mother around." Dick winked at me like we were sharing some secret.

"And why would you need to talk to us without Mom here?" I asked.

"Can I get you something to drink?" the server asked, interrupting before Dick could explain.

"Water for me," I told her.

Dick and Arthur ordered their drinks. Arthur thanked the server and asked if we could order lunch. The two of them told her what they wanted, then she turned to me. I ordered my lunch and asked for Goldie's to be put in a to-go bag when we were almost finished.

When the server left, I focused on Dick again. "What do you need to tell us about Mom? Is she sick?"

"Gosh, no. She'd tell you boys that herself. I just wanted to talk to you. Man to men."

Bile rose up inside me. I knew where this was going. I wasn't sure I'd be able to sit there and listen.

"Oh, God," I whispered.

"Yeah, that's sort of how I feel," Dick said. "I love your mother, and I can't imagine my life without her. I know I'll never replace your father, and I wouldn't want to, but I think of you two as my boys. And I want to ask your blessing to marry your mother."

Arthur looked at me with his mouth hanging open. He closed it once, then it fell open again. I wasn't much better.

The server came back with our drinks, and we barely managed to thank her before she walked away, leaving us to figure out how to answer Dick's question.

"Do you really think Mom wants to marry you?" I finally blurted.

"Well, I sure hope so. I mean, that's the part about asking someone, isn't it? You know, you decide you love them and want them in your life. But they might not be the same as you. It's scary to ask someone, but when it's right, it's right. You know?"

I didn't know. I couldn't follow any of what he was saying. And more than that, I did not want him to marry my mom.

"Of course you have our blessing," Arthur said. "We only want Mom to be happy. Right, Patrick?"

He growled the last two words and glared at me. I glared right back. How could he agree to let that man marry our mother?

Dick slapped him on the back and stood, dragging Arthur from his chair into a hug. He slapped Arthur again, then pushed him back into his seat and came around for me, dragging me up into a hug that knocked the breath out of me. I gasped for air as he shoved me back down and beamed at us.

"Thank you, boys. You just made me the happiest man alive. It means the world to me to have your approval."

We exchanged a glance and forced smiles on our faces and wondered what in the hell we just did.

13

GOLDIE

My stomach growled as I looked up at the clock. It was later than I expected Patrick to be back from lunch. I debated texting him just as I heard him say something to Eve.

I finished what I was doing and closed the program I was in. He walked into my office and dropped the bag of food on my desk, then turned to walk back out.

"Are you okay?" I asked.

"Yeah. Great." He forced a smile and moved toward the door again.

I was up out of my chair and rounding my desk before he made it out of my office. "What's wrong? Is your brother okay?"

Patrick laughed mirthlessly. "He's fine. Everything's fine."

I took a step back at his dismissive tone. "I don't believe you. Talk to me. What's going on?"

He shook his head. "I'd really rather not."

I flinched. "Um, okay. Did I do something?"

He scoffed. "Not everything is about you, Goldie. I have

other people, other things in my life than the woman who doesn't see me as a part of her life."

"Patrick, I never—"

He held up his hand to stop me. "I...I can't do this right now. I apologize, boss, but I need to walk away before I say something I can't take back."

I stared at his back as he walked away from me. Boss? What the hell happened? We were fine. I thought we were fine. I explained to him why I didn't want everyone at work knowing we were seeing each other, but did he really understand? He only called me *boss* when he was upset about something.

My food was cold by the time I stopped obsessing over what he was thinking and dug it out. I ate it anyway, knowing I needed the energy to get through the rest of the day. And my evening.

I checked my phone as I finished lunch, hoping for something from Patrick. Instead, I found a text from Charles.

> Why are you keeping Paul from me? We talked about him coming to visit.

I sighed. He didn't understand how his lies hurt our son. It bothered me that I never noticed how self-absorbed he was when we were together. Charles would lose himself in whatever grabbed his focus, often to the point of Paul and I not seeing him or having real conversations with him for days. He would sit at dinner but would stare off like he was somewhere else.

Once he admitted he'd been lying about who he was, Paul was crushed. He adored his father. They were close. But Paul was as hurt by the lies as I was. He felt like he didn't know his dad anymore. It didn't matter how many times I told him Charles was still the same father he'd always had, Paul couldn't get over the fact that Charles lied.

I felt guilty for thinking it, but it would have been easier if Charles never admitted that he always knew he was bisexual. If he'd told us it was a new discovery. It still would have hurt for my marriage to end, but I wouldn't have felt like the entire thing was fiction. And Paul wouldn't have felt like his father had tricked him.

It was like when he found out there was no Santa. He cried for an entire day. Nothing we said could console him until I told Paul we believed Santa was a part of all of us, and that the true magic of Christmas was in giving to others. Santa embodied that, so we kept the story going for him. He was still upset, but he understood and made a point of giving to others from then on.

> I have never and will never keep Paul from you. He's fifteen years old. He makes his own decisions.

I turned my phone over, but it buzzed a second later with a new text. Charles again.

> We're his parents. He is still a minor. He needs to listen to us.

> Maybe we need to listen to him. He's hurt. He doesn't trust you to be honest with him right now. I've forced him to visit you before because I want you two to have a relationship, but how many times have you made an effort to reach him where he is? You haven't been back here since you left. You haven't even tried to come to see him. You just sit there and demand he comes to you. How is that a healthy relationship?

My blood pressure rose with my words. They'd been building inside me for a long time, and maybe it wasn't the best thing to say to him, but he needed to hear them.

I stared at my phone and waited for a new text to pop up. I was sure it was going to be something about calling his lawyer. I cringed at the thought. My lawyer would not be happy with me for that outburst.

> You're right. I'm sorry. I've been selfish in creating a life I wanted after hiding who I was for so many years.

> I'm happy you've found your happiness. I really am. But you don't see the impact it has had on Paul.

> Or you, I imagine.

> I'm not important here. Our son is. I'm moving on from us, but he doesn't get that option. You're the only dad he's ever going to have, and he needs to know you actually care about him.

> You're moving on? Wow.

> What does that mean?

> Nothing. I promise you. Just a twinge of jealousy that I have no right to feel. I'm happy for you, Goldie. Truly. He must be an amazing man.

> Our son is an amazing man, Charles. He's the one you need to be worrying about.

> You're right. I have no right to get involved in your personal life. I apologize. And you're right about Paul. I haven't been a very good father to him the last few years. Do you think he'd be okay if I came up to visit?

I think you should ask him, but that's a good idea.

Should I come alone?

Paul has never had an issue with Leslie. Paul likes him and knows he's a good fit for you. That has never been part of it.

Thank you, Goldie. I really wish things had been different for us.

We have an amazing son. That was our contribution to the world as a couple. Now we can create other amazing things to add beauty to the world.

Any chance I'll get to meet the man you're moving on with when I visit this summer?

Bye, Charles.

LOL. Bye, Goldie. And thank you.

I smiled and locked my phone. Hopefully he reached out to Paul and Paul agreed to having him visit. Either way, it seemed Charles was willing to see he was not blameless. Which was definitely a good thing.

I dove back into work, securing a few more vendors for events toward the end of summer. The calendar was nearly full and so were the local hotels and inns. It was a great thing to see, even if I hadn't yet figured out how I was going to meet the new budget Mayor Levine handed down.

With a groan, I pulled out the budget again. That big of a cut was painful, and not something easy to manage. The fiscal year for MacKellar Cove followed the calendar year, which gave me a few quiet months to get creative, but when eighty percent of my budget was spent in the summer, there wasn't a lot of room.

I spent the rest of the afternoon buried in the budget. I had a few ideas, but none of them were all that appealing. Cutting head count wasn't an option, and reducing salaries, including mine, held little appeal. We scaled back on a few of the events, but since we promoted them before summer, people booked trips to the area to celebrate. We couldn't cancel events without risking tourists canceling their trips.

The sounds of the office filtered in late in the day. Eve called out that she was leaving, and Theo was right behind her. Patrick asked Theo to wait up and left without a word to me.

What the hell?

"You heading out soon, Goldie?" Howard asked, stopping by my office on his way out.

"Right behind you. Everything locked up?"

"All set. Have a good night."

"You, too, Howard. Thanks."

I shut down my computer and packed up my stuff. I debated bringing my computer home, but I decided not to bother with it. If Charles reached out to Paul, we would have some things to discuss.

I checked my phone for any messages from Paul before I left and noticed I had a message in Book Boyfriends Wanted. I'd almost forgotten I'd signed up for the dating app months ago. After so many of my friends met their significant others there, I joined. A few crappy dates later, I debated deleting the account entirely. I was matched with men who were not interested in dating a single mom, and who were not interested in dating a woman my age. I changed my profile description to reflect who I was, including a disclaimer that I was past my thirties with a teenage kid. My matches fell off significantly.

When I opened the app, I saw I had three new matches and two messages. I opened the first message and immediately deleted it. Just because someone couldn't send dick pics didn't mean they didn't try to tell you how amazing theirs was. Gag. I removed him from my matches.

The second message was from weeks ago from Lucky-Charm. I don't know why I didn't notice it.

LUCKYCHARM

Hi MagicMama. I was raised by a single mom. It's a tough job. And not one that scares me off, even though you kind of sounded like you were trying to. I hope to hear back from you.

My cheeks heated. If I'd seen his message, I would have replied. I felt bad and debated answering. Was it fair to Patrick?

I shook my head. Patrick and I were just starting to date. I could be honest with the guy about a real life relationship. And apologize for ignoring his message.

MAGICMAMA

Hi LuckyCharm. Don't know why I'm just seeing this, but sorry about that. Scaring men off seems to be my superpower, whether intended or not. I guess you don't scare easily.

I closed the app and tucked my phone away. I'd check again later and see if he replied, but I didn't count on it.

Paul was finishing homework when I got home. I asked how his day was and was pleasantly surprised when he said Charles called him.

"Yeah? What did he have to say?"

"He apologized, Mom. Can you believe it?"

"That's good. He owes you an apology."

"Yeah. He said he hasn't been a great dad lately. It's true, but I felt bad. It's not like he meant for it to happen."

My defenses rose. If Charles guilt tripped Paul, I was going to have to light into him. Paul didn't need, or deserve, that. "No," I said calmly, "but he's still your father and should be thinking about you and doing what he can to be there for you."

"I know. And he said he's sorry for not being here. He asked if he and Leslie can come visit us this summer. He wants to meet Sam and see what I've done with my room and stuff. Is that okay?"

"Of course it's okay. Your father is always welcome to visit you. And you are always welcome to visit him."

He nodded, but the smile slipped a bit.

"Why don't you want to go see him?" I hadn't been brave enough to ask the question point blank before. I knew there was a reason. There always was with Paul.

"I don't feel like I know him right now. He calls every week, but it's been a while since we've really talked. When I visit, Leslie is always there, and he's great, too, but he's not my dad, you know? I guess I just miss him."

"Maybe you should tell him that."

Paul shrugged. "He'll probably get mad."

"And if he does, you tell him how that makes you feel. Just because he's your father doesn't mean he gets to charge in and tell you how you should feel."

"Like you're doing right now?" Paul lifted one brown eyebrow, giving me the look his father used to give me when he was questioning my contradictory advice.

"Do as I say and all that," I told him with a laugh.

"Uh huh."

I ruffled his short hair, making him duck even though it didn't move. I kissed the top of his head, again earning a frustrated teenager sound. "Any thoughts for dinner tonight?"

"Nope. We can order a pizza."

I shook my head and walked toward my room to change. Pizza was always Paul's suggestion. The kid burned calories like it was his job. He was blessed with his father's lean build, which was why he was a star on the cross-country team, even as a freshman.

I checked my phone as I changed out of my work clothes and found a new message from LuckyCharm.

LUCKYCHARM

Good to hear from you. I figured I scared you off. But I want to be up front and let you know I've started seeing someone since I first reached out.

MAGICMAMA

You didn't try to describe all the ways you can use the appendage you would share pics of if only I'd give you my number, so not scared off yet. And same. On the seeing someone else. Although I'm not sure how long it's going to last.

LC

Uh oh. That's not good. Sorry to hear it.

MM

Thanks. I don't have a lot of hope for relationships, so I guess I expected it, but it's a bit of a blow. Especially because I'm not even sure what happened.

LC

Why do you think it's over then?

MM

It's complicated, but we work together. He went out to lunch today and came back angry and didn't say anything to me for the rest of the day. Maybe I'm being too sensitive, but that's not usually me. It just feels like he's done.

LC

Maybe he got some bad news.

MM

It's possible, but he wouldn't talk to me. Anyway, I'm sorry. I shouldn't be complaining to you about someone else. What do you like to do for fun?

LC

I'm sorry, but I need to ask you something. I know this is against all the rules and stuff, but is this Goldie?

I gasped and threw my phone on the bed. How did he know that?

LC

Maybe I shouldn't have asked, but you sound a lot like someone I know. If it's not you, I apologize.

I stared at the message for a long moment and debated. If he knew me, admitting it wasn't a big deal. Unless it was someone trying to manipulate me into a bad situation. Like Mayor Levine. Although why he would admit he knew me so quickly made no sense.

I drew a breath and thumbed out a response.

MM

Yes, this is Goldie. Who's this?

I chewed on my nail and stared at the screen.

LC

Patrick

I dropped onto the bed. What? How? Why?

MM

I'm confused. Did you know who I was before?

LC

No. The app doesn't give any identifying info. I had no idea until you started talking. I thought it was possible when I saw your profile, but I didn't actually know. I forgot I'd even messaged you until you replied today. I don't really blame you after how I acted this afternoon, but I'd hoped you would give me a little time to work through what's going on.

MM

I didn't do this because of your mood. It was just weird timing. As for giving you time, you didn't tell me you needed time. You didn't tell me anything. You just walked away from me.

LC

It was a rough lunch. I need to process everything.

MM

Okay. I will be here when you decide what you want to do.

LC

You. Always. It's family stuff, but it doesn't mean I want you any less. Please believe that.

MM

Okay.

LC

Can I take you to lunch tomorrow?

MM

I thought I was supposed to buy on our next date.

LC

Then you can take me to lunch.

MM

Sounds good. I hope you have a good night.

LC

It's better now. Thank you.

MM

See you tomorrow.

LC

Looking forward to it.

I smiled as I closed the app. I wasn't sure what the odds were that I was paired with Patrick, but it definitely made me feel better to know he was still interested.

14

PATRICK

I COULDN'T STOP SMILING THE NEXT DAY ON MY WAY TO WORK. When I was first paired with MagicMama on Book Boyfriends Wanted, a part of me wondered if it was Goldie, but I thought the odds were not in my favor. When she didn't reply, I forgot about it altogether.

But when she started talking, I knew it was her. And I knew shutting her out after lunch with Dick and Arthur was bad. I had to talk to her and try to explain. I tried to reach out to Arthur, but he ignored me. I had to protect my mom, which meant not having her end up with a guy who was no good for her.

Goldie rushed in just in time for our morning meeting. She was definitely frazzled looking, and as soon as our meeting started, I learned why.

"Our entertainment for the weekend canceled. I got the message last night," she said.

"Is it real?" Eve asked.

Goldie nodded. "I called them this morning. Their guitar player broke his hand. It's just bad luck. We need to see if we can find another group to play."

"Were these guys big headliners?" Theo asked.

"Headliners, yes, but they weren't big," I provided. I was the one who found the band and booked them. "They're out of Boston and set up their own small tour of the northeast. They're good. Lots of talent. Will they reschedule for later in the summer?"

"They're not sure how long it'll be before the guitar player is back at it. Sounds like it wasn't a bad break, but it might require more extensive healing time than a normal person because of how much he uses his hands." Goldie looked like she was going to fall apart at any moment.

"We will figure it out," I assured her. "I'll make some calls and check with some of the bands and singers we've already been in touch with. There were a few that wanted to come but we'd already filled spots. Maybe one of them has an opening this weekend."

Goldie nodded as I stood, effectively ending the meeting. I filed out ahead of everyone else, my phone already in my hand as I scrolled through numbers to find someone who could fill in at the last minute.

An hour, half a dozen phone calls, and some serious negotiation later, we had the spot filled. The band was from Syracuse and supposed to be off for the weekend after having spent the last month on the road. They'd replied to earlier requests, but by the time they chose a weekend, it was already booked with other events. They were looking forward to the chance to come to MacKellar Cove, even if it was on the heels of one trip and right before a new one.

I took the information about the band, along with the contract they already signed and emailed back to me, and headed to Goldie's office.

She was on the phone when I stopped in her doorway. She waved me in, so I took a seat across from her desk while she finished her call. After a minute, she hung up and raised her brows at me.

"I got a band," I said without preamble.

"Oh, thank God. I thought we were going to be in big trouble."

I shook my head. "All handled. Contract is signed and everything. We're good."

"Thank you so much. The mayor already heard about the cancelation and was threatening me. This saves my ass."

"And what a fine ass it is."

She breathed a surprised laugh. "You're too much."

"Not even close. So, um, about yesterday…"

"Yeah, what were the odds we were matched?"

I was going to tell her about Dick, but if she wanted to talk about us, I could get on board with that. "Well, good, apparently. We do work well together, both at work and not at work."

"We've only been on one date."

"True, but date two is very, very soon. And I'm hoping I can convince you to agree to date three next week."

"Waiting until next week? Are you playing it cool?"

I snorted. "Hardly. I just know weekends aren't really options for anything through the summer. Hedging my bet that you will be willing to go out during the week again instead of rejecting me over the weekend."

"Smart man."

"I do know you, Goldie. I know a lot about you."

"Yes, you do," she whispered. "Thank you for helping with this today."

"It's my job. I hope you know I do my job because I enjoy it, not because you're my boss."

"I've never wondered about that. I consider myself lucky

to have such an amazing team. We all work very well together."

"And that's why you don't want them to know about us?"

She nodded and chewed the inside of her lip. "I am worried about Levine firing me, and I know he'd do it. I don't think anyone will go to him, but if it's public knowledge, he'll find out."

"I understand."

"Are you sure? Because yesterday you were angry. I thought we were okay, but after lunch—"

"That had nothing to do with you," I interrupted her.

"It didn't?" Her eyes narrowed, and she tilted her head.

"No."

She was silent for a minute, studying me. "Bad news. You said in our messages last night maybe he got bad news. Did you get bad news?"

I sighed heavily. "Sort of. My mom's boyfriend asked Arthur and I if we would give him our blessing to ask Mom to marry him."

Her brows shot up. "Wow. That's... Dick. And you don't like him."

"It's not that I don't like him, but he's just not right for my mom."

"I'm sorry, Patrick. You told him you couldn't agree?"

I shook my head. "I didn't get a chance to say anything. Arthur said yes for both of us, and I didn't know how to say no. I thought he was on my side. And he's not answering my texts. I even went to O'Kelley's last night, but he left work early."

"He's avoiding you."

"Yep. But none of that had anything to do with you. I apologize for making you feel like it was your fault."

She shook her head, her blonde waves tumbling over

her shoulders. "It's okay. I'm relieved to know. And I'm sorry you're in such a tight spot."

"I'll figure it out." I stood and closed my tablet. "What time do you want to leave for lunch?"

"Noon?"

"Sounds good."

She smiled as I turned and walked out of her office. Noon couldn't come fast enough.

GOLDIE WAS beautiful when she laughed. It didn't happen often at work, but getting her away from the office made her light shine just a little brighter. She was gorgeous.

"I can't believe you did that," she said, trying to calm the laughter that still bubbled through her.

"I was not a great kid. My dad and I were close, and when he died, I kind of took advantage of my mom being overworked and exhausted all the time. Skipping school as a fifth grader was the least of her worries. Even though I got caught and blamed the dog we didn't have."

"Wait a minute, you didn't even have a dog? You told the school you were home because your dog was sick and you didn't even have a dog?"

"I told you I wasn't a great kid," I said with a laugh.

Goldie chuckled again. "I'm really happy to hear you've changed."

"Who said I've changed?"

"Well, you've never called in to work because your nonexistent dog was sick."

"I have other motivations for going to work these days. School was not nearly as much fun."

Her cheeks turned red. She ducked her chin.

I grinned and waited for her to look up again. When she did, I said, "My fifth-grade teacher was not nearly as sexy as my boss is."

Her cheeks darkened. She bit her lip. My cock rose. Damn, this woman. She had no idea the effect she had on me.

"I want to say thank you, but my fifth-grade teacher was this really old lady who hated kids and had been teaching forever and was miserable, so she was a low bar."

I laughed. "My fifth-grade teacher was cute. She was nice and sweet and very positive."

"Jeez, I'm feeling a little jealous."

I scanned her figure and shook my head. "Trust me, you have nothing to be jealous of."

Her eyes widened at my tone. She sucked in a quick breath. She met my gaze as her lips parted. "You make me feel like I'm half my age and half my size."

"I wouldn't want you as much if you were either. You're exactly who I want to be here with right now."

Her lips turned up at the edges. "Thank you."

"I mean that, Goldie. I will keep telling you until you believe me."

"I'm starting to get it."

"Good. So, when can we do this again? Preferably at night when I can kiss you senseless and take advantage of you."

She breathed a laugh and shook her head. "It's only taking advantage of me if I say no, and so far I haven't been saying no."

"Good. Then say yes again and let me take you out next week."

"Okay."

"Tuesday and Thursday?"

"Two nights?"

"Yep. If you're agreeing to go out, I'm taking advantage of it and getting two nights with you."

"I thought you went to guys' night on Thursday."

I reached across the table for her hand and slid my thumb over her wrist. "If you really think I'd rather be with them than you, I have not been clear about my intentions. They're not at all honorable, but they will be a lot of fun."

She laughed, her breath hitching when I tightened my grip on her wrist.

"I want to take things slow with you, but I'm not sure I'm strong enough," I admitted. "I want you so much, Goldie."

"I don't want you to go slow."

"Why don't you come to my place for dinner on Tuesday?" I asked.

She took a deep breath and nodded. "I'd really like that."

"Good. Me, too."

THE EVENTS PLANNED for June were relatively tame compared to Memorial Day weekend or July and August, but June was still busy. The band made it into town without any issues, and things were moving along well. Since it was a quieter weekend for events, no one was scheduled to work, even though we were all available if necessary.

My mom insisted on attending every single event to support me. When I mentioned I was off for the weekend, she insisted I give her the inside tour of what was going on and refused to listen when I said there wasn't anything going on that wasn't public. So, I was spending my Saturday afternoon with Mom, Dick, Arthur, Sharon, and the kids.

I wasn't complaining, though. The kids ran around and

had fun in the park. All three of them wanted their faces painted, then whined when they almost immediately rubbed it off. Sharon rolled her eyes and took them back for touch-ups. With half the other kids in town.

Dick went to get food, leaving Mom, Arthur, and I alone for a few minutes. I still hadn't spoken to my brother since our lunch, but I obviously couldn't do that in front of Mom.

"Dick asked me to marry him," Mom said once the others were gone.

"What did you say?" Arthur asked.

She looked between us. She smiled and looped her arms through each of ours and started walking. "He said he spoke to you boys."

"He did," Arthur answered for us. Again.

"And that you said you only want me to be happy."

"We do, Mom. That's what matters to us," Arthur said.

Mom smiled at him. "Thank you, sweetie." She turned to me. "It's not like you to not have anything to say."

I shrugged. "Arthur is saying it all."

She chuckled softly. "Which means you don't want to tell me what you think. Because you don't like Dick."

I almost laughed out loud at her unintended comment, but I kept it in. "It's not that I don't like him, Mom. I just don't know if he's right for you."

She nodded. "I understand that. He's very different from your father."

"Yeah. In every way."

"True. He's loud, and he inserts himself into things. He doesn't really know when to stop talking or when to hold his opinions. And he's always sneaking things to the kids when we tell him not to."

"See? Exactly." She got it.

"Life would have been so different if your father hadn't

died. I wish for that all the time, but it's not reality. He isn't coming back."

"I know, Mom," I said. The pang in my chest still ached when I thought about my dad. I didn't have a lot of memories of him. More feelings that were tied to memories that had faded over the years. What I knew was he adored my mom, and Arthur and me. He lived for us. And when he died, it nearly destroyed my mom.

"Dick asked me out for a long time before I agreed to date him. He's the kind of man who wears you down."

"And you want to be with someone like that? Someone who has to convince you to date him?"

She shrugged. "I wasn't willing to see who he was. I resisted letting someone into my life."

"Well, now he's here to stay."

"Maybe not. I haven't given him an answer yet. I wanted to talk to you boys. Find out what you were really thinking." She tightened her grip on our arms.

"If he makes you happy, that's what matters, Mom," Arthur said diplomatically. "We don't have the right to choose your happiness for you. We're no longer children. You have your own life."

She put her head on his shoulder and said, "Thank you, Arthur. That means a lot."

I felt the pressure of the truth bearing down on me. I could tell her how I felt, or I could bow out and hide behind my brother. If I admitted the truth, Dick would be gone. That was the best thing for everyone.

"I—"

"Hi, everyone," Goldie said from off to the side of us. "I'm Goldie. I saw the three of you and wanted to say hello."

As much as I was happy to see her, the timing sucked. Still, I forced myself to smile at her and introduce my mom and brother. "Goldie, this is my mom, Teri, and my brother, Arthur. Have you two met?"

"We haven't," Arthur said, releasing Mom to hug Goldie. "I have been wanting to meet you for months. Thank you, again, for passing my resume on to Hudson."

Goldie laughed. "You're so welcome. I'm glad it all worked out. Hudson is an amazing person."

"He is. He's a great boss. Which I hear you two have in common. My little brother sings your praises constantly."

My cheeks burned. I forced my face into a sour smile that no one believed.

"Oh, you're that Goldie," Mom said. "Patrick is always talking about you. He adores you. Um, working for you." Mom winced as she looked at me, which fooled absolutely no one.

"Thank you," Goldie said. "This is my son, Paul." She grabbed the arm of a tall boy a few feet away.

I never would have guessed he was her son. He had dark hair and dark eyes. Everything about him was different, except his height. But then he smiled, and I saw Goldie in him. "Hi. Nice to meet you."

"Nice to meet you, Paul. You're so tall," Mom said. "How old are you?"

"Fifteen." Paul looked more than a little uncomfortable with the questioning. And with being there in general.

"He is horrified to be here with me. Because teenagers aren't supposed to have parents. They just appeared out of nowhere, without anyone to take care of them for the first decade plus of their lives." Goldie rolled her eyes at her son.

"Mine were the same way," Mom said. "It'll change when they get a little older. Arthur's still pretty independent, but Patrick's my mama's boy."

"Mom!" I blurted. The last thing I needed was for Goldie to think I wasn't my own man.

"Oh," Mom gasped, as if remembering who she was speaking to. "I just meant he's no longer worried about me being around. He won't pretend not to know me these days."

"Who's this pretty young thing?" Dick said, walking up from behind us and shouting loud enough to turn half the heads in the park.

"I'm Goldie. And this is my son, Paul. Patrick works for me at the tourism department." Goldie smiled and waited for Dick to introduce himself.

Dick went all in and wrapped Goldie in a hug. "Well, damn, it's good to finally meet you." He stepped back, the drinks he'd brought over still in his hands. "I hope I didn't get anything on your clothes. I was just so excited. Patrick talks about you all the time."

Arthur snickered. Mom stepped forward and pulled Dick away from Goldie. Goldie shot me a look, and I nodded, confirming that was exactly who she thought it was.

"Patrick is a wonderful man," Goldie said.

"He is," Sharon said, joining our little group with her hands full of children. "I'm Sharon. Arthur's wife."

Arthur reached for Katie, the two-year-old, and she went willingly to him.

"Nice to meet you. I'm Goldie, and this is Paul." Goldie grinned at my nephews, neither of whom were paying her any attention. Henry went straight to Dick, and Nicholas, the four-year-old, hung on Sharon's leg.

"You're Goldie? Patrick's Goldie?" Sharon asked, her grin wide and bright. Until she realized what she said. "I mean—"

"Patrick's Goldie? What does that mean, Mom?" Paul

asked.

"Patrick and I work together, so they know my name from that. It's all she means, honey." Goldie smiled at her son, ignoring us for a minute.

Paul shrugged. "Okay. Weird, but okay. Can I go find Sam now?"

"Yes, go find Sam. Text me if you guys go anywhere other than the park."

"Okay. Bye." Paul disappeared into the crowd, barely waving before he left.

"Teenagers," Goldie said with her flaming cheeks.

"It's just how they are," Mom said. "Why don't you wander with us? Patrick was going to give us the behind-the-scenes tour for today."

I rolled my eyes and shook my head when Goldie gave me a questioning look.

"I'm sure that'll be wonderful, but I'm actually meeting up with a friend. Her daughter is my son's girlfriend, so we're going to pretend we're not spying on them together."

Mom laughed. "Good plan."

"You got yourself a smart one, Patrick. I like her," Dick shouted.

I nodded and flashed Goldie a look of apology. She smiled back.

"Well, it was nice meeting all of you. I'm sure I'll see you around. Enjoy your behind-the-scenes tour."

I widened my eyes at her, but she just grinned and winked at me before following Paul into the crowd and disappearing.

"I can see why you're in love with her," Mom said. "She's very nice."

"Nice to look at, too," Dick added.

I rolled my eyes. Kill me now. I agreed with Dick.

15

GOLDIE

I'D JUST FINISHED TELLING VALENTINA ABOUT MEETING Patrick's family when we knocked on the door to Book Boyfriends Unlimited for book club the next night. Valentina, bless her, understood why I was freaking out and screeched, "They called you *his* Goldie?"

"Whoa," Finley said as she opened the door. "Who called you his Goldie?"

"Patrick's entire family," Valentina answered for me. "She met them all yesterday."

"I guess your date went well if they're all calling you his," Finley said with a wiggle of her shoulders.

"If by good you mean they got dirty on the drive home from dinner, then yes," Valentina told her.

"Valentina!" I hissed.

"Who's talking about getting dirty? I need to hear this story," Elise shouted from the back of the bookstore.

"Goldie and Patrick had a really good date," Valentina said as we walked back to join the others.

Elise, Blake, Melody, Willow, Piper, Sofia, and Haley

were already there. We all said our hellos before they jumped on me again.

"We're talking dirty, dirty kind of good?" Elise asked.

"Elise," Finley admonished.

"Oh, please," Elise said, "not one of you is surprised I'm asking. Tell me everything, Goldie. Don't leave a single detail out."

"You act like you haven't had sex in years. What's going on?" Willow asked Elise.

"I like sex. A lot. And there's nothing wrong with enjoying it with my husband, or wanting my friends to have lots of it. It's been—" Elise looked at her phone "—two hours since I've had sex."

"I did not need to know that," Anna said as she joined us. She worked with Finley and had her own keys. Right behind her were Trinity and Laura.

"How long has it been for you?" Elise asked her.

Anna's red cheeks said not very long at all.

"Good for you," Elise said, offering a fist to bump.

Anna returned the gesture and shook her head. "How did I sink to your level?"

Elise cackled. "It's a great place to be where orgasms are a-plenty and the men live to please. I hope Hudson qualifies."

"He does," Anna said without hesitation.

"Damn, girl. Nice." Elise nodded approvingly before turning her gaze to me. "Now, back to you. How dirty are we talking? Sex in the car dirty or something else?"

"We did not have sex in the car," I answered.

"Okay, so something else. Want me to guess? I mean there's—"

"Dear God, please stop her," Melody said, reaching out to clamp a hand over Elise's mouth as she laughed.

"I always thought men would be the ones who talked about sex all the time. I never expected it to be so bad from a group of women," Haley said.

"Clearly, you've been hanging around the wrong women." Elise tapped her chin. "Of course, you haven't picked any winners for men either." Elise glanced at Valentina and grimaced. "Sorry, Valentina."

Valentina shook her head. "No sorry necessary. I am choosing to move on with my life."

"By moving under someone?" Willow asked.

"Yes!" Elise high-fived her.

I shook my head but hoped Valentina would answer the question. She deserved good in her life. A good man, and a good time.

"No men. I've been with Dawson for most of my life. Brantley introduced us our freshman year of college. We've been together since we were eighteen. I haven't dated anyone since then. I need a break." Valentina sighed and shrugged, but her lip wobbled just a touch. It was the only indication she was having more trouble with the end of her marriage than she was willing to let on.

"Well, good for you. I can give you some vibrator recommendations if you need them," Willow said.

Valentina snorted. "I've been married to a man who was screwing someone else for over a year. I'm all set in the vibrator department."

"Man, I love you guys," Elise said. "This is my happy place. Well, one of them. The other is—"

"No!" everyone shouted together.

Elise laughed loudly and shook her head. "You guys know me too well. Okay, Goldie. You still haven't told us about Patrick. How dirty was the drive home?"

"It wasn't that bad," I hedged. I loved them all, but I

wasn't used to sharing all the details of my sex life with anyone. Even Valentina and Anna didn't get everything, and they were my closest friends.

"Give her a break, Elise. Not everyone wants to share everything," Blake said.

"You're no fun," Elise said. She leaned closer to me. "A little under the skirt action or over the shirt action?"

"Under," I said.

Elise nodded approvingly. "Good for you. Although rumor has it Valentina and Willow can share vibrator recommendations if you need it."

"I'm all set there, too. But I'm hoping I'll be able to give my batteries a rest one of these days," I confessed.

"Love it! Yes! We should all give the batteries a rest once in a while. Okay, so now that we know about the dirty, what were you guys talking about when you walked in?" Elise asked. She looked between Valentina and me.

"Goldie met his entire family yesterday. They called her his Goldie," Valentina said.

"Is that a problem?" Finley asked. "I mean, the whole possession thing is a little off-putting for me, but I'm hoping they just meant it in terms of you two are together. Do you not want people to know?"

"No, it's not that. I mean, no, I don't want to tell everyone at work, but I knew his family knew we were going out. I was just surprised at how they addressed me. Instead of his boss or even someone he works with, I was just *his*." I shrugged, struggling to explain how weird it made me feel. And how weird it was that it didn't bother me as much as I felt like it should have.

"Do you think they see him as the boss instead?" Piper asked.

I shrugged. "I'm not sure. And part of me isn't worried

about that. It was more than they seemed like they knew me. Like they knew a lot about me. More than if I was just his boss."

"You think he's been talking about you," Anna said. "Want me to see if I can find something out from Arthur?"

I shook my head. "No, I don't want it to be weirder than it already is. I guess it's not a big deal, but we've been on two dates. One was just lunch. And it felt like they were saying he's been talking about me a lot longer."

"You said he's been flirting with you forever. Almost since you hired him," Laura said.

I nodded. "True. But it's just strange. I don't know."

"I think all the times you thought he was joking, he wasn't. It sounds like he really likes you. A lot. And you've been running from it while he's been trying to get you to notice him," Anna said.

Could she be right? It fit, but was it possible? And if it was, what did that mean? Things with Patrick were fun. We were enjoying spending time together. Was it possible he was that serious?

"Or maybe I'm wrong," Anna blurted. She pasted on a smile I didn't believe. "You guys are having fun. You don't need to worry about him being serious. It's fine."

I looked at her, then scanned the rest of them. "What is going on?"

"You're spinning out," Trinity answer for the rest of them. "Anna saw you starting to go. She's trying to pull back so you don't freak out because Patrick is more in this than you are."

"You think he is?" I shouted.

Trinity nodded and patted my hand. "I think you like him a lot more than you want to admit. I've been there. The hard part of that is you both need to find a way to be honest with each other. If you can't be, it doesn't matter how serious either of you are, it isn't gonna work out."

I sucked in a breath that didn't feel big enough. They were all staring at me, which only made my lungs feel tighter. I blew out the breath and, God bless her, Blake asked Piper how Zoey was doing. Zoey hadn't been to book club much since she had her baby, the third in their busy household.

The others talked around me while I tried to make sense of what was happening. If Patrick was serious, was I leading him on? Or was I serious about him?

But maybe the biggest question was if I could take the risk of letting him in without knowing if he was going to crush me.

I WAS STILL TRYING to figure out the answer to those questions on Tuesday night when I knocked on Patrick's door. He lived in a converted building on the north side of town. It held eight units, according the to mailbox in the lobby. He was on the second floor, unit D.

He answered the door a minute later, barefoot in shorts and a golf shirt with a bright smile. He leaned forward to kiss my cheek before pulling me inside. "Hi."

I couldn't help but smile back. "Hi."

The corners of his eyes crinkled behind his glasses as his smile widened. "I'm glad you came."

"Me, too." It was an honest answer. I was happy to be there. Even as I was trying to figure out where things were going, I was enjoying our time together. I told myself I didn't need all the answers about the future right now.

"Dinner should be ready soon. Do you want a glass of wine or something else to drink?"

"Just water, please. I don't like to drink when I'll be driving."

He nodded and led the way to his kitchen.

His apartment was neat. No shoes were at the door but were tucked neatly into an entryway closet he opened for me to put my stuff. He had a hook for his keys and a small basket in the closet where his wallet was. The rest of the apartment was small, but it was clean and smelled amazing. Candles burned around the open living room, dining room, kitchen combo space. A door on the far side led to a bedroom, and another closed door must have been the bathroom.

He filled a glass with water from a pitcher in the fridge and handed it to me. "I didn't think to ask if you have any food allergies or things you really don't like."

I shook my head. "I'm pretty much equal opportunity with food. I enjoy salad as much as I enjoy chocolate." I paused. "Well, maybe not quite as much."

He shook his head and moved closer to me. He wrapped an arm around me and leaned down. His lips pressed lightly to my neck, then his tongue slid over my heated flesh. "You're beautiful, Goldie. I'm barely keeping my hands to myself right now because I owe you dinner before I make us both crazy in my bed, but don't ever doubt how stunning you are."

His raspy words strummed every chord in my body like he owned them. I shivered in his arms, resisting the urge to beg him to forget about dinner and go straight to dessert. Dessert was always the best part of the meal anyway.

He kissed my jaw again, then took a head-clearing step back and smiled at me. He was a few inches taller than me barefoot. Looking up at him was different since I typically wore heels at work. I liked it. I liked the feeling of him being able to protect me, even though I would never admit I loved the thought of being taken care of.

"Okay, so we have risotto with shrimp and asparagus. The asparagus was too good to resist. I hope it's okay."

"Sounds delicious. Smells delicious."

He closed his eyes and smiled. When he opened them again, his gaze went straight through me and lit me up.

The intensity of it made my breath stutter. My pulse raced, my heart skipped. I couldn't remember the last time someone looked at me like that. Probably never. It was intoxicating. Who needed wine when I had a man who looked at me like I was all he needed to survive?

The need to define what we were doing pressed on me, but I pushed back on it. I didn't want to ruin things. I wasn't ready for that. I wanted more time with him. More time to enjoy life exactly as it was.

"Okay, before I lose my mind, let's eat." He gave me a sheepish grin that was both boyish and devastatingly panty-melting.

"Sounds good."

He handed me a heavy stoneware plate and gestured for me to go ahead of him to the steaming pan on the stovetop. I filled my plate, not thinking twice about how I looked with an appetite. This was Patrick. He knew me. He'd seen me eat more than a few times. And I was not willing to pretend I didn't enjoy a good meal.

We sat across from each other at the table, digging into our food. I groaned. "Oh, my God, this is so good."

He breathed a laugh. "Thank you."

We devoured our food, the conversation flowing easily from work to summer to growing up. I laughed at a story

Patrick told me about him getting into trouble with Arthur.

"Arthur was nice. Your entire family was."

Patrick groaned. "Oh, my God, they were so embarrassing."

"They were sweet."

"I was bracing myself for you to run screaming in the other direction. They were a little...pushy."

I chuckled. "They clearly love you very much."

"Love is a very fuzzy word with them."

"You're lucky to have them."

"Thank you. They're crazy and overbearing, but I love them."

"Even Dick?" I asked with a grin.

He laughed. "Are you trying to get me to say I love Dick?"

I barked a laugh, nearly choking on the food I just slid into my mouth. "That's a touchy thing to say to me after my divorce."

He winced. "I shouldn't have said that. I'm sorry."

I shook my head. "No. I'm mostly just joking."

He smiled. "Dick finally asked my mom to marry him."

"Wow. That's big. Of him. Big...Dick."

He snorted a laugh. "That was good. And bad. Ew. I am not willing to think about that."

I chuckled. "Sorry. So, what did your mom say?"

"She's thinking about it. That's what we were talking about when you saw us Saturday. She was asking what we thought of Dick asking her to marry him."

"And what did you say?" I sympathized with his mom as a single mom, but I also knew Patrick. He wasn't the kind of person who would be wary of his mom getting involved with someone unless there was a reason for his hesitation.

"I didn't say anything."

I waited for him to continue. When he didn't, I asked, "What do you mean, you didn't say anything?"

He shrugged. "She told us, and Arthur repeated what he said before, that he wants her to be happy. Which is not really an answer at all. She pushed us to answer, but before I could say anything, you walked over."

"I'm sorry. If I'd had any idea you were in the middle of that, I—"

"No, don't do that." He reached across and took my hand. "I don't want you to feel bad. There's no way you could have known."

"So, what would you have told her if I hadn't interrupted you?"

He sighed heavily. "I don't know."

I squeezed his hand. "You don't?"

He gave me a smile that said he didn't want to admit it. "I love my mom. She's been the one constant in my life. Arthur got married and had kids, so a lot of the time it's just been me and Mom. She and Dick started seeing each other a little while after I started working for you. I'm not even sure if she loves him or if he's just convenient."

"Do you really think your mom would marry someone she didn't love?"

"I don't know. I guess not. But why would she ask us? If she's so sure about him, why would we get a vote?"

I drew a breath and took my time before answering him. "I think she knows it has an impact on your life. If you hate Dick, it'll strain the relationship you have with your mom. She doesn't want to lose you."

"I guess. Maybe."

"She also could need an excuse. Maybe she wants to say no and doesn't really know how."

"You think?"

I shrugged. "I don't know. I only met her for a minute. But as a mom, I know the most important thing in our worlds is our kids."

He smiled and nodded slowly. "You know, I really didn't want to spend our entire date talking about my family."

"And Dick."

He snorted. "Well, maybe a little of that, but not that Dick."

"Oh, is that so?"

He nodded and stood, tugging my hand until I was standing with him. He guided me forward into his arms and sealed his lips over mine.

All thoughts about his family went out the window as he tested the seam of my lips and I opened for him. I sighed, and he moaned. His hands cupped my butt and yanked me against him. Close enough that I could feel his erection growing between us.

He pulled back and brushed the hair from my face. "Should we take this into the other room?"

16

PATRICK

I held my breath as I waited for her to reply. When she nodded, I thought I was going to pass out with relief.

I'd wondered what it would be like to kiss her for a year. I wondered about seeing her in my bed, too. I was about to get my wish. And all of a sudden, the moment got so much bigger in my head and I started to panic a little.

We made it to my room, and I spun to face her. She didn't look anxious or unsure. She smiled at me, and all my nervousness dissipated like she lit it on fire. I leaned into her, spreading my hand wide on her back to touch as much of her as I could at once.

She showed me again why I was so enamored by her and took control. She tilted her head and licked into my mouth, groaning when my hands slid down to cup her butt. She arched against me, rubbing herself against my body and making me crazy with desire.

I needed her like I'd never needed a woman in my life. My first time, it was lust and desire and teenage hormones. Every other woman I'd been with was fueled by similar things. But with Goldie in my room, soon to be in my bed, it was so much more. All those things were there, but I wasn't going to be done with her after tonight. I wasn't going to be done with her ever. I wanted her in my life for good. I needed her in my life.

But I was smart enough to know I couldn't admit that to her. Not now. Not anytime soon.

She guided us toward the bed and broke away from our kiss to reach for the edge of her top. She eased it up her body, holding my gaze until the shirt snapped our connection, and I let my gaze slide to the exposed skin.

She was stunning. Soft, creamy skin on display for me. A sexy, pink satin bra held her barely contained breasts up for me like they were on a platter and ready for me to feast. She moved her arms to cover her belly, but I grabbed them and held them apart while I dropped to my knees.

I kissed the softness of her belly, licking and sucking her flesh. Worshipping her and trying to tell her without words how much I wanted her. I loved her body. The curves she tried to hide that turned me on so much I nearly swallowed my tongue on a daily basis. But tonight... tonight I could touch and taste and tease her. I could have my way with her. I was allowed, and I wasn't going to waste a second.

Her hands eased into my hair, tugging me back so she could meet my gaze. Her lids were heavy with lust but sparkling with desire. I licked her belly button while she watched me, her lips parting with pleasure.

"I want to taste every inch of you, Goldie," I confessed softly.

"Please."

She didn't need to ask. I unzipped her crops and eased them down her legs. She widened her feet so her pants would slip between her thighs. I slid a hand up her thighs once her crops were on the floor. She trembled at my touch.

I kissed the edge of her pink panties. I ran my tongue over her skin, pressing her thighs apart with my hands. Her breath shook as she inhaled.

"Patrick."

I didn't answer, choosing to put my lips on her instead. I inhaled deep, drawing the scent of her desire inside me. I licked her through her panties, making her moan. Her hips shifted with my movements, then she whimpered.

"Please."

I hooked my fingers around the edges of her panties and slid them from between us, letting my tongue hit her skin the second the air did. She gasped and bucked and moaned.

She kicked her pants and panties away. I pressed her thighs wider and licked her. She backed away from me, which made me panic for a second, then she sat on the edge of my bed.

"I don't think I can stand while you do that."

"I don't think I can stand it if you tell me to stop."

She shook her head. "Please don't stop."

I smiled and crawled over to her. She watched me, her eyes widening. I was so hard I was barely contained in my shorts. I might not last long enough to get inside her, but it would be the most satisfying orgasm of my life if I got to come with my lips on this woman.

She unhooked her bra and tossed it aside as I pressed her thighs wide. There was already a wet spot on my bed. More come leaked from inside her. I leaned forward and licked it up, pressing my tongue into her entrance.

She sighed heavily, her body shaking with the release. I looked up over her belly and saw her hands cupping her breasts. Jesus. I hardened even more. I was going to hurt myself.

I kept my tongue on her while I freed myself from my

shorts. Zipper down but boxer briefs on, my cock could breathe. Then I went back to what I wanted to be doing. Making my woman crazy.

I licked through her folds, her hair tickling my face as I did. I loved that she didn't change for me. That she let me see the real her. I wouldn't have cared if she shaved or waxed, but seeing her natural was a huge turn-on. She was real, and she was letting me in.

Her clit was plump and sensitive when I ran over it with my tongue. She jumped at the contact, squeezing her nipples hard and tugging her breasts up. I wanted to make it last for her, but I was an impatient, selfish asshole who needed to see her come. I lashed at her clit relentlessly, watching her play with her breasts the entire time. She pulled her nipples and swung her breasts, letting them bounce with every flick of my tongue.

Before she came, I thrust a finger deep into her. That was all it took for her to lose her control and fall. She clamped down around my finger and fucked my face. Her breasts were pulled tight, and her face twisted in perfect agony. She moaned loudly, like it surprised her and delighted her at the same time.

I didn't let her go with just one. Her channel rippled around my finger, so I added a second one to stretch her out and kept going. It wasn't long before she was panting and begging me to make her come again.

I fucked her hard with my fingers, slamming them in deep. I sucked her clit. My body fought me, trying to let my release arrive with hers, but I forced back the need to come and focused on Goldie until she let go.

"Patrick!" she screamed.

Fucking hell, my name on her lips made me crazy. As she lost her mind, I lost my sanity. I grabbed her hand and put it between her thighs so she could tease herself a bit more. I yanked my clothes off as quickly as I could and grabbed a condom from the new box I put in my nightstand earlier that day. Thank God I had the foresight to open the box. I rolled the condom on and moved back to her, only to realize she was watching me.

"I need you," she whimpered.

Her fingers pinched her clit, her channel dripping. One hand was still on her breast, stroking over her nipple.

"I'm sorry, but this is going to be over far too quickly. You're so much better than every fantasy I've ever had about you."

"You've fantasized about me?" She sounded surprised, like she didn't think this was a big deal for me.

"Fuck yes, Goldie. So many, many times. I never thought I'd see you in my bed, ready and waiting for me after two orgasms."

She breathed a laugh and licked her lips. "And now that I am, what are you going to do with me?"

My cock swelled at her teasing words. "Fucking hell. I need you." I moved toward her, not giving her a chance to respond before I slammed into her body.

She moaned and wrapped her legs around me, her back arching. "Oh, God, yes. Touch me while you fuck me. Please."

I pressed my thumb to her clit, wanting to feel her come on my dick. I was already close after watching her, and I knew feeling her would send me right over the fucking edge, but I needed it.

"Boobs. Grab your boobs," I grunted.

She cupped them again, rolling her nipples between her finger and thumb. She moaned and thrust against me. "Oh, God."

I fucked her harder, faster. I was losing control, but she was right there with me. She rippled around me as our bodies slammed together. My thumb slid over her come-slick clit. Her hair stuck to her neck and her eyes fell closed. I watched her, memorizing every second of it. I would remember the moment forever, watching her fall apart with me inside her for the first time.

She tensed, flopping with my movements as I fucked her. Then she came, her core sucking me in as her legs fought to push me out. She yanked her boobs hard, her nails biting into her nipples.

And I was right there with her, the release making me dizzy after holding back for so long. I shouted her name, erupting inside her and wondering how I was ever going to be the same again.

She twitched around me as we both struggled to breathe. Her lips curled up in a grin before her eyes opened. "That was amazing."

I huffed a laugh. "Agreed."

We shared a secret smile as our bodies tried to figure out how to function again. My dick was still hard and ready for another go, but she squirmed and I knew she needed to get up.

I took a step back and helped her to her feet. Before she could hurry to the bathroom, I pulled her naked body against mine and kissed her hard. I missed having my lips on hers. She returned my kiss eagerly, panting again when we finally stepped apart.

She smiled and moved around me toward the bathroom. She closed the door between us, and I snapped out of the spell I was in.

I just had sex with Goldie Spear. I just made the woman I love scream my name. I just came inside her. Holy fuck.

And I was ready to do it all again. But I knew the night was almost over. Dinner was gone, and she needed to get home before too much longer. I checked the clock. Yep. Already after nine.

The toilet flushed, and water ran in the sink. I wasn't sure what I was supposed to do, so I trashed the condom in the kitchen, then pulled on my shorts.

She walked out of the bathroom and looked around. She spotted me in the kitchen and smiled. "I should probably go."

I nodded. "I figured you'd need to when I saw the time. Get dressed while I pack up dessert."

"There's dessert?"

"Of course there's dessert. Besides you, I mean."

Her cheeks darkened. The flush spread down her neck and across her breasts. My dick rose at the sight.

"Down boy," I hissed.

Goldie didn't hear me and returned to my room. She bent to pick up her clothes, and I almost came right then. Next time, I needed her like that. Fucking hell. Next time I needed a lifetime. But I was going to take what I could get from her.

I opened the fridge and pulled out the strawberry cream pie I bought from Cove Bakery that afternoon. Valentina was there and gave me a knowing grin when she handed over the pie. I didn't tell her a thing, but she knew who I bought it for. She probably even knew strawberries were Goldie's favorite fruit.

"That looks amazing," Goldie breathed from right next to me.

I nodded. "Valentina made it. I know you love straw-berries."

"I do," she whispered. "Thank you."

I handed over the entire thing.

"Don't you want some?"

I shook my head. "I get much more enjoyment out of it knowing you will love it. Does Paul like strawberries, too?"

She grinned. "He does. He'll love this. But I feel guilty."

"Why would you feel guilty? I bought that because I knew you'd like it."

"But you aren't going to eat any?"

I pulled her close and licked the shell of her ear. "I already had my dessert. And it was delicious."

She shivered against me. "You are really good at that."

"At what?"

"At making me feel like I'm the only woman in the world you want."

"You are," I admitted.

She pulled back and smiled sadly. "Thank you. And thank you for the pie. I think I still owe you a date."

"And I'll be happy to let you take me out any time."

"Thursday, right?"

I nodded, more than a little happy she remembered. "I can't wait."

She studied me for a long moment, then said, "Neither can I."

I kissed her once more at the door, only stopping when she almost dropped the pie. We said goodnight, and I watched until she was down the stairs and out of sight before I closed the door.

I smiled while I cleaned up the kitchen and as I slid into bed that night. It still smelled like her. It was the best kind of torture.

THURSDAY MORNING I got a text from my mom asking if I would meet her at Just Tacos for lunch. Before I left, I checked in with Goldie and let her know where I was going. She said to have fun and that she brought lunch when I asked if she wanted me to bring her back something.

Goldie and I hadn't spoken much since our date, but the secret glances were enough for me right now. I still struggled with not telling our coworkers about us, but I was respecting her decision and keeping it to myself.

Mom wasn't there yet when I arrived, so I ordered for us and grabbed a table in the quickly filling restaurant. She got there just as they called my name.

"Stay at the table while I pick up the food," I told her as I kissed her cheek and rushed past her.

I set the tray down and went back to get our drinks. When I finally returned, Mom had figured out what food was hers and had things laid out for us. "I didn't mean for you to buy my lunch," she said.

I shook my head. "It's the least I can do. How are you?"

She shrugged. "I'm okay, I guess."

My neck tingled. "What's wrong?"

"I turned Dick down."

"You did?" I tried not to grin.

"I did."

"Why? I thought you really liked him." Something about this felt off.

"I love him, but if I'm going to marry him, he needs to fit into the family."

"You don't think he does either. I'm sorry, Mom. I hoped he would, but he's just a big personality."

She nodded and nibbled at the edge of her taco. "That's why I said yes to dating him in the first place. He asked me out so many times, but I wasn't sure. But he never gave up. A different man would have."

"You have a right to say no," I defended her.

"I do. But I was scared. I haven't dated much since your father died. I didn't really know Dick, but when he didn't turn his nose up at my refusal and instead stuck around and got to know me, I knew he was different."

I didn't like the tone of her voice. I also didn't like the way her words made me feel. Dick was the enemy. He was the guy who swept in and tried to change her. He wasn't the hero.

"Persistence isn't a reason to marry someone," I argued.

"No, it's definitely not. But he wasn't like that in a nasty way. He was just sure he wanted to be with me. He told me he was falling in love with me while we were becoming friends. When we finally went on our first date, it was like we'd been together forever."

"What about Dad?"

She reached across the table and patted my hand. "He would have wanted all of us to be happy. We talked about it before he died. It was purely hypothetical, but he said he wanted me to date again if something ever happened to him. After he died, I couldn't bring myself to do it. I couldn't imagine anyone else ever making me feel the way he did. But Dick has a lot of the same qualities as your father."

"Like what?" I scoffed. I couldn't see it. I didn't remember my dad that well, but I knew he was nothing like Dick.

"Dick loves Arthur's kids the same way Dad loved you boys. He'd do anything for them. And he gets me out of my comfort zone. He makes me more confident and bold. Your father did the same thing, always complimenting me."

"Okay, but there's a lot more than just that."

"Of course. It's like your relationship with Goldie. It's a

feeling that starts things, but eventually it grows to be more than that. It's knowing that this person is someone you don't want to spend your life without."

"So, why did you say no?" I asked, my throat tightening.

She looked up at me and smiled sadly. "I couldn't imagine my life without you, Patrick. I know you don't like Dick. Arthur tolerates him a little better because the kids adore Dick, but you don't like him at all. I couldn't agree to marry him when I knew you boys would be so unhappy about it."

"It's your life, Mom," I argued. My defenses rose, and I got angry. "You can't blame me for your choices."

"I'm not, sweetie. Not at all. I made my own decision."

"Good. Then I guess I'm happy for you."

She stared at me for a long moment. It was the look she would give me when I was a kid and she thought I was lying about something. The one that made me squirm in my seat and want to confess all my secrets, even when I didn't have any.

"So, how are things going with Goldie?" she asked after a minute.

"Good," I answered, happy to be on safer ground. "We have another date tonight."

"That's good news. Tell her I said hello. I think she's good for you. Gets you out of your comfort zone a bit. I hope you're good for her, too. You were persistent with her. I know that means she's special to you."

"She is," I said, unsure why her words made me so uncomfortable. "She's very special."

"Then you need to do whatever you can to hold on to her. Make sure she knows how you feel. Don't let her go. The special ones don't come around all the time."

I nodded. "You're right. They don't."

Mom smiled and finished her tacos. We talked about Arthur and the kids. She worried about how to tell them about Dick not coming around anymore, and I assured her she'd find a way to explain it to them.

When we left, she hugged me a little tighter than usual and asked me to call her tomorrow to let her know how my date with Goldie went. I watched her drive away with a sick feeling in my stomach and a soul deep knowing that my mother was not okay.

And it was all my fault.

17

GOLDIE

I LEFT WORK THURSDAY AFTERNOON LATER THAN I'D HOPED. I wanted to get home and spend some time with Paul before my date with Patrick, but Mayor Levine called to confirm the upcoming events for the town. I marked all the ones I told him about so I could double check with the vendors and reiterate that no one outside my office would be making changes. All of that made me late leaving work.

I rushed inside and hurried to my room. I considered changing, but I didn't have time. I left my computer bag on my bed and went back to the living room where Paul was watching TV.

"Are you done with homework already?"

"Yeah. Teachers aren't giving us anything new. It's all just review for exams."

"Are you ready for exams?"

He snorted. "Yeah. I was ready for exams a month ago."

"Good."

"What are we having for dinner?"

"Um, I'm going out for dinner."

"Again? Are you going out with Patrick?"

"How do you know Patrick?"

He rolled his eyes. "I met him over the weekend, and you've talked about him a lot over the last year. I figured you were dating a long time ago."

"No, we weren't."

"But you are now?"

I nodded and sat beside him on the couch. "We are. Are you okay with that?"

He shrugged. "Doesn't bother me. You should be happy, Mom. He seemed like a cool guy."

"You barely spoke to him."

"Maybe, but he was nice. He smiled when he looked at you."

"He did?" My cheeks heated.

Paul nodded. "He likes you a lot. Which is good because I'd have to kick his ass if he wasn't nice to you."

"Language," I scolded.

"Kick his butt."

I breathed a laugh. "Better. And thank you."

"Does that mean he's nice to you?"

I nodded. "He is. He's a good person."

"Good. Then I hope you have fun tonight."

I smiled and stared at him while he watched the TV. I felt silly asking my son about dating, but he was the most important person in my world. "Do you think he's too young for me?"

"Patrick? Is he under eighteen?"

"Of course not!"

"Then no."

"But he's fourteen years younger than me."

"And?"

I stared at him like he wasn't getting it.

"Mom, men date women half their age all the time. He's

not half your age, but if he was, that would be fine. Age isn't all that important. Not when you're an adult."

"But what if he wants kids? I'm not interested in having more kids. I'm not even sure I could."

"Does he want kids?"

"I don't know."

"Then you might want to ask him before you talk yourself out of a relationship because of something that might not even be an issue."

I stared at my son for a long moment. "When did you get so smart?"

"I've always been smart, Mom."

I grinned. "Yes, you have been. And you're growing up. I don't want to miss that."

"You aren't. I know you're here for me. Even if I don't always want you to be."

I laughed. "Good. And thank you for the advice."

"Just don't ask me about sex. I don't want to know."

"You better not know anything about sex yet."

He shook his head.

I didn't like the non-answer. "Paul."

"I've taken health class."

"Paul!"

"No, Mom, I don't know anything about sex from personal experience."

"Good. Let's keep it that way until you're my age."

He snorted.

"At least let me pretend."

He grinned. "Okay, Mom."

I hugged him and kissed the top of his head before letting him know there were leftovers in the fridge and I transferred money to his account if he wanted to order food in. He nodded and went back to his show.

A few minutes later, I was out the door, feeling rushed and a little guilty for not spending more time with Paul. Summer was going to be busy, and I was running out of summers with him at home. After the busy summer season, I needed to take some time off to spend with him.

I didn't want to wait that long to spend time with him. The end of school was coming soon. I needed to check my calendar and find a day I could take off now. I owed my kid that.

I parked in front of Patrick's apartment and pulled out my phone. I wanted to mark off a day to spend with Paul before I forgot about it. I was still looking at my phone when the passenger door opened.

"Gah!"

"Hey," Patrick said.

"You scared me."

"Sorry. I saw you sitting here and wondered if you changed your mind about going to dinner."

I shook my head and blocked off the next afternoon. It was the last day of school for Paul, a half day. Exams were the following week, but it would be nice to have a little time together.

"Are you okay?" Patrick asked.

"Do you want kids?" I blurted. I hadn't planned to ask him the question, but it popped out.

"Um, what?" He chuckled.

I dropped my phone back into my handbag and met his gaze. "I don't want more kids. I have one, and he's amazing, and I was just scheduling a day off so I can spend time with him, but I don't want to start over with babies. I didn't want more kids when I had Paul. I'm content with just one, but you're young. You have lots of time if you want kids. And I don't want my age or my lack of desire to hold you back. I don't want this to become something that breaks us up in five years because you resent me for never wanting more kids and not telling you. So I wanted to ask you now, because if you want kids, and I don't want kids, then I know this won't work and we can just agree now to let it be fun and easy and when we decide it's getting too serious or whatever, then we move on, but if you don't want kids..."

"If I don't want kids, what?" he breathed.

I sucked in a breath and let myself have a little more of that hope I grabbed onto when we started talking about dating. Hope that made me think maybe this could work. Maybe I didn't have to be scared. Maybe I deserved a man in my life who looked at me the way Patrick was. Like my next words meant the difference between getting everything he wanted and not.

"If you don't want kids, then I don't know. But I don't want you to tell me you don't want kids if you really do. I don't want you to not have something you want. I—"

"I want you, Goldie. And I don't tell a lot of people, but I don't want kids."

I drew a breath to speak, but he held up his hand.

"You can believe me or not. Most people don't. I haven't ever wanted kids. Not because I hate kids or anything, but because I never saw myself as a dad. I love my niece and nephews. I love kids. But it's not the path I want for my life."

"What do you want?"

"I want to do work I'm proud of. I want to enjoy my job. I want to have the freedom to travel if I decide to and retire when I'm young enough to enjoy my life. My dad died when I was only seven. He never got to retire. My mom has worked constantly since then to support Arthur and me, and now herself. I live in an apartment because I don't want to have to worry about a big mortgage payment or tax bill. I want to take you out for nice dinners and buy nice things and love my life. And I'm not saying kids would ruin any of that, just that kids have never been a part of the future I saw for myself."

"And you're not just saying that?"

He shook his head. "I'm not. When my oldest nephew was born, my mom asked when I'm going to give her grandchildren, and I said never. She argued with me, so I don't say it often, but it's the truth. I like being able to spoil them and do things for my mom. I like that I can work at a job I truly enjoy and find fulfilling without worrying about how much money I make."

My cheeks warmed. I knew what he made, and I always wished I could give him more. "I'm sorry about that."

"I don't want you to be. I don't need more than I make. Not saying I would turn down a raise, just that I am comfortable. I have everything I want and need. Especially now that I have you in my life like this."

I sucked in a breath and nodded. That hope was settling in and getting comfortable. "Thank you."

He leaned across the console and kissed me softly, his lips barely brushing mine before he pulled away and smiled. "Thank you for trusting my answer and not judging me for it."

"I think a lot of people have kids who don't really want them because it's what most people do."

"There's a lot of pressure to have kids. My mom is convinced I'll change my mind one day."

"Do you think you will?"

He shook his head. "No. It's ended a few relationships in my past, but we're on the same page, so hopefully that's a good thing."

"I think so," I admitted.

"Good. So, are we still on for dinner? Do you want me to drive or do you want to drive since we're already in your vehicle?"

"I'll drive, if you're okay with that."

"Of course. I have no problem with you being in control."

My cheeks heated at the sexy tone of his voice, and I wondered if he would feel the same in the bedroom. I backed out of the parking space and turned south toward the restaurant. We talked about work and Paul while I drove. When we were seated, I asked how his lunch with his mom went. I'd forgotten to ask earlier and didn't see him before he left work that afternoon.

"It was good," he said.

"Then why do you sound like it wasn't?"

He shrugged. "She told Dick she didn't want to marry him."

"Is that not a good thing anymore? I thought that's what you were hoping she'd say."

He nodded. "Yeah, but it feels crappy."

"She made the decision. You didn't tell her to turn him down."

"I know, but she said she told him no because she knows I don't really like him."

"That's not fair to you."

"It's fine. She said the same thing you did that she made the choice. It's okay."

"But it's bothering you."

"It just seemed like she was disappointed. Like she didn't want to tell him no, but felt like she had to because of me."

"Sometimes we can't see when something isn't right. With my marriage, I knew we weren't in a great place, but I didn't know he was going to ask me for a divorce. I thought we'd figure it out. Valentina said she felt the same. She was frustrated with Dawson and all the traveling he was doing for work, but she didn't know for sure he was cheating on her. We don't always want to see the truth, but the people around us have a different perspective. If you see Dick in a way she doesn't, she just might be disappointed she missed something."

Patrick nodded. "Maybe."

"Should we go? We don't have to stay here if you'd rather not be out."

"No," he said firmly. "I want to be with you."

"We can go back to your place."

The server came over and asked if we were ready to order. I raised my brows at Patrick and he nodded.

"We're ready." He looked at me. "We're staying."

DINNER WAS AMAZING. Patrick stopped worrying about his mom, and we laughed and talked and kissed. We left with our bellies full and our faces smiling.

Patrick rested his hand on my thigh during the drive back to his place. He didn't tease me at all while I was driving, but his hand was a constant reminder that I wanted him. And after our talk earlier, I was less worried about where things were going between us.

"Do you want to come in?" he asked when I parked in front of his building.

"Yes," I answered. "But I'm not sure I should."

"You want to get home to Paul?"

I shook my head. "It's not just that. I like you. And it's more than just sex. I enjoy talking to you and spending time with you."

"I enjoy that, too."

"I didn't expect that."

He laughed. "You thought we'd sleep together a few times, and you'd get it out of your system?"

"Actually, I thought you would. And it was a safety net for me. I wouldn't get too attached to you if I knew things would end."

"And now?"

I shrugged. "Now I'm getting attached."

He leaned across the console again, stopping when his lips were a breath away from mine. His eyes were dilated but clear. "I was attached a long time ago, Goldie. There's no safety net for me."

"What are you saying? Are you saying...?"

"I'm not going to say it right now. I know you're not ready to hear those words. But I don't think you need to hear them to know they're true."

I sucked in a sharp breath and drew him to me with it. He captured my exhale with a demanding kiss that filled me with all the things he wasn't saying. Love. Lust. Passion. Forever.

We kissed until the windows fogged up and the console between us was at risk of being ripped out of the car, then we scrambled from the seats and rushed inside, barely keeping our hands to ourselves before Patrick slammed the door behind us.

He yanked at my skirt, the zipper grinding as he drew it down. The only other sound in his apartment was our uneven breath. He dropped to his knees in front of me and pushed me to the door, sucking my clit through my panties.

I gasped for breath and held his head in place. He shoved my thighs apart and tugged my panties to the side before sucking on my burning flesh.

"Come for me," he whispered against my core. "Just like this. Like you can't wait until we get to the bedroom before you have to come all over my face. You can't wait until I take off my clothes. Come, Goldie."

His whispered plea was punctuated by his tongue teasing my clit, my entrance, and my folds. I was halfway there before he pressed two fingers into me and sucked my clit into his mouth. It wasn't long before he was supporting my weight as my knees gave out and my orgasm took over.

"Fucking hell, that was hot," he gasped. His fingers were still inside me, my body slumped on top of his. He was on his knees with me barely contained on his lap. "I need more of that. I need all of you. I know this isn't just sex, Goldie. It never has been for me. But right now, I need to fuck you. I need to be inside you when you come again. I want to touch you and taste you and feel you on my dick. Please, Goldie."

"Yes," I whispered. I couldn't refuse him. I wanted the same thing. I needed it just as much as he did.

He helped me to my feet and followed me, his hand slipping from between my legs. I moaned at the loss but was rewarded with his other hand on my breast.

He unbuttoned my shirt as we stumbled our way to his bedroom. My skirt was somewhere near the door, and my shirt was somewhere between there and the bedroom. My panties and bra were discarded as soon as we stepped into his room.

He walked past me to the nightstand, yanking his clothes off as he dragged open the drawer. I stopped him before he ripped the condom open and dropped to my knees in front of him.

"Fucking hell," he groaned, staring at me on my knees. "You don't have to."

"I want to taste you, too."

He closed his eyes and shuddered. I wrapped my hand around his cock, loving that it was average length but thick. When he filled me, I felt him against my walls. And he wasn't so long he hurt when he let go and fucked me hard. He was perfect for me.

I licked the tip of his cock, and he jerked. I looked up at him and found him watching me, his eyes glazed and full of desire. I sucked him into my mouth, letting him hit the back of my throat before I withdrew and groaned. Salty and musky and Patrick. My thighs grew slick as I sucked him, my head bobbing back and forth.

His hands eased into my hair, brushing it back from my face and tipping my chin up so I would meet his gaze. I saw it right there. The four letter word he wasn't willing to say yet.

18

———————

THERE WAS A PART OF ME THAT WANTED HIM TO SAY IT, BUT HE was right. I wasn't ready to hear it. But I saw it. In the way he touched me. In the way he supported me. In the way he did everything for me.

Oh, God. I was about to come just thinking about it. Just thinking about Patrick caring so much about me was a huge turn on. One I wasn't sure I could stop myself from acting on.

I slid my hand between my legs. My cheeks heated when Patrick's gaze followed my hand. His eyes widened and dilated more, the blue almost completely overtaken by black.

His cock swelled in my mouth, and he pulled back. "You need to stop. Fuck, Goldie, I need to be inside you. Watching you is…"

"I shouldn't have—"

"No. Fuck, no. Don't say that. You never have to stop with me. I want you to do what feels good." He yanked me to my feet and kissed me hard. His tongue pulsed inside my mouth and his entire body thumped with the same need. He held me so close our hearts synced and beat together.

He pulled back with a gasp and grabbed the condom he'd set on the nightstand. He rolled it on and laid on the bed, reaching for me. "Use me. Get yourself off with me. You're in control tonight, beautiful. Fuck me however you need to."

My breath hitched. I was the boss at work, but in the bedroom, I rarely took charge. I wasn't sure how, but with Patrick's confidence in me, I was willing to try.

I climbed onto the bed with him and straddled his hips. He held his cock still while I positioned myself over him. He dipped a finger inside me before he eased me onto his cock. We groaned together when I sank onto him.

"You're so beautiful," he whispered. His gaze slid across my body, his cock twitching as he looked at me.

I lifted up on my knees and sank down, getting used to the feel of him inside me. I was wet and ready, but being on top was different. And I didn't hate it.

I started slowly, letting my body adjust to his width before speeding up. He didn't try to control me at all, just trailed his fingertips over my body. Nipples to my clit to my collarbone and down to my hips. My breath hitched and my pulse sped up with his teasing touches.

"Use me, Goldie. Touch yourself. I want to watch you. Show me what you do when you think of me."

I closed my eyes, blocking out the sight of him, and let my mind wander. The feel of his thick cock inside me was almost enough to send me over the edge, but I liked to play with my clit, too. I slid a hand there and eased my finger across it. I jumped when he added his hand to mine, but he didn't try to take over.

My body was slick with come and I used it to slip and

slide over my clit, faster and faster while my hips pumped his cock deeper into me. He groaned and thrust up with my strokes, adding to the fantasy and the erotic moment.

"Patrick."

"I'm right here, Goldie. Right here. Come for me, beautiful."

My fingers flew faster, my hips pumping mindlessly over him. I opened my eyes and met his gaze, and the way he looked at me sent me over the edge. "Oh, God. Patrick, yes."

He powered into me, fucking me as I screamed. His body tightened, clenching as I came. His fingers pinched my clit, tugging it slightly, and I went over another peak. He went with me, shouting as he came.

I collapsed onto him, my body weak from the exertion even as it twitched for more. My hands were trapped between us, his still teasing my clit as I came down from the highest peak I'd ever been on.

"That was amazing," he whispered. He kissed my neck. "Tell me you're willing to do that again sometime."

"Any time you want."

He laughed. "Be careful what you promise. I will definitely take you up on that."

I chuckled with him and eased our bodies apart to free my hand and his. "I've never done that before."

"Done what?"

"Been on top. Touched myself with someone watching like that."

He kissed me hard, his tongue sealing all the promises he made with his lips. "Thank you for sharing that with me. For being willing to be vulnerable."

"I don't know what it is about you that makes me throw caution to the wind."

"I know exactly what you mean," he said. There it was again. That unspoken word.

I don't know why I didn't notice it before, but it was there between us. It had been there for a while. I wasn't there yet, but I could see myself going there. Falling in love with him and not worrying about the safety net I wanted to have between us.

Patrick was different. He wasn't what I expected. He knew who he was in a way I was still figuring out. But I wasn't willing to question it. I wanted him in my life. I wasn't sure if it would last, if it would be forever, but I wanted the chance to find out.

"You're thinking awfully hard over there," he said softly. "Should I be worried?"

I shook my head. "Not even a little."

He smiled at me. "Good."

We cleaned up and teased each other a little more before he told me to go home and dream about him. When I said he should dream about me, too, he said, "I always do."

We kissed goodnight, and I went home to see my son. Paul was already asleep when I got there, so I snuck into his room to say goodnight and went to my room and got ready for bed.

In the morning, I woke up with a smile on my face and a pulsing between my thighs. I definitely dreamed about Patrick. All night.

THE WEEKEND EVENTS were on track, so I felt okay leaving early Friday. Mid-June was a quieter time, but we still had things going on. When school was out in another week and

July Fourth arrived, we would have bigger events, but for now, it was quiet.

I worked a few hours in the morning and handed things over to Patrick for the afternoon before leaving to get Paul from school. He was waiting with some friends when I got into the line with all the other parents getting their kids early from the half-day.

He spotted my car and pointed it out to his friends. They waved, and Paul hurried over.

"What are your friends doing today?" I asked, feeling guilty for taking him away from a day he could have spent with them. It never occurred to me he might have had plans.

"Just hanging out. They were talking about going into town, but they didn't really have anything in mind."

"I should have asked if it was a good day for us to spend time together. Would you rather be with them?"

He shook his head. "No, I'm good. Where are we going for lunch?"

"It's up to you. Your choice today."

"Is it a yay day?" He'd been asking me for a yay day for years. I always said no, but it was feeling like a good day for an adventure.

"You know what? I think it is."

"Wait, what? Are you serious?"

I shrugged. "Sure, why not? But there are rules, even on a yay day."

He rolled his eyes. "What are the rules?"

"It's not going to be a day to spend money on stuff. We're not buying video games and all the things I tell you I won't buy every other day. Today is about experiences and fun, not more things."

He nodded. "I'm good with that."

"And I can veto anything that's too expensive or dangerous."

"You're no fun."

"We can just not have a yay day at all."

"You're the most fun mom ever."

I laughed and pulled out of the lot. "Where to?"

"Cracked."

"We go there all the time. You can go anywhere you want and that's where you pick?"

"Yep. Because today you can't tell me I can't have the loaded French toast."

I groaned. He was right. I always said no to that because it was sugar on a plate. It would have been better if he just ordered a bowl of sugar. I couldn't deny it looked really good, but the volume of food it was made me sick just thinking about.

"You promised," Paul argued before I could say anything.

"You're right. Loaded French toast it is. Maybe I'll have one, too."

Paul laughed. "Yeah, not likely. You're going to get an egg white omelet, coffee, and a side of sourdough toast."

I glared at him. "Maybe I should shake things up a little."

"I'll believe it when I see it." He buried his nose in his phone while I drove to Cracked. It wasn't busy yet, but the streets were. I ended up parking a few blocks away, and we walked over to Cracked.

Blake was working and showed us to a table in her section. "Coffee to start? And water?"

"Please," I said automatically.

"Told you," Paul said as he opened his menu.

"I like coffee."

"Who doesn't? I'll be right back to get your orders." Blake winked at me before she walked away.

"You're going to be on a sugar high the rest of the day," I told Paul.

He nodded. "Yep. It's going to be awesome."

I laughed and shook my head. He was also just as likely to go for a run in an hour or two and burn off all the calories he was about to eat.

"Coffee and water. Are you guys ready to order?" Blake asked.

Paul told her which of the loaded French toasts he wanted while I studied the menu. I wasn't sure I could handle all the sugar of the loaded French toast, but trying something new was a good idea. The strawberry waffles caught my eye and reminded me of the pie Patrick bought for me.

"Goldie? Egg white omelet?" Blake asked, waiting for me to answer before she recorded my order.

"Actually, I'm going to have the strawberry waffles."

"Nice. They're fantastic. Bacon or sausage?"

"Bacon. And extra whipped cream."

Blake grinned. "My kind of lunch. You two are going to be ready for the rest of your day."

"We're having a yay day," Paul told her. "Mom agreed to it."

"What's a yay day?" Blake asked.

"It's where I have to say yes to anything he wants to do. Within reason, of course."

"Within reason kind of ruins it, doesn't it?" Blake asked.

"That's what I'm saying," Paul said.

I laughed at the two of them. "I'm not buying him a new car or something like that. That's what I mean."

"So you'll buy me a motorcycle?"

I rolled my eyes as Blake and Paul laughed.

"I think we'll stick to activities. Doing fun things we don't do all the time."

"That sounds like fun, too. If you need a boat, let me know. Ian isn't using his today."

"A boat?" Paul asked. "Can we go out on a boat?"

"Do you know how to drive a boat?"

"No, but you know how to drive a car. How different can it be?" Paul countered.

"I think dry land might be for the best," I told Blake.

She nodded and grinned as she left to put in our orders.

"So, what do you want to do today that doesn't require a boat we don't know how to drive or a vehicle you aren't allowed to drive?" I asked.

"Sam said they might all go to the movies today. MacKellar Theater is open early today since it's a half-day."

"That would be fun. What are they playing at the theater?"

Paul shrugged. "I don't know. I can ask Sam. I think she's going to be with her mom and sister. They've all been spending a lot of time together."

"That's good for them. Has she heard from her dad at all?"

He finished his text, then shook his head. "The guy's a jerk. He hasn't called her once."

"Wow. That's really bad."

"Yeah." His phone buzzed, and he checked it. "Oh, hey, she said they're going to the one o'clock movie. She doesn't remember what it is, but they'll be there for that one."

"Sounds good to me. I'll see if Anna and her boys want to meet us there, too."

Paul nodded.

I pulled out my phone and sent a text to Anna and

Valentina, letting them both know about the movie and our plans to crash Valentina's afternoon.

> Paul's talked me into a yay day. I need backup in the form of something to kill a few hours. He wants to meet up with the Hayes family at the movies at one. Valentina, is that okay? And Anna, want to join us?

VALENTINA

Sam just told me. Looking forward to seeing you. I could use some adult time. Do they sell wine at the theater?

> Sounds good. And yes on the wine.

ANNA

Yes to wine and time with you guys. We'll be there. Joey didn't work today and wanted to go to the movies, too. I have a feeling it's going to be a busy day. Might want to get there early to get tickets and seats.

VALENTINA

Good to know. Thanks. We'll do that. See everyone then. Whoever's first, save seats.

> Good idea. See you guys soon.

ANNA

I was dreading it but now I'm excited. Glad you reached out, Goldie.

I put my phone away as Blake set plates in front of us. Mine was piled high with whipped cream and covered in strawberries. My stomach growled just looking at it. Then I looked at Paul's plate.

"That is huge," I said.

The grin on his face was almost as big as the French toast. "It's going to be so good."

"I can smell the sugar from here."

Blake laughed. "You need to try it once. It is really good. Sweet enough to make you sick if you're not careful, but delicious. Do you guys need anything else?"

We shook our heads, then dove into our lunches.

My waffles were light and fluffy and perfect. The whipped cream and strawberries added a touch of decadence that tipped it over the edge.

"Want a bite?" Paul asked. He held his fork up for me to take a tiny bite of his French toast.

I smiled. "You know me too well."

He handed over the fork. I slid the bite into my mouth and handed his fork back while I chewed.

It was like an explosion of flavor. Better than I expected it to be. The sweet cereal crunch was surprising and delicious. The softness of the French toast underneath was a good contrast. And the overall sweetness was powerful but balanced in a way I didn't expect.

"That's actually good. Very good," I finally said.

"See? You should let me get this more often."

"Uh huh. We'll see about that. Want to try my waffle?"

"Yeah." Paul helped himself to a sizable bite and nodded as he chewed. "That's awesome. Not as good as the pie, but good."

"I agree."

We finished our food, talking about exams and summer and Charles coming to visit in a few weeks while we ate. When we were done and paid, we decided to head to the theater since we expected it to be busy.

The line was already around the block when we arrived. Valentina and her girls were closer to the front and told everyone behind them they were buying our tickets anyway, so we jumped ahead to wait with them.

"I was just about to text you guys. This line is crazy," Valentina said.

My phone buzzed. I pulled it out and saw a text from Anna.

ANNA

Trying to find parking. Anyone here yet?

In line with Valentina. We will buy tickets for you guys. 3?

ANNA

Yes, 3. Thank you. It looks like we're going to have to walk a little bit.

VALENTINA

Shouldn't you get employee parking or something? You work for MacKellar Investments.

ANNA

LOL! I need to ask about that. Found a spot. Walking that way now.

At the front of the line. Not letting anyone in yet.

ANNA

We see you!

I turned around and spotted them walking past everyone waiting in line. We waved to each other just as the door to the theater opened to let people in.

"Hurry!" we shouted.

Anna and the boys took off and made it to us before we walked into the theater.

"I'll buy tickets so it's just one transaction," I told them.

"Good idea. I'll get next time," Valentina said.

"Me, too. We'll work it out," Anna agreed.

I nodded and swiped my card. It was good to have friends like them.

Valentina offered to buy snacks and Anna said she'd get drinks. I wasn't sure how Paul was still hungry, but he accepted both offers. I took the five kids into the theater so we could find seats.

Valentina and Anna joined us a few minutes later, and the kids promptly deserted us to talk to their friends.

"Nice to know we matter," Anna said.

"Right? I think they're all excited to be out of school. Even though they have exams," Valentina said.

"I agree. It's nice for me, too. I'm ready for this year to be over. It's been a wild one," Anna said.

"Yeah, you have a different life than a year ago," I told Anna.

She smiled. "I do. And it's amazing. I never would have imagined Hudson Grant would be the guy for me, but I'm lucky to have him."

"He's lucky to have you," Valentina said. "And I'm happy to be single."

"When does your divorce finalize?" I asked.

"Probably soon. My lawyer said maybe by the end of the month. He's not fighting anything and neither am I. We're both pretty clear on what we want. The hardest thing is the girls are getting left out in the cold." Valentina glanced to where her girls were talking to friends.

"What do you mean?" Anna asked.

"Dawson hasn't reached out to either of them. He's gone radio silent. The only time I hear anything from him is through his lawyer. He doesn't call me or them and when they reach out, he doesn't answer." Valentina looked more hurt than angry.

"Wow. Divorce is hard, but it doesn't have to be that

hard. Of course, my ex wasn't a picnic either. Joey and Matty never hear from Nick. Haven't in years." Anna shook her head.

"I just don't get it. I don't understand how someone can look at those kids we have and not want to be in their lives." Valentina teared up. She quickly wiped them away and sniffed, but she was definitely upset for her girls.

And I didn't blame her. I felt the same. Charles was in contact with Paul, but he wasn't around like he used to be. I guess it was better than what the other kids were going through, but it sucked that we all chose men who couldn't be bothered to be full-time fathers.

"Hudson is twice the father Nick ever was. You'll find someone who's better for your girls than Dawson. Someone who'll teach them how to expect to be treated," Anna said. She patted Valentina's arm.

Valentina nodded. "Eventually. I'm not ready to date yet, but if I ever am, I will go into it with my eyes wide open."

"Yes, you will. And you'll find the right one for all of you." Anna leaned her head on Valentina's shoulder. They both nodded.

"I'm just happy we have each other. I felt really alone when I went through my divorce. I'm glad we can be here for you," I told Valentina.

"Me, too. I don't know what I would do without you guys. Thank you."

"Any time," Anna said.

"Always," I replied.

It was good to have friends.

19

PATRICK

I checked my phone for the tenth time on Sunday afternoon. Still nothing from Goldie. I'd been texting her all day to make sure things were going as planned and hadn't heard back from her. I volunteered to help out, but after taking half a day off on Friday, she insisted on the rest of us taking the weekend off. It was a small event, local restaurants and fun for the kids. It was supposed to be over by early evening. So why wasn't she returning my texts?

"Uncle Patrick, watch!" Henry shouted, drawing my attention.

I shoved my phone away and pasted a smile on my face. "I'm watching."

Henry repeated his actions for me with the other adults in the room looking at me instead of the six-year-old who was entertaining us. I glared at them when Henry wasn't looking, then clapped for my nephew.

"Was that good?" he asked.

"Absolutely. It was amazing."

Henry beamed, then turned to Mom. "Where's Papa Dick? I want to show him."

If I wasn't watching her, I would have missed the way my mom's face twitched before she forced a smile to her lips. "He couldn't be here today, honey."

"Again? He wasn't here last time, either. Is he coming to see me later this week? He never misses seeing us. Even if he's driving, he always stops by when he gets home." Henry's face was set. In his world, Papa Dick was someone he could count on.

I flashed a look at Arthur. I didn't know Dick visited the kids after a trip. Arthur nodded, confirming what his son said. How did I not know that?

"Come sit with me," Mom said to Henry. "All of you kids. I need to talk to you."

Henry led the way with a smile on his face. He was waiting for an exciting story, something about Dick's trip. Mom always shared pictures with them and told them about where Dick was. That was what they expected.

"Where Papa Dick?" four-year-old Nicholas asked.

"Papa Dick is on a trip right now," Mom said carefully. "He's driving far across the country. He's going to go all the way through New York, then he's going to Pennsylvania, and down to West Virginia, then he'll end up in Kentucky. Then he's going to Indiana and Missouri, then he stays on the very edge of Iowa up to South Dakota and North Dakota. Then he's going west again and driving all the way across Montana. He'll go through the skinny part of Idaho and into Washington state."

"Wow," Henry asked, like he could actually picture it.

I could picture it. It was the longest trip Dick had taken since I'd met him. He was supposed to be slowing down and staying home more.

"He's going to go all the way out to the Pacific Ocean,

then he's going to go a little south into Oregon and come back toward here."

"That's a long trip," I said.

Mom nodded and kept her focus on the kids. "It's the longest trip Dick's done in a while. He wanted to see the country a bit. Get away for a while."

"Why didn't you go with him, Grandma?" Henry asked.

"Because Dick and I are not seeing each other anymore."

"Cuz he on twip," Nicholas said.

"Yes, and because we've decided not to spend time together anymore. But Papa Dick said he still loves all of you. And he hopes it'll be okay for him to visit when he gets back, but he's going to take some longer trips. He won't be here as much."

"Why not?" Henry still didn't get it.

Nicholas and Katie nodded, not understanding what Mom was saying, but Henry knew enough to understand that things were different.

"I thought he wanted to be here," Henry said.

"He does. And he will be back to visit. He will always be there for you. You can call him anytime you want, Henry."

"I want him to be here. He makes me laugh." Henry pouted.

"He makes me laugh, too," Mom whispered.

"Then why isn't he here?" Henry cried.

"Why don't we have some dessert?" Sharon suggested. Her voice was loud and falsely bright and not fooling anyone over the age of seven.

"Dessert!" Katie yelled, throwing her arms up and jumping off Mom's lap to follow Sharon to the kitchen.

Nicholas was right behind his sister, enticed by the promise of something sweet. But Henry wasn't falling for it. "Can I call Papa Dick right now?"

"We will call him tomorrow," Arthur promised.

"Why isn't he here?"

"He has to work," Arthur said. He stood and picked up his oldest, holding him close and speaking softly to him as he carried him into the kitchen for dessert with his siblings.

I watched my mom. She stared at Henry, her face slowly collapsing as he got farther away. "I knew it was going to be hard to tell him," Mom whispered.

"He'll understand eventually," I said. I moved to sit next to her on the couch. "It's never easy. I was only a little older than him when Dad died, and I thought he'd be back soon. It took a while for me to really get it."

"He's a smart kid. He'll get it eventually. It's just going to be tough since Dick won't be here with all of us. He asked if I would be okay with him still visiting with the kids. I couldn't tell him no. I know it puts Arthur and Sharon in a tough spot, but I wasn't going to say Dick couldn't call. If they're not okay with it, they can tell him. I just couldn't bring myself to cut him off from those kids. He loves them so much."

Mom wiped a tear from her cheek and smiled up at me. My heart split open. I couldn't remember the last time I saw her cry. Probably when my father died, but I didn't remember it. Back then, she had to be strong for Arthur and me. She told me in the years since that she had to be mother and father to us when we needed our father. But this time, Dick was still around. He was the only grandfather Arthur's kids knew on our side of the family. Sharon's parents were involved, but Papa Dick was the one who got on the floor and played with the kids, from what Arthur said.

"He'll still see them," I told her, knowing it was true. Dick always kept his word. He wouldn't let those kids down.

She nodded and sniffed. "I know. But I know it's not the same for anyone."

"They'll figure out a new normal," I said.

"Who will?" Arthur asked, joining us from the kitchen. The kids sounded happy with whatever dessert Sharon had for them.

"Dick asked if he could call you guys and still come by to see the kids. I couldn't tell him no. I hope that doesn't put you in a tough position," Mom explained.

Arthur shook his head. "The kids love when he visits. Henry's going to be asking me every day when he'll be back. Of course, Nicholas is going to be asking what he's going to bring them."

Mom chuckled. "He always had fun picking out something special for each kid. He refused to come home until he found them a gift."

I didn't know any of that about Dick. I never liked him for my mother, but there was a lot more to him than I knew. He was a grandfather to Arthur's kids. He spoiled them in a way I didn't ever know. And Mom was miserable without him.

"He'll still be around. He already called to talk to us," Arthur said.

"Good. Before he left, he told me he'd reach out to you. I just hope he's safe on this trip. He hasn't taken a trip like this in a long time. He prefers shorter ones where he can get back home in a night or two."

"Why did he take such a long trip?" I asked.

Mom teared up again. "He said he needed to be away for a while. I guess he thought I'd say yes, and it crushed him when I didn't. He couldn't face any of us right now."

"He is always welcome here," Arthur said. "Sharon has been texting him to see where he is."

"Is he okay?" Mom asked quickly.

Arthur nodded. "He's good, Ma. I would have told you if that wasn't the case."

"Grandma!" Henry shouted from the kitchen.

Mom pushed herself to stand. "I'm coming."

I watched her walk toward the kids as she wiped her tears. Her voice was bright and happy when she stepped into the kitchen and saw them.

"She's fucking miserable," Arthur snarled.

"Why did she turn him down?" I snapped back at him.

"Because of you, you spoiled snot."

"What?" He could not be serious.

"You don't like Dick. You've made that clear. You think he's not good for Mom. She turned him down because of you. This is all your fault," Arthur hissed.

"What are you talking about? You don't like him either," I whispered.

Arthur shook his head and met my gaze. "He's not Dad. He'll never be Dad. But Mom loves him. My kids love him. Dick is a good man. He might not be my favorite person on the planet, but that doesn't mean I want him to disappear from our lives. He would do anything for Mom and anything for us."

"Why didn't you tell me all this before? Why didn't you say something when he asked if he could marry Mom?"

"I did," Arthur snapped. "I said he could ask her. I stopped you from telling him no. I tried to jump in every time Mom said something. But she knew. She knew you didn't like him and that you wouldn't be okay with her marrying him no matter how many times I said it was okay with me. You're to blame for all of this."

"He forced her to date him. He asked her out for months before she said yes. He inserted himself in our family and is all handsy with her. He's loud and irritating. Why do we want him to marry her?"

Arthur huffed a mirthless laugh. "You're serious, aren't you? God, you're so oblivious. He didn't force her to date him. He got to know her when she said no. And she said no because of you. Her grown ass son who shouldn't get a say in her relationships because he's not a child anymore. Her grown ass son who did the same fucking thing to his own boss and pushed her to go out with him for months until she finally agreed."

"I didn't..." I couldn't argue that point because he was right. I did the same thing to Goldie. I pushed her. He didn't even know how far I pushed her, but I did. I made it almost impossible for her to say no to me. Even after she said no, I kept pushing until she said yes. I acted like a child, pouting when she didn't agree to go out with me after I pushed so hard.

I wasn't just like Dick. I was worse. I was judging the man for things I'd done. Things I found acceptable for me.

And I ruined my mother's relationship because I was a child. I was jealous and stubborn and thought I knew what was good for her. I never bothered to ask her what she wanted or why he made her happy.

"Shit," I breathed.

"Finally," Arthur growled. "Are you seeing the truth yet?"

I swiped my glasses off and rubbed the bridge of my nose. "Yeah, I see it. I'm an idiot and a jerk."

"To put it mildly."

I nodded. "You're right. I never gave Dick a chance. I decided he wasn't good enough for her a long time ago and refused to consider that I was wrong. That she was smart enough to make her own choices. And now he's gone."

"He's coming back. But you need to fix this. She told him we didn't want her to marry him."

"She did?"

Arthur nodded. "Dick asked me about it. Said he was sorry he pushed things with us and that he didn't give us a chance to tell him no when he spoke to us. I told him that wasn't the case, and that I was okay with them being together."

"You threw me under the bus?" I snapped.

"Fuck, yes, I did. Because you're the one who did this. And because I wanted Dick to know he was welcome in my home. I wanted him to know he could see my kids, those little people in there who adore him. I'm not going to take him away from them because you're a spoiled, selfish prick."

I winced. He was right. Again, I was trying to blame someone else for my fuckup. I couldn't do it. I had to make things right with Dick, and I had to make things right between him and my mom. It wasn't fair to any of them that I wasn't willing to see Dick for the man he was.

"I'm sorry," I told Arthur.

He shook his head. "I'm not the one you need to apologize to. You need to apologize to Dick and Mom and my kids."

I nodded. "I will. But I need to talk to Dick first. He deserves the biggest apology of them all."

"Yep, he does. You might want to call him tonight. He's at a hotel and he can talk. And maybe he can get out of the rest of his trip and come home soon."

I nodded again. Arthur was right. I needed to call Dick sooner rather than later, and I needed to convince him to come home. Because he was better for our mother, for our whole family, than I ever thought. And she deserved that.

She deserved someone who loved her and would care for her and would always be there for her.

And that man was Dick. So help me God.

I MADE my excuses and left dinner. I didn't tell Mom or the kids that I was going to reach out to Dick. I didn't want to get their hopes up that I'd be able to fix everything. Not when I wasn't sure I could.

I had two texts from Goldie when I got home, but I ignored them and called Dick first. I hated doing that, but I knew Goldie would understand.

The phone rang three times before Dick answered with a very confused sounding, "Hello?"

"Hey Dick, it's Patrick."

"Is your mother okay? The kids?" His voice was immediately worried.

"Yes, everyone is fine."

"Okay. Okay. Good."

He wasn't going to make the call easy on me. Not that I blamed him. "I wanted to talk to you about my mother."

"I'm not sure there's anything we need to say about her."

"There are a few things I need to say. The first of which is I'm sorry."

"Excuse me?"

"I have been an asshole to you. I haven't given you a fair chance. I'm sorry for that."

"Well, damn. That's the last thing I expected to hear from you."

I huffed a laugh. "And I'm sorry for that, too. I wasn't willing to see you as yourself. I judged you because you weren't my father. And you never should have tried to be."

Dick sighed heavily. "When I met your mother, I thought she was the most beautiful woman I'd ever seen. I asked her on a date, and she told me she couldn't because her son needed her. I assumed her son was young, a teenager. When she told me you were twenty-five years old, I laughed. I thought it was an excuse not to date me."

I scowled at the phone.

"She said you were looking for a job and were stressed about it. I asked her more about you, and we started talking. When you got your job, she was so proud of you. She gushed about you. And then you started working, and your time was not as free. She had fewer updates about you because she saw you less often. She had more free time. She was willing to go out to dinner with me because you weren't there."

"I didn't desert her," I argued.

"No, son, you didn't. You got a life. And she was happy for you. She knew you loved your job. She was a little worried about you falling for Goldie, but she wanted you to be happy. The first few times we went out to eat, all she talked about was you and Arthur and the kids."

I mumbled something incoherent.

"She started calling me after a month or so. I think she was lonely for the first time ever and she liked having someone to talk to. I never pushed her for more than a friendship, but I didn't hide my interest in her. I could see you guys were her world. I'll admit I was a little jealous of that, not because of her, but because I wanted the same thing. The first time we kissed, I told her we needed to slow things down. I wanted her to make sure she wasn't using me as a replacement for you. Not in a weird way, but she wasn't as busy with you."

He was right. When I started working for Goldie, I

stopped having dinner with Mom as often. I was working weekends and evenings and when I wasn't working, I was thinking about Goldie and trying to figure out how to convince her to go out with me.

"We took things slow. We got to know each other. I know you don't like me, son, and I can't change who I am, but I love your mother. She will be the greatest regret of my life."

"I don't want that to be the case," I told him.

"Your mother loves you, Patrick. She will do anything for you. Even give up what she wants. I don't tell you that to make you feel bad, just it's the truth. Maybe she didn't want to marry me and you were an easy excuse, but I don't think that's the case. She chose you over herself."

"And she was wrong to do that."

Dick laughed softly, the quietest laugh I'd ever heard from him. "I'm not your father. I'm not anyone's father. I don't know what it's like to surrender yourself for another person. But what I've learned from your mother is that's exactly what you do when you're a parent. You put your children ahead of yourself every single time."

"I was wrong about you, Dick. I should have supported her. You're the person she needs to choose right now."

"Don't you put that on me. She'll never choose me. Not as long as you don't want her to. And I don't want her to choose me. I want her to make the choice that's right for her. If she loves me and wants to spend the rest of her life with me, I'm happy to do that. That's what I want. But I don't want her to choose me just because I'm an option. I want her to choose herself."

"I want that, too," I whispered. He was right. And he was a better man than me, by far. I could definitely learn a few things from him. "Thank you for loving my mother."

"I will always love her. It's up to her if she wants me to love her from here or there."

"I'm going to fix this, Dick. I promise you."

"We'll see, Patrick. We'll see. Have a good night, son."

He hung up, leaving me to stare at my phone. Everything he said was right. I just needed to grow the hell up and make it right.

I needed to talk to my mother, but that would have to wait. I clicked over to the texts Goldie sent me, hoping for good news about the day. My heart sank.

> Just finishing things now. Complete disaster. Betty's brought a fryer. Grease fire sent one employee to the hospital. Two booths burned.

An hour later, she sent a second text.

> I'll be late in the morning. Mayor Levine insisted I'm in his office first thing. Hopefully I'll be in after that. Going to bed now. Stressful day. I hope yours was better.

Goldie was going to get fired. Shit.

20

____

GOLDIE

I sat in my car and stared up at Town Hall. I did not want to go inside. I knew what Mayor Levine was going to say. He was going to fire me. And I had no defense. There was nothing I could say to change that. It still hurt.

I drew a deep breath and forced myself out of my car. I smoothed my hand over my blouse and straightened my spine. I debated wearing a skirt to the meeting, but fuck him and his misogynistic views. I was not going to show up looking like a female who needed his guidance in order to garner his favor and keep my job. It would only make my life worse if I did that. He didn't get that power over me.

Jane was sitting outside the mayor's office when I arrived. She gave me a sad smile and said, "He's not ready for you yet."

"He told you to say that so I'd have to wait?"

She nodded. "I think so. He's not in a meeting."

I sighed. "Thank you for all your help. I know I wouldn't have lasted this long in this job without you looking out for me."

"Not that it helped in the end," Jane said sadly.

"I know, but I appreciate it. I wish there was something I could do to make things better for you."

She shrugged. "I'll be okay. He has power over me and knows it so he mostly ignores me."

I rolled my eyes. "A boss shouldn't be like that. A boss should inspire and motivate their people."

"Not all bosses are willing to do that. Most I've had are only interested in looking like they're good at their job."

"Too bad we can't get a mayor who loves this town. It's too amazing of a place for it to be led by someone who doesn't love it."

"I wish you could be mayor."

I laughed. "Nope. I don't want that job."

"Why not? You'd be great at it."

I shook my head. "I love what I do. What I did, I guess."

"What are you going to do now?"

"I don't know. I haven't really had a chance to think about it. I'm hoping maybe I can convince him not to fire me."

Jane grimaced.

"Yeah, I kind of figured that, too. He already warned me."

Jane's desk phone buzzed. She held up a finger and lifted the receiver. "Yes, sir."

She lifted her gaze to me as she listened.

"She is here, sir. I'll send her in."

She hung up the receiver and rolled her eyes.

"He's ready for you."

I nodded. "Thanks, Jane. I'll see you soon."

She flashed me another sad look and returned her focus to her computer.

I opened the door to the mayor's office and forced a

smile to my face as I walked across the room on the plush carpet he brought in when he took the office.

He watched me as I moved, glaring at me the entire way until I sat. "Ms. Spear."

"Mr. Mayor."

"I'm sure you know why you're here this morning."

I swallowed roughly. "I am assuming you're looking for an explanation of what happened yesterday."

He laughed. "An explanation. Do you really think you can tell me what happened and all will be forgiven? This is not the first time your events have been ruined because of your inability to lead a team."

"My team had nothing to do with this," I snapped.

His brows rose. His lips curled up into a tight smile. He looked evil, like he was waiting for me to say something to defend my team. "Well, I'm glad you brought that up."

Dammit. I walked into his trap. Not that I knew what his trap was, but I was in it.

"You were alone at the event yesterday, is that correct?"

"Yes."

"So the fault for the accident rests on you?"

"It was an accident," I argued. Not that I didn't feel a significant measure of guilt. The event was supposed to be an easy one. That was why I told the rest of my team to take the day off. We had everything set and ready. The restaurants each had booths and the kids' events were all arranged around the food so it would be easy for the parents to grab food and let the kids enjoy the fun.

It never occurred to any of us that there would be a grease fire in one of the stations. All the menus were all approved ahead of time. None of the vendors were permitted to use grease. But one snuck in a fryer.

The grease fire was small compared to what it could

have been, but it was bad enough that the station was ruined and the booth next door was destroyed. Even worse, one of the employees was burned.

The event ended early when the fire broke out. Families were scared and upset. Betty's, the restaurant that brought the fryer, was potentially facing a lawsuit, and the tourism department was likely to be named, too.

What I hadn't figured out yet was why Betty's had a fryer. It was in the contract they signed that there was to be no grease because of the risks associated with it in the type of event we were holding. The restaurants were permitted to bring fried foods, but only if they prepared them in their location off-site and not at the event.

"That accident if going to cost the town a lot of money. The injured employee spent the night in the hospital. I went to see her last night, and she's talking lawsuit. How can I allow you to stay in your position when you're going to be a defendant in a lawsuit?"

"Every vendor signed a contract saying they would not use grease. Betty's violated that contract. They have no grounds to include me or the town or the tourism department in a lawsuit."

"Did you do an inspection of each booth before the event started?"

"No," I admitted. I did spot checks, but without the rest of my team, I couldn't inspect every single booth. Some events we did, but not for an event fully booked by local people we assumed would follow the rules.

"Maybe you should have. I'm sure it's something that would have been easy to see."

"I'm sure it would have been, but I didn't have time to go through every single booth to confirm the local vendors were following the guidelines set out by the contract they signed."

"So you're blaming them."

"They're the ones at fault."

"It was your event, Ms. Spear. You were responsible for it. And you already confirmed what Mr. Hill told me."

"Patrick?"

"Yes. He was here this morning. Said he wasn't even there. No one was except you."

My heart sank. Patrick went to talk to the mayor. He went to defend himself and throw me under the bus. How could he?

I drew a breath and pushed down the hurt. If Patrick was more concerned with his future than anything else, that was on him. He said over and over he loved his job, but maybe that was just bullshit so he could get close to me and help the mayor push me out. I couldn't worry about that at the moment.

"That's true. I was the only one there because my budget has been slashed and all the vendors were confirmed. One violating the terms of their contract was not something I could have foreseen nor something I could have prevented just by having others there."

"You could have if you did inspections before the event started. If you'd done your job."

"I did my job. I did everything right. I hold no responsibility in this."

"Tell that to the young woman in the hospital."

I sucked in a sharp breath. He was right. She wouldn't care who was to blame. She was injured. It didn't matter who was to blame.

"I can't overlook this, Ms. Spear. I can't allow you to stay in this position when you were the sole representative for the town in attendance and there was a fire that sent someone to the hospital. I can't let it go."

"You never had any intention of allowing me to hold on to this position."

"Because I knew you weren't qualified. This incident proves it. You should have confirmed all the stations met requirements. I have no doubt Mr. Hill would have. He said as much when we spoke."

"He did?"

Mayor Levine nodded. "You are able to stay in your position through the summer, but it will be in name only. Mr. Hill will be taking the senior role for all events. You'll be answering to him."

Losing my job was bad enough, but losing it to Patrick was twice the blow. He manipulated me and stole my job right out from under me. I thought I could trust him. Hell, I thought I could love him. But again, I was wrong about the man in my life. I was wrong about who he was and what I meant to him.

"When the summer is over and all the events are finished, you are, too, Ms. Spear. Consider these last two months your severance pay."

I nearly laughed in his face. If I didn't love MacKellar Cove so much, I would have told him where he could shove his severance pay and his opinion. I wanted to. But I kept my mouth shut and nodded.

"You can go now," Mayor Levine snarled.

I stood and glared at the weaselly man. I wanted to slap the smug look off his face. But he won. I was done. I had two months to find a job in the area that would pay me enough to keep my house and allow me to support my son. And we both knew no such job existed.

I left his office and came face-to-face with Jane. She had

that sad expression of a person who knew exactly what happened inside that office. She opened her mouth to say something, but I waved her off. I needed a minute. I couldn't speak. Not yet. I was going to cry or scream, or maybe both.

Probably both.

I forced a smile for Jane and left the building. I cranked up my engine and pulled away from the building, not wanting Mayor Levine to look out and see me sitting there.

I wasn't ready for work yet. If I went there with my emotions so close to the surface, I was going to punch Patrick.

I pulled over a few blocks from Town Hall and sent a text to Anna and Valentina asking if either of them were free.

ANNA

Yes but not home. I'm on my way to Detroit.

VALENTINA

I'm at the bakery. You can come in the back with me if you need to hide for a minute.

Sold. Be there soon. Anna, we'll call you. I just got fired.

I dropped my phone into my handbag as it buzzed with rapid-fire texts from both of them. I ignored them while I drove, putting all my focus and energy into holding my emotions inside before I could let them out at Cove Bakery.

The happy striped awning welcomed me to the adorable bakery where Valentina worked. Harriett waved at me as I walked in. The line in front of her wasn't long, but it was long enough that she was busy. I walked around the end of the case and headed straight for the kitchen and my friend.

As soon as I was behind closed doors, I fell apart.

Valentina was there, picking me up off the floor and helping me into a chair.

"What's happening? Is she okay?" Anna asked through the phone.

"Nope," Valentina answered for me. "Shit."

I sobbed, cluing Anna into my exact mood.

"What happened?" Anna asked.

Valentina stared at me, gaping, as all I did was cry.

"She's not okay," Valentina said. "She can't speak yet. She's just crying."

"He lied to me. He made me think he loved me." I hiccuped.

"Who is she talking about? The mayor?" Anna asked.

"Patrick," I cried. "He said he was attached. That he wasn't going to say he loved me because he didn't think I was ready to hear it, but he lied. He didn't mean it. He didn't mean any of it."

"Um, what did I miss?" Anna asked.

"I don't know, but I missed it, too," Valentina told her. "Goldie, you said you were fired. Why are we talking about Patrick? And why do you think he lied?"

"He stole my job," I hissed. "After the fire yesterday, Mayor Levine wanted to see me. I texted Patrick last night that I'd be late, and the snake went to see the mayor early this morning. Told the mayor he wasn't there yesterday. That it wasn't his fault. The mayor is going to let me finish the season, then I'm gone, but Patrick is in charge. He's the one making all the calls. I report to him."

"Seriously?" Anna said.

"Fucking men," Valentina said.

"Why would he do that? I thought he said he liked his job," Anna said. "Arthur says all the time how much Patrick loves working for you."

"Then I guess he's a liar, too, because Patrick went behind my back and stole my job. I told him earlier this summer that Mayor Levine wanted to fire me. That he was looking for any excuse. He cut my budget and said if I don't meet it, I'm fired. He said if anything goes wrong, I'm fired. Shit's gone wrong. A lot. But now someone was hurt and Patrick went in and told the mayor he had nothing to do with it and knows everything happening and he secured the spot. He stole my damn job."

"Have you spoken to him?" Anna asked.

I shook my head. "I couldn't face him. Not when I'm so upset."

"Maybe there's an explanation."

Valentina scoffed. "Please. He's an asshole who saw what he wanted and stole it out from under her. He got close to Goldie and made sure he was aware of everything going on, and the first chance he got, he positioned himself to take advantage of the situation."

I nodded even as I ached to argue with her. The man she described wasn't the Patrick I thought I knew. It wasn't the man I thought I was falling in love with. I hated that it was the man he had become. The man who swiped my job. Maybe that's who he was all along. God knew I couldn't read a man. I had the divorce papers to prove it, and now the figurative pink slip to match.

"I really think there's an explanation. We all know how Mayor Levine is. He's a manipulator. He's going to twist things. Maybe—"

"But why would Patrick go there?" Valentina asked. "Why did he go see the mayor at all? What reason could he have for that? He wasn't there. He couldn't defend Goldie because he wasn't there. He couldn't say she did everything she could do. The only reason he would have gone was to volunteer to fill in and take the job."

"It just seems strange. He's been so devoted and so sweet to Goldie. Why is this happening now?" Anna asked.

"Because he had the opportunity. My husband was screwing someone else. He still would be if she hadn't shown up in town. Men are assholes," Valentina argued.

"I know, hun, and Dawson is a dog. He isn't worthy of you. But we were all so happy about Goldie and Patrick," Anna said.

I leaned back in my seat. They were happy for me. They believed Patrick was good. Because I did. Because I trusted him and thought he was a good man.

"He pretended to be someone he isn't," Valentina said. "He pretended to love her. He told her he did but wouldn't say the words for her benefit. I believed all his lies. I believed he was a good guy."

"And I still think he is," Anna argued. "I don't think we were wrong about him. Goldie, you need to talk to him. Hear his side of things. Maybe there's an explanation. You owe it to yourself, and to him, to find out what really happened. Don't just take Mayor Levine's word for it. Talk to Patrick."

I sighed and met Valentina's gaze. "She's right."

Valentina nodded. "I know. But be careful. Because right now, we don't know which Patrick is the real Patrick. If he stole your job, you deserve better. If he lied or manipulated you, you deserve better. Don't settle."

"I won't. Been there, done that. I'm not going back."

"Let me know what happens," Anna said. "I need to get on a flight, but I'll check in tonight. I love you, hun. Both of you."

"Love you," Valentina and I both said. "Bye, Anna."

"Bye, guys." Anna hung up.

Valentina looked at me and offered a sad smile. "I hope she's right. I really do."

I nodded. "Me, too, but I'm just not as confident as she is."

Valentina shook her head. "Neither am I."

21

PATRICK

I walked into the office and looked around. It was quiet. Too quiet. An eerie quiet that set me on edge and made me wonder what was going on.

Goldie's office was still dark, which meant her meeting with the mayor wasn't over yet. Good. She would be happy when I talked to her and told her about my morning. But first, she needed to show up.

I logged into my computer and went through my morning routine of checking emails and reaching out to the vendors on my list. We had another quiet weekend coming up, but obviously quiet weekends were not as quiet as we'd hoped, so I was still going to check with everyone involved.

It was almost eleven when Goldie finally arrived. I heard her speak to Eve, then Theo. I stayed in my office, expecting her to stop by before she went to her own, but she didn't.

Strange, but okay. She had stuff to do. And her meeting probably wasn't good if it was that long.

I gave her a few minutes before I got up from my seat. I grabbed my tablet but really I just wanted to see her. To make sure for myself that she was okay.

I knocked on the doorframe and waited until she looked up at me. I started to walk in, smiling, but stopped when I caught the look on her face.

"Close the door, please," she said. Her voice was icy and crisp. Angry. Furious if I had to guess.

I closed the door and took a seat across from her. "How did your meeting go?"

"Not well. I've heard I will be reporting to you for the rest of my employment."

"What?"

"Mayor Levine informed me that you are my replacement. He's asked me to stay on through the end of summer to be available for the remainder of the events planned, but you will be the one calling the shots and in charge of everything."

"No. There's no way. I don't want that."

"Well, it seems as though your meeting this morning convinced him that you're the right person for the job. Since you weren't in attendance when the events went wrong, when a fire occurred and someone was injured, you're an excellent candidate for taking over for me."

"I never told him that," I argued. She was making it sound like I went to the mayor to steal her job.

"If that's the case—"

"If that's the case? What are you talking about? Goldie, you know I love my job. You know I don't want your job."

She shook her head. "I'm not sure what I know. There were a lot of things I thought that no longer seem to be true."

I sighed heavily and stared at her. She wasn't the woman I knew. She was cold and stiff. Her spine was straight. She was rigid. Her mood, her figure, her face. She actually believed that I tried to steal her job.

"He lied to you. Whatever he said, he lied."

"So you didn't meet with him this morning?"

"I did, but—"

"And you didn't tell the mayor that you weren't there yesterday?"

"I did that, too. But—"

"And you didn't tell him you would have performed inspections on all the booths if you'd been there?"

Shit. I said that, too. "Yes, but—"

"Then I'm struggling to find where Mayor Levine lied to me." She raised a brow, daring me to contradict all the things I just agreed to.

"It's not what it seems."

She folded her hands on her desk and tilted her head to the side. "Please, enlighten me. Tell me exactly how you telling the mayor you weren't there and that you would have done things differently during your meeting early this morning before I was there was not what it seems."

Fuck. She was right. All I wanted to do was help. I knew he was looking to fire her. I knew he was going to push things. He would use what happened to prove Goldie wasn't fit for the position she was more than qualified for.

After her texts the night before, I found out more details about what happened. I couldn't believe it. That was why I was up early, and why I went to the hospital after I saw the mayor. To protect Goldie and her job.

But it wasn't enough. Not if Mayor Levine already fired her.

"I wanted to tell the mayor that you weren't to blame. I said I wasn't there to show him that we need more staff at the events. I said I would have done inspections because that's what you have us do when we're all there. He's the reason we had less staff than usual. He's the reason you've been working yourself to death instead of taking time off."

"I'm going to have plenty of time off in a few months," she whispered.

"Goldie—"

She shook her head. "We have work to do. I can't deal with this right now. I'm going to schedule a meeting for after lunch with the entire team so I can update them all on what's going on and what to expect for the rest of the season. I will send you all my notes for the rest of the events. I believe you're up to date on everything I've been working on and all the events, so our transition should be easy enough to manage."

"There's no transition, Goldie. I'm not taking your job."

"You don't have a choice, Patrick. Mayor Levine—"

I jumped to my feet. "Fuck Mayor Levine! I don't care what he says. I don't want your job and I'm not taking it. You are the best thing that's happened to this town. You're the one who needs to be in this job. You need to keep your job. Mayor Levine said he wanted to get rid of you. If he's behind all of this, it's on him. He's the one who needs to be fired."

"There was a fire, Patrick. Even Mayor Levine couldn't have orchestrated that. Nor do I think he would have. A woman is in the hospital. I'm to blame for that. I'm the reason she's there. If I'd checked the booths, if I'd looked in on all of them, I would have seen the fryer. I would have been able to shut them down."

"They signed a contract."

"And it doesn't matter when someone's hurt."

"I spoke to her this morning. She said she's not going to sue us."

"She has no grounds if she wanted to. But she still got burned. Her life is forever changed."

"I'm sure it is, but that doesn't mean Mayor Levine wasn't behind it. You said you thought he was behind all the issues we had Memorial Day Weekend. Why wouldn't he be behind this?"

She sighed. "Patrick, he didn't set out to hurt someone. There's no way."

"But—"

"It's over, Patrick. We're over. Everything's over."

"We're over? Goldie, no. Why?"

She shook her head. "I can't do this. I can't trust you. I don't know what to believe right now, but I can't focus on whether or not I can trust you. I need to start looking for a new job and putting Paul first. I can't do this anymore."

"I love you, Goldie. Don't end this. Don't push me away."

She blanched. "No, you don't. You don't know how you feel."

I leaned back in my chair. Shocked. Hurt. I'd spent most of my life being told I didn't know my own mind. I was too young, too immature, too something to know what I really wanted. How I really felt. I never thought Goldie would be someone who would say something like that to me. I never thought she saw me the way so many others did. She trusted me. She believed in me. She hired me to work for her and made me believe in myself in ways I never had in any other job.

But now she said she didn't think I knew my own heart.

"Don't do that," I snapped. "Don't tell me I don't know how I feel."

"You don't," she said. "You told me you weren't going to say that. I know it's because you weren't sure. You knew you didn't love me. Don't throw it at me now when I'm trying to do what's right for me."

"Ending things with me is what's right for you?"

She swallowed roughly. After a second, she nodded. "Yes. It is. I need to find a new job. Paul's dad is coming to visit. I need to focus on that."

I nodded and stood. "Okay. I understand. Please let me know what I need to do, boss. I will be available to help you as much as possible."

"I will do what I can to make sure things go well for the town the rest of the time while I'm here."

I sucked in a breath. She made it seem so final. She was done. We were done. Everything was done.

I stumbled out of her office and went back to mine. I couldn't argue with her. She wasn't willing to listen to me. All I could do was follow orders.

And hope we could figure it out.

THE MEETING GOLDIE held in the afternoon was not good. Eve, Theo, and Howard were angry about Goldie getting fired, but they were even more angry when she told them I would be her temporary replacement.

To her credit, Goldie did her best to be the person I knew her to be. She told them not to be upset with me and that it was all because of Mayor Levine, but after the meeting, she refused to speak to me again.

I spent the rest of the day reviewing everything about the position so I could fill in for her, but when I went home, I carried work with me so I could find out how to save her job.

I was angry with the owner of Betty's. He signed their contract. He knew the rules. What I wanted to find out was why he didn't follow the rules, even though he knew them.

It was late, but not so late that Betty's might be closed. I got in my SUV and drove over there. Lights were still on and people were walking out. I walked inside and smiled at the hostess.

"Good evening. Our kitchen is closing soon, but we can seat you if you'd like."

"Actually, I'd like to speak to the owner if he's here."

Her smile faded ever so slightly, but she nodded and asked me to wait there.

I looked around the restaurant. It was a nice, local place. Pictures of local events and graduating classes the last few years. I hadn't been there to eat before, but if the food was half as good as it smelled, I had a feeling I'd enjoy it. If things worked out with Goldie, maybe I could convince her to go there sometime.

"Hello. Can I help you?" a man asked from behind me.

I turned to face an older man with brown hair and kind eyes. "Hi, Rodney?"

He nodded. "Yes, and you are?"

I extended my hand. "I'm Patrick Hill. We've spoken on the phone a few times."

"Yes, from the tourism office, right?"

I nodded and shook his hand. "Yes, sir. I was wondering if we could speak for a few minutes."

Rodney gestured to a booth a little away and sat on one side. I took the seat opposite him.

"What can I do for you, Patrick?"

"I was wondering if you could tell me what happened yesterday."

He sighed and rubbed his head. "My attorney said I shouldn't be speaking to anyone about this."

"Really?"

Rodney nodded. "Yeah. I don't like to be like that, but I don't know how bad Clara's injuries are or if she's going to be filing a lawsuit. My lawyer said I could say something to make it worse."

"I just want to know what happened. We spoke many times. Even last week. You never said anything about a fryer."

He inhaled deeply and met my gaze. He chewed the inside of his lip and looked around. "Is there a way this can be off-the-record?"

I leaned back. That meant he had something to tell me, but he was worried about how it would look or what it would mean. "I don't know, Rodney. The situation I'm in is my boss is getting fired because of what happened. She's being held accountable by the mayor. I don't want that to happen because she's an amazing boss, and she's smart and creative. She's responsible for all the events this summer. But because of what happened yesterday, the mayor is going to fire her."

Rodney shook his head. He pursed his lips. "My lawyer is going to hang me for saying this, but the mayor is the reason I had the fryer there in the first place."

I straightened. "Excuse me?"

"I knew about the clause. I saw it when I signed the contract. I had no intention of bringing the fryer out. But last week, Mayor Levine came in here with his wife. He asked if I was going to be serving at the event. Said his favorite thing was our onion rings. I told him we wouldn't be serving them because of the fryer rule. He told me I should bring it anyway. Said no one would know. He wouldn't tell anyone."

I blew out a breath. Wow. The mayor was behind it. And we had proof. We had a witness. "Have you told your lawyer this?"

He nodded. "Yeah. He said it'll be something we need to

use if Clara sues us. She's a good employee, a good person. I hate that she was hurt. I never imagined anything like that could have happened. I feel so guilty about it. I wish I could go back and not listen to him."

"I wish you could, too. Is there any chance you would be willing to go on the record? Reporting the conversation you had with the mayor?"

"I don't know. If I do, I could lose everything."

"Actually, I think the opposite is going to be the case. Mayor Levine has been manipulating events all summer. This is something he's liable for. I understand he didn't force you, but when a man like him, a powerful man, tells you to do something and implies his approval and that he will look the other way, it's something that is very strong in the eyes of the public. If nothing had happened, maybe it would be no big deal, but a woman was injured. Public property was destroyed. Someone needs to be held accountable, and it shouldn't be my boss."

Rodney looked around at his restaurant. Customers were eating, some were paying their bill and heading out. "I poured myself into this place. My wife and I started it almost twenty years ago. Liz is the head chef. She loves to cook. I'm the people person, the one who talks to the customers and makes sure everyone has everything they want. She's the one with the magic. Liz made a special menu for the event. She wasn't going to include anything fried. But when I told her what Mayor Levine said, she was excited. She knew those foods were our biggest sellers. Having them available would mean we'd have a better day."

I nodded. I sympathized. It was hard to not offer their customer favorites, but it was for a reason. A reason they learned the hard way.

"Liz debated. She slept on it. That's how she functions.

When she woke up, she said it only made sense to allow us to have a fryer when so many things we serve are fried. We have one that's smaller, but that would still work well. Or so we thought. We weren't counting on the wind and the environment we were working in. We had no idea. We should have known, but we didn't."

"I understand. We should have included more warnings in our contracts. We should have made sure you understood the risks and the reasoning behind it."

"It was our decision. We knew the rules. But when the mayor—"

"And that's why I want you to go on the record. Because he needs to be held accountable. He needs to be removed from office. He needs to know he can't put people at risk, mess with people's lives, and get away with it. Will you help me, Rodney? Please."

He held his breath for a second, then nodded. "Yes. Yes, I will. You're right. Mayor Levine shouldn't fire your boss when he's the reason Clara is hurt and we're worried about our business. I'll help."

I sighed. It was all going to be okay. Mayor Levine was done.

22

____

I debated all night about telling Goldie what I learned when I spoke with Rodney. In the end, I decided to keep the information to myself. She didn't trust me. She believed I was trying to sabotage her job. It hurt more than I thought it would to know she thought I could do something like that, and I couldn't open myself up to more judgement and anger from her.

The next few days were quiet around the office. Theo and Eve barely spoke to me. They were just as angry as I was, but they decided I was the bad guy, so they were taking it out on me. Goldie was only communicating through email. We weren't speaking when we passed each other, and I worked with my door closed most of the time.

If I didn't find a way to fix all of this, I was going to need to look for a new job. Hell, maybe if I did fix it, I needed to look for a new job. I wasn't sure I could stand being there with all of them when they didn't believe in me and thought so little of me.

Wednesday afternoon, I left early to meet with Rodney's lawyer. Once he found out we'd spoken, he was angry, but when Rodney and I explained I was trying to help, he was willing to listen. Rodney approved my involvement in everything, up to and including the conversations the lawyer, Weston, had with Clara.

Everything was falling into place. It felt like a victory. I wanted to share it all with Goldie, but I was too raw and she was too angry.

"Mr. Hill. Thanks for coming," Weston said when I arrived. "We're all waiting for you."

"All?"

Weston was an older man with a kind smile and sharp green eyes. He wore a too-big gray suit and sneakers, which made me smile. His voice was deep and commanding, the kind of man you'd listen to in a courtroom, or anywhere else.

I followed him into the conference room where Rodney and Clara were already sitting, talking and smiling.

"You're out of the hospital. I'm so happy to see that," I said to Clara. She had her curly hair tied up away from her face and a bandage on her left hand. Her brown eyes were bright and happy. Aside from the bandage, you'd never know she spent two days in the hospital.

She chuckled. "I'm out. They mostly kept me longer as an extra precaution. I could have been treated and released the same day, but since it was my hand, they wanted me to stay and make sure I didn't have any mobility or nerve issues."

"Which they should have done," Rodney argued sternly. "We are going to cover everything."

Clara waved him off, but Weston stepped in and said, "Let's discuss all of this."

I took a seat across the table from Rodney and Clara,

with Weston at the head. Weston handed out stapled packets of paper to each of us.

"What you have is all the evidence we have in this case. The first page is an affidavit from Rodney stating Mayor Levine asked him to serve fried food using a fryer. It details the conversation to the best of Rodney's memory, stating he mentioned the violation of the contract and Mr. Mayor stating that no one would check and the food would be better."

I read through the paperwork and knew that alone was enough to run the mayor out of town. If even one news station picked it up, he'd be done.

"Next we have the contract that Rodney signed. It was clear that fryers were not allowed. That's to show we're not trying to hide anything. Rodney admits he violated the terms of the contract he signed but only did so when he received encouragement from the mayor prior to the event."

I scanned over the contract I'd read dozens of times. It was the same one we had all vendors sign. Being in the park, the risk of high winds meant restricting anything that could blow over and burn someone. The fact that it only happened the one time was a relief, but it still happened.

"Next are Clara's medical records from the hospital. Clara is here because she's agreed to be a part of this and has given us permission to use her medical records as evidence against the mayor."

"What about your injuries?" I asked her.

"I've been working in restaurants my entire life. I love it. Burns are a part of the job. Not that it was fun, but it's expected and I'm not upset by it. I knew what the contract said, and I didn't argue about it. I'm just as liable as Rodney."

"But you're the one who was hurt," Rodney said, putting his hand on her uninjured one. "I'm so sorry for that, Clara."

"I know you are. And I appreciate you offering to pay my bills."

"It's not an offer. We're going to cover it. I think that's the next page, right?" Rodney looked at Weston for confirmation.

"It is," Weston agreed. "Rodney and Liz have agreed to cover all of Clara's medical expenses related to the incident. The restaurant's insurance will also cover the damage to town property. We've already spoken to their agent and everything is going to be handled appropriately."

"So, where does all of this leave us with the mayor? He's the one who made everything happen. Why is he getting off without punishment?"

Weston closed his packet of paper and folded his hands on top of it. He looked at Clara and Rodney, then back at me. "That's what we'd like to ask you about. Rodney's insurance is covering the damage. He's taking the hit for it. Clara is not looking to sue anyone. We can ignore all of this as far as the mayor is concerned, or we can push the issue and force him out of office."

"He doesn't deserve that office."

"Agreed," Rodney said. "But if I go after him, it'll be my word against his and I'm not in a position to prove my innocence."

"Which is what we want from you. You said there were other incidents that you believe the mayor influenced? Is that something you can share with us?" Weston asked.

I drew a breath. "It's all suspicion. We have no proof. Memorial Day Weekend, we had one chef who didn't show up because he was asked to come the next day. The same night, the band we booked was told we'd found a better replacement and didn't want them to come either. We haven't been able to prove it, but both people were contacted from a generic number in Town Hall."

"And you believe it was the mayor? Why would he do that?"

"He doesn't like my boss. He feels as though women shouldn't be in charge and wants to push her out. He cut our budget by fifteen percent two weeks before our kick-off event and told her if she didn't hit it, he was going to fire her."

Rodney whistled. "That's a big hit. But is that enough to go after him?"

Weston shook his head. "No, but it might be enough to scare him. Patrick, how good is your deception?"

I shrugged. "Okay, I guess. Why?"

"Because I think I know how we can get the mayor to resign without anyone else getting hurt."

"I'm listening."

THE REST of the week was busy. Weston and I were in touch daily with anything we could find out about Mayor Levine. He wanted time to dig into the man's background before I confronted him, so we agreed I would request a meeting with the mayor at the end of the following week, which was right before July Fourth.

The weekend events went well. We had no issues and no concerns at all. Everyone showed up, and even the weather cooperated.

Goldie still didn't speak to me. She sent me texts if there was something I needed to know quickly, but otherwise we didn't communicate. The entire time, I tried to tell myself it was okay, but it wasn't. It hurt like hell. I loved her, and she dismissed me like I was nothing. Like what we had was never that important to her.

The only bright spot was Mom was a little happier when I saw her Sunday night. I missed dinner with everyone, but Mom was smiling a little more. When I asked her about it, she said she enjoyed her time with the grandkids.

"I was really hoping you and Goldie would give me another one or two," she said with a twinkle in her eye.

I shook my head. "Mom, I don't want kids. And Goldie doesn't want me."

"You'll change your mind, and you two will work it all out."

"Mom," I said firmly. "I need you to hear me. I know you don't want to accept it, but I don't want kids. I've never wanted kids."

She teared up at my harsh words. "I'm sorry. I push too hard. I just always hoped you would decide you did. If you met the right woman. You're such a good man, and you'd make such a great father."

"I'm sorry I snapped, Mom. It's been a long week."

"Goldie will come around. The ones we love always do."

"Have you heard from Dick?"

She shook her head. "No. And I won't. He's moving on. He won't put me in a position to turn him down again."

"Maybe you shouldn't turn him down again."

She smiled sadly. "I know you don't like him. I'm not going to choose him over you."

"I had no right getting involved in your relationship, Mom. And if I was going to stick my nose in it, I should have at least made sure I knew what was going on. Dick's a good man, Mom."

"I know."

"And he's not Dad, but he's kind and he adores you. That's what really matters."

"Not if you won't come around when he's here."

"I will. I've seen a different side to him. I didn't want to see who he was before, but I was wrong to think of him as the bad guy. He was there for you when I wasn't."

"You're supposed to have your own life, Patrick. You don't need to hang around your old mom forever."

"And you need to have your life, too. Call Dick, Mom. Tell him to come home."

"He won't."

"Yes, he will. He told me he would if you decided you wanted him to."

"You spoke to him?" she gasped.

"I did. Because I realized after he left that I was wrong about a lot of things, and that I needed to apologize to him and make things right between you. He said my apology isn't enough and that you have to decide what you want. He's not going to make you refuse him again."

Tears spilled down her cheeks. She patted my hand. "Thank you, Patrick. I know that wasn't easy for you to do."

"I never should have been so hard on him in the first place. Or on you. You deserve to be loved, Mom. And you picked a man who loves you with his entire being."

She smiled. "Yes, I did. And you'll find a woman who's the same."

My heart stung at her words. I thought I had when I fell for Goldie. When she let me in and said I gave her hope and she might be feeling the same way I did. But love didn't seem to be in the cards for me. Maybe one day, but I couldn't imagine risking my heart again. Not after the pain I was in. It was better to just stop trying. Find a new job and move. Leave the hurt behind and make the most of a new life. One far from Goldie and MacKellar Cove.

MY MEETING with the mayor was scheduled for late Friday afternoon. Weston and I decided meeting with him going into the weekend was the best. It would take a little while for the news to become public, giving Levine a chance to get out of town. We hoped.

I didn't bother telling the others I'd be leaving early since none of them spoke to me anyway. After I settled things with Mayor Levine, I would find a new job and submit my resignation. But first, I needed to get Goldie's job back.

Mayor Levine's assistant, Jane, was at her desk when I walked in. She gave me a tight smile and said he was ready for me.

I knocked on the door and let myself in when I heard him call out. Mayor Levine stood and approached me, holding out his hand for me to shake. He was treating me like an equal, someone worthy of his approval. And he was expecting the same from me.

"Good afternoon. I heard the events last weekend went well. No doubt because you were in charge."

"Actually, Goldie was the one who had everything set and ready for the weekend. She's the one who deserves credit when everything goes according to plan."

The mayor's lips tightened and thinned. His eyes blazed with anger. "Yes, well, if that were the case, errors wouldn't have happened under her watch. Let's sit and talk about how we're going to change things within the tourism department for the better and make MacKellar

Cove an even more attractive tourist destination next summer."

I nodded. "That's exactly why I came here."

He grinned and rounded his large desk. He sat down and leaned back in his chair. "Well, the first thing I'm assuming you want is to have your budget back. I'm not sure I can get all fifteen percent for you, but I'll see what I can do. If we're going to improve the town, it'll cost some money."

"Yes, it will. But you won't be the one approving that budget."

"Excuse me?" Mayor Levine leaned forward and glared at me. He threaded his fingers together and rested his hands on the desk.

"You're going to resign. Today. You're going to tell everyone you got a new job or you're having a personal issue or you were never qualified for this job and are leaving. I don't really care what you tell people, as long as the words *I resign* are a part of it."

"Why in the hell do you think I would do that?" he snarled.

"Because if you don't, I'm going to expose you for the snake you are."

"What are you talking about?"

"I'm talking about you calling Chef Julian and telling him that he needed to come in a day later and you would pay the extra five percent. And I'm talking about you calling Unhinged and telling them you found a better band. And I'm talking about you telling Rodney from Betty's that he could bring a fryer to the event two weeks ago, even though you knew it was a violation of his contract."

"If he chose not to follow the contract, that's not on me."

"Actually, according to his lawyer, as a representative of MacKellar Cove, your request and assurance that no one would know constitutes approval of that violation. That means you will be named as a defendant for the injuries and property damage in the event of a lawsuit."

"That'll never stick," he growled. "And you can't prove anything. It's his word against mine, and no one will believe that fool over me."

"Actually, I think a lot of people will. And I think you know that, but even if you don't, I don't think you're willing to risk your reputation on the chance that you're right."

"I am right."

"Well, you might be right, but you have two options. You can take your chances with the public and let the people of MacKellar Cove decide if they trust you or Rodney, who has the support of myself, Ms. Spear, and the entire tourism department, not to mention his attorney and all his staff. Or you can resign with whatever excuse you want to come up with."

Mayor Levine glared hard at me. I could see the caged animal in his gaze. He was trapped, and he knew it.

"You've made an enemy, Mr. Hill. You're not going to succeed at your job now."

I laughed. "I don't want the job you assigned to me. I never did. Goldie Spear deserves that job. And our new mayor will reinstate her the minute you're out of office."

On cue, there was a knock on the door. It opened before Mayor Levine had a chance to say anything and Vice-Mayor Omar Knight walked in. "Good afternoon, gentlemen."

Omar was everything Mayor Levine was not. Forward thinking, supportive of women and nonbinary people being in charge, and competent. He was in his mid-thirties. He hadn't been in politics long enough and was not next in line when Mayor Sanchez stepped down, which was the only reason Omar didn't get the job over Levine. But I saw that as a good thing.

"I did not tell you to come in," Mayor Levine spat. It was clear they did not get along.

Omar met my gaze, then slid his back to Mayor Levine coldly. "Well, considering this is going to be my office very shortly, I don't care what you did or did not do."

Mayor Levine sputtered. "You don't deserve this office."

"Actually, sir, you don't deserve this office. You put the town and the residents at risk with the stunts you've pulled the last few months. You do not get to sit there and judge anyone else. It's past time you submitted your resignation and left the building." Omar crossed his arms and stared down at Mayor Levine.

Mayor Levine rose to his full height, which was still a few inches shorter than Vice-Mayor Knight. The two men squared off silently. Levine turned red and looked like he was going to pop while Knight remained calm and did nothing more than raise a single brow.

"You'll regret this," Mayor Levine snarled.

"If you ever say anything disparaging about anyone in this town, including Ms. Spear, Mr. Hill, myself, or anyone else you've tried to manipulate in your schemes, you will be the one who regrets this. Legal action will be taken against you for your part in the ruined events this summer. And that legal action will draw all your demons out of the shadows, sir." Vice-Mayor Knight refused to sink to Levine's level. He was telling the truth, not making empty threats. He was aware of everything that had happened and didn't hesitate to believe it all.

Mayor Levine growled at us and slammed his chair back, letting it crash into the wall. He rushed around his desk and headed for the door. When he opened it, Officers

Rucker and Masterson were waiting to escort the mayor off the property.

Jane watched the scene with shock and a barely contained smile. Mayor Levine turned back to Vice-Mayor Knight and me, but thought better of saying something and instead stormed out of Town Hall with the officers following closely behind him.

It was finally over.

23

GOLDIE

I DESPERATELY NEEDED A PIECE OF CAKE. MAYBE A WHOLE cake. I couldn't remember ever looking forward to book club as much as I was.

"Have you figured out what you're going to do about your job?" Valentina asked as I shoveled my first bite of cake into my mouth.

I shook my head. We'd talked about it. She knew I couldn't challenge the mayor, no matter how much I wanted to rub his nose in the things he'd done to put me in the position I was in.

"You should confront him about the band and the chef," Finley said. "Trent will go with you."

I shook my head again. "I'm a big girl. I can fight my own battles. No offense, but I don't want Trent or Patrick or any man to try to fix things for me. If Mayor Levine is going to fire me, which he did, then I'm done."

"But you don't deserve it," Valentina argued. "He doesn't deserve his job either."

"Who doesn't deserve their job?" Trinity asked. She took

a seat next to Laura and cut herself a piece of cake. Less for me. Damn.

"Mayor Levine," Valentina answered for me.

Trinity snorted. "Then I guess it's good he's leaving."

I choked on my cake. "He's what? No. There's no way."

Trinity paused with her fork halfway to her mouth. She glanced around until her gaze landed on Willow. She raised her brows.

Willow shrugged. "She's right. Rowan and James were there Friday to walk him out of the office. Rowan didn't really have any information, but the Vice-Mayor doesn't usually ask police officers to walk out a person who resigned. I have a feeling some shit went down. I figured you'd know, Goldie. I was going to ask you."

I shook my head again. "I didn't know about it at all."

"James said Patrick was there," Trinity said.

"Patrick? My Patrick? I mean, my ex Patrick?" I blabbed.

"Yep. I sort of got the feeling he had something to do with the mayor leaving. Vice-Mayor Knight is going to be the new mayor until the election. I like him a lot." Trinity took a bite of her cake and nodded. "Yum."

"Omar is a really nice guy," Blake said. "He comes in for breakfast most days and is a really good tipper. He tipped huge when I was pregnant."

"He was probably grateful you didn't give birth while he was eating," Finley teased.

Blake laughed. "Probably true. I think his tips alone bought the crib."

"He's going to be a good boss, Goldie," Willow said.

"Mayor Levine already fired me. He told me I was done at the end of the summer. Why would Vice-Mayor Knight go back on that?" I asked.

"Because he's not a dick," Finley said. "He actually uses

his brain and is a good man. I think he'll give you your job back."

I wished I had her confidence. Omar was a good man. The few interactions I'd had with him, he was competent and intelligent. He was someone I had a lot of faith in. He would be good for MacKellar Cove. But that didn't mean he was willing to give me a job I'd been fired from after a fire that left a woman injured and damage to town property.

"I think you need to get a meeting with the new mayor this week. Find out. Let him tell you he doesn't want you for the position."

"If Patrick was there, it was probably to make sure he kept the job," I said, my gut churning as I said the words. I hated saying them. That wasn't the man I knew. But it was hard to argue with the evidence I'd been given.

"You need to talk to Patrick," Finley argued. "I'm with Anna that you need to give him a chance. There could be an explanation."

I nodded, but they all knew I wouldn't actually do it. I told them all the week before about Patrick stealing my job. I couldn't imagine another option. And Patrick being there when Mayor Knight took office was just another thing that made it seem as though he was securing his job.

And that hurt.

BEFORE WORK THE NEXT MORNING, I saw an email asking me to come in for a meeting with the mayor. Not knowing which mayor I was meeting with, I gave myself a pep talk and headed to Town Hall.

Jane was smiling when I got there. "Did you hear Mayor Levine resigned?"

"That's true?"

She nodded eagerly. "He's gone. He's not coming back. An announcement is going out shortly, but Mayor Knight wanted to speak to you first thing. He's ready for you."

"Thanks," I told Jane. It was good to see her smiling.

I knocked on the office door and waited for Mayor Knight to call out for me to enter. When I opened the door, he stood from his desk and walked around to shake my hand. "Ms. Spear, it's so nice to see you. Thank you for coming in here this morning. I wanted to catch you before the news goes public."

"It's a small town, sir. News is already public."

He chuckled, his straight white teeth on full display. He looked kind and pleasant, not like he was going to eat me alive like the last man who occupied that office. "I tend to forget about that. Well, then I guess you know Mayor Levine has chosen to step down as mayor. His resignation will be announced today at ten. He's already left town, but that's okay. He wasn't too happy to be leaving, as I'm sure you can imagine."

"Yes, I'm sure he wasn't."

"So Patrick filled you in?" he asked.

"Patrick? No. We haven't spoken. I assume he will retain the position as head of the tourism department, and I'll be ready to leave by the end of summer."

"Is that what you want? Because Patrick told me he has no interest in the position."

"He what?"

"Sit, Ms. Spear. It seems as though we have some things to discuss."

He sat in the matching chair on the visitor side of the desk, facing me. He leaned forward, his forearms on his thighs. He wasn't wearing a suit jacket, just a pink button-down shirt rolled up at the sleeves with a navy tie. He looked casual and professional at the same time.

"Patrick has been working the last two weeks to get rid of Mayor Levine. He found out that Mayor Levine gave Rodney verbal permission to bring a fryer. Not explicitly, but close enough that a lawyer said it was perceived approval."

"What?" My mind spun. Why didn't Patrick tell me that? Why did he keep it from me?

As I asked myself the question, I knew the answer. We weren't speaking. I wasn't speaking to him. He tried to talk to me multiple times, but I refused to have a conversation with him. I cut him off and didn't give him a chance to explain himself.

Shit.

"Patrick was the one who made all of this possible. He found the evidence needed to get rid of Mayor Levine for good. He's the one who confronted him. And when he came to me with the entire story, I knew he was telling the truth. I wasn't the slightest surprised to find out Mayor Levine was manipulating things and blaming you. And that's only part of why Patrick insisted you get your job back."

"He did?"

"He did. He was very specific about that requirement. He said you're the best thing that's ever happened to MacKellar Cove. He wants you running the tourism department. And he's convinced me to return your original budget and to give you an increased budget for next year." Mayor Knight laughed.

I shook my head slowly, struggling to make sense of what he was telling me.

"Can I be blunt with you, Ms. Spear?"

"Please, call me Goldie," I said, nodding for him to speak his mind.

"Patrick is your biggest fan, Goldie. He refused to do anything if it meant you wouldn't be reinstated. He adores you. He told me more than once that working for you was the best decision he'd ever made. I got the feeling his feelings run deeper than a boss and employee, and I have no judgement on that. But if you can see how good of a man he is, I also want you to know he's very dedicated to you."

My throat tightened. I nodded, knowing I wouldn't be able to get words out.

Mayor Knight grabbed my hand and squeezed it. "I think you feel the same, Goldie. I hope you two can work out whatever has happened that put this distance between you."

"I hope so, too. Thank you for telling me what happened, Mayor Knight."

He grinned. "Omar, please."

I nodded. "Omar. Thank you."

He stood with me and walked me to his office door. He left it open when he went back inside. Jane just smiled again. She was a whole new person. It was a whole new office. In the very best way.

I couldn't wait to get to the office and speak to Patrick. A part of me felt guilty that he was going to be forced to give up the job, but if what he told Omar was true, then he wouldn't be upset by it.

"Meeting!" I called out as I walked into the office. I tossed my stuff on my desk and went to the conference room. Eve and Theo were right behind me. They glared at Patrick as he joined us. Howard wasn't far behind him.

"What's going on?" Eve asked when everyone was seated.

"What I'm about to tell you doesn't leave this room," I

said, meeting the confused gazes of everyone except Patrick, who refused to look at me.

The others all nodded.

"Mayor Levine is gone."

"What? How?" Theo asked.

"Patrick worked with a lawyer and the owner of the restaurant that had the fire and got Mayor Levine to resign. It'll be announced shortly."

"Dude. You did that?" Theo asked.

"Why would you do that? You got Goldie's job," Eve said.

"Because he's in love with her," Howard answered.

Patrick snapped his mouth shut and crossed his arms.

"Patrick did it because he never set out to steal my job. We all know how Mayor Levin was. We all understand that he was the bad guy here. What the rest of you didn't know was he threatened to fire me more than a month ago. He said if we didn't hit our budget, he was going to let me go. He never wanted me in this position. He never wanted a woman in this position. I blamed Patrick because Mayor Levine made it seem like he was to blame, but I was wrong. And I owe him an apology."

Patrick finally looked up at me. He shook his head. "No worries. You don't owe me anything."

My eyes narrowed at the sharp tone of his voice. "I definitely owe you an apology. I should have given you a chance to explain. I was hurt and angry, and I took it out on you. It wasn't right and it wasn't fair, and I am very sorry for the way I treated you the last few weeks."

"Me, too," Theo said. "I was a dick, man. I fell for the mayor's bullshit, too."

"So did I. I'm sorry, Patrick," Eve said.

"It's all good. Is there anything else?" Patrick asked.

I shook my head, wondering why he didn't seem relieved

to have the truth out in the open. "There's nothing else. Mayor Knight will be holding the press conference. It sounds as though Mayor Levine will be resigning officially, but no one is going to publicize what he did. We're putting it behind us."

"Damn. I would have thrown him under the bus," Eve said.

"It's better to just have him gone," Patrick said. He stood and walked out of the conference room.

Theo, Eve, and Howard asked me a few more questions that I didn't have the answers to. In the end, they agreed it would be better without Mayor Levine, and that was good enough.

I followed the others out of the conference room and went to Patrick's office. His door was closed, as it had been the last two weeks. He was still shutting me out, literally.

He lifted his head when I knocked but didn't smile at me. I waited until he waved me in before I let myself into his office. I closed the door and sat down opposite his desk.

"What can I do for you, boss?" he asked.

"I'm sorry for the way I've treated you, Patrick. I should have listened to you when you tried to tell me you didn't try to talk Mayor Levine into giving you my job. I shouldn't have assumed I knew what you would do."

"But you did. You did assume. You thought I was the kind of man who'd steal your job right out from under you."

"And I was wrong."

He nodded slowly. "You were. But you were only wiling to see that after Mayor Knight told you I fought so hard to get your job back for you."

"Patrick, I—"

"Listen, boss, I get it. You were hurt and angry and you blamed me. You thought I was just as bad as Mayor Levine.

You believed I was only with you for my own greed. I'm happy you have your job. I'm happy you know the truth. I'm happy things are working out for you. But I can't go back to the way things were before that quickly. I just can't."

"What are you saying?" I whispered.

"I'm saying nothing has changed between us, Goldie. You saw me as the bad guy, and I can't be with someone whose first instinct is to think that of me. I deserve better."

I sucked in a shaky breath and nodded. "You're right." I rose to my unsteady feet. "You're right, and I'm sorry about that. I should have trusted who I thought you were instead of who I feared you were. And that will be a regret I carry forever. You definitely deserve better, Patrick. And I hope you find it. I hope you find everything you deserve."

He nodded. He swallowed. He didn't speak.

So I walked out. It was over. And it was all my fault.

TWO DAYS LATER, Charles and Leslie came to visit. They wanted to stay for the long holiday weekend so they had extra time with Paul. Paul was awkward at first, but after a few hours, everyone was talking like we'd all been a family all along.

Leslie was a wonderful man, kind and sympathetic to what our family had been through. He connected well with Paul, making him feel important to both Leslie and Charles. And the two of them were sweet together. I was happy to see Charles happy. And for the first time, it didn't hurt to know I wasn't enough to make him happy.

Leslie excused himself to go to bed a few hours after dinner. Paul stayed up and watched a movie with Charles. It was good to see them together, and nice to not have to watch the terrifying movie myself. I sat on the opposite side of the living room and read a book while they scared themselves shitless.

Paul went to his room after the movie, and Charles picked up the snacks they'd eaten and started the dishwasher. I followed him into the kitchen.

"Thank you. You didn't have to do that."

Charles shrugged. "It's the least I can do. Thank you for letting us stay."

"You're always welcome."

"Is Patrick okay with it?"

"How do you know about Patrick?" I blurted.

Charles smiled. "Paul mentioned him. He sounds like a good man."

I smiled. "He is. But we're not together anymore."

"You're not? I'm sorry, Goldie. Can I ask what happened?"

"I didn't trust him."

"I'm sure I'm partly to blame for that," Charles said with a wince.

"You can't blame yourself. I'm the one who was presented with false evidence that I believed. I thought he was out for my job."

"He works for you, right?"

"Yeah." I breathed a laugh. "I should have known Paul would tell you everything."

"He clearly didn't tell me everything. I didn't know it was over. I'm sorry, Goldie."

I shrugged and tried not to let my emotions out. "I'll be fine."

Charles smiled. "I know you will be. You were always independent and sure of yourself. It's part of what makes you a great boss."

"But not a great wife?" I asked.

He shook his head. "I didn't say that."

"No, but that seemed to be what you meant."

"We weren't right for each other, and that was my fault. You were an amazing wife when I was willing to let you be."

"What does that mean?"

"It means you can take care of yourself. There were times when I wanted to be the person who was there for you. The one you turned to to solve things. But you didn't need me for that. You didn't need anyone for that. You were rarely willing to be vulnerable. And I wasn't willing to ask you to be."

"You think that's what I did with Patrick?"

He took my hand and held it loosely. "I can't answer that for you. But if you pushed him away at the first sign of a challenge, maybe you have your answer."

I didn't like that truth.

"All I can say, Goldie, is that you have an amazing heart. You're a wonderful woman and you deserve the kind of love that makes you willing to expose yourself. If it's not with Patrick, then it'll be with someone else, but the way Paul talked about him, he made you happy. That's something worth holding on to, even if it means being more vulnerable and telling him exactly how you feel about him."

I sucked in a breath. Was he right? And could I do it?

And what would it cost me if I couldn't?

24

———

PATRICK

IN THE DAYS SINCE GOLDIE APOLOGIZED, NOT MUCH HAD changed. Sure, my coworkers were talking to me again, and Goldie was trying to be herself, but I couldn't let go of it all. I was still too hurt, and I couldn't imagine letting go of that pain and being okay with it all.

Which meant I had to tell my family I would be moving. I didn't know where I was going to go yet, but I had to leave. I wouldn't go too far so I could visit them often, but I couldn't stand being in the same small town as Goldie or working the same job as her and the people who believed I was capable of the things they accused me of.

Since it was July Fourth weekend, we all got together Thursday night for dinner. My niece and nephews played and danced for us. Mom was smiling and laughing and looking like herself again. The light was back in her eyes. I hoped that meant she'd spoken to Dick, but he wasn't there.

Mom just announced it was time to sit down for dinner when the doorbell rang. "Who could that be?" Mom's grin said she knew exactly who it was. "Come on, kids, let's go see who's here."

The kids followed her, Katie holding her hand while the boys led the way to the door. Before they got there, Katie raised her arms for Mom to pick her up.

Henry opened the door and shouted when he saw Dick standing on the porch. "Papa Dick! You're here!"

"I'm here, little man. How've you been?" Dick scooped Henry up and tossed him over his shoulder. He bent down for Nicholas and tossed him over the other shoulder. He leaned in and nuzzled Katie with his cheek and gave Mom a quick kiss.

"Papa Dick!" the boys shouted as he carried them to the living room.

Dick bounced them on his shoulders as he trotted around the room like he was doing a victory lap. They giggled and squealed, and for the first time, I saw the man the rest of them loved. The man who was a grandfather to those kids and a husband for my mom.

"You're back," Sharon said, standing to hug him. "How was your trip?"

"Lonely without all of you. It's good to be home." Dick met my gaze and nodded.

I nodded back, fighting the emotion I felt. I was happy he and Mom worked it out. I hated that I caused their split, but I was grateful he was willing to give her another chance.

"Did you bring us presents, Papa Dick?" Henry asked.

Dick tickled his belly and growled, "Presents? Is that all you want? Presents?"

Henry and Nicholas squirmed and screamed.

Dick carefully handed the boys to their parents and went back to the front door. "Of course I brought you presents!"

The kids all cheered and oohed and aahed over the gifts Dick brought from his trip.

Mom walked over to me and rested her head on my shoulder. "Thank you for making this possible."

I wrapped an arm around her. "I'm sorry I made it an issue in the first place. He's a good man, Mom."

She nodded and lifted something up. "He is." It was a ring hanging on a necklace.

"Is that the ring?"

"It is. He got home last night but wanted to surprise the kids. We wanted to tell you guys together that we're getting married."

"You're getting married?" Arthur asked loudly.

"What? Congratulations!" Sharon shouted. She jumped up and hugged Mom, then Dick. "I'm so happy for you both."

"We are, too," Mom said.

Arthur hugged her, then shook Dick's hand and hugged him.

"I'm really happy for you, Mom. He's the right man to spend the rest of your life with."

She smiled and patted my cheek. "Thank you, sweetie."

I hugged her, aching inside at the idea of leaving. I tried to tell myself I could stay in town and just find another job, but I wasn't sure I could do that either. It would be too hard. I was more like Dick than I realized. He took off when Mom said no, and I wanted to do the same when things ended with Goldie.

Dick approached us and gave me a tentative smile. I extended my hand to him, and he shook it, then tugged me in for a hug that included a sharp blow to the center of my back.

"Congratulations, Dick," I said when I pulled back. I met his gaze. "Take care of her."

"I promise you that."

Mom handed Dick the ring, and he dropped to one knee. I took a step back so they could have the moment to themselves. Dick asked if she'd make him the happiest man alive and marry him, and she said yes.

He slid the ring on her finger and stood, wrapping her in his arms and spinning her around. Mom squealed with delight and gently smacked his shoulder. "Put me down."

Dick kissed her soundly, then finally set her down. "Thank you."

Mom moved all of us toward the dining room for dinner. I still hadn't worked up the nerve to tell them about my decision. We ate and were almost finished when the doorbell rang again.

"Who could that be?" Mom asked. She actually did look confused this time. Mom went to the door and her voice was polite but hushed when she answered.

The rest of us looked around at each other and tried to listen to whoever was at the door. After a minute, the door closed and footsteps came toward us.

"We have a guest," Mom said. She stepped to the side to take her seat again and revealed Goldie standing behind her.

My breath stalled. God, she looked amazing. Her hair was loose and flowing around her shoulders, catching the light and making her look like she had a halo of gold around her. She wore a pair of white crops and a red and blue top that hugged her curves and made my mouth water.

Jesus, she was like a drug. I wanted more of her, always. But I couldn't do it. I couldn't let my dick rule my life. No matter how much I wanted to.

"Patrick," she whispered.

"What are you doing here?" I asked, not too kindly.

"I wanted to speak to you. I got some advice that made it

clear I haven't been honest with you. I know what I have to say won't change anything, but I need to say it."

I sighed. "You don't have to say anything, Goldie. We've said all we need to say."

"I love you," she blurted.

My entire world froze. No. She couldn't say that. I knew it wasn't true. My head buzzed, and I realized she was still talking.

"I know you don't want to hear that, and I'm sorry for just throwing it at you. The last year working with you has changed me, and the last few weeks together have given me something I never thought I'd have. I thought I knew what love was, but I was wrong. And it took me a long time to realize that. I wasn't willing to let you in, not really, because letting you in meant being vulnerable. I'm not good at that."

She paused and gave me a sheepish smile. I didn't return it even though I agreed with her statement.

"I wasn't fair to you at the end. I never should have considered that Mayor Levine was telling me the truth. And that's on me. I don't accept help very well, and when you went to him, it felt like you were saying you didn't think I could handle my job on my own. Like you agreed with his assessment about my inability to do the job, and him making it seem like you were trying to steal my job fit. I've fought my entire career to prove I'm as good as I believe I am against men like Mayor Levine. Men who think I'm worthless just because I'm female. If I can't stand on my own, if I need a man to defend me, it has always felt like I'm saying those men are right about me. So, I immediately got defensive when you tried to help me. I wasn't willing to see beyond the men in my past who tried to take care of me because I was incapable of taking care of myself, and..."

She paused and looked around the room. She drew a

breath and straightened her spine. Refocusing and centering herself.

"I didn't come here to throw all of this at you. I came here to apologize to you. To tell you I'm sorry for the way I treated you, for throwing something so amazing away. And to tell I love you and I'm sorry I threw those same words back at you when you said them. You're the person I always wanted in my life, and I couldn't handle it when I had you. And that will be my lifelong regret."

She forced her lips up into a smile. She looked around the room at everyone.

"I'm sorry I interrupted your dinner. Patrick mentioned you were all getting together tonight, and I was rude to interrupt, but I hoped you would let me in. Thank you for that. It was good to see you all again. Enjoy the rest of your night." And with that, she turned and left.

The room was silent until the front door closed behind Goldie, then they all started talking at once.

"Go after her."

"I like her."

"What are you doing?"

I shook my head and ignored them all. It was too much. What she said, how I felt, I couldn't do it.

"Patrick," Dick said softly.

I lifted my gaze to his and saw kindness and understanding reflected back at me.

"Trust is an important thing. She broke yours, and that's hard to overlook. But you also broke hers."

"Excuse me?" I said.

He smiled. "You heard her. You went behind her back to her boss. You tried to fix things for her that you had no business fixing. How would you feel if I did that for your mother?"

I fell back in my chair like he hit me. I scowled. He was right.

"Exactly," Dick said. "Women like Goldie and your mother are strong and independent, but they're always having to prove to others, to men, that they're also capable. Most men don't believe they know their mind or their power. We assume we have to defend them and care for them and do things for them. But we don't. Goldie reminds me a lot of your mother. She's smart and strong and beautiful, and she loves with her whole heart. And you're the lucky son-of-a-gun she loves. But you've got to pull your head outta your butt and accept that. You need to know she can handle her own stuff, and she will, without your interference. She might need you as a sounding board, but she doesn't need you as a shield. She's her own shield, son. There might be times she needs you to help hold that shield, but she doesn't need you to be that shield."

I tried to absorb Dick's words. He was right. Every word was right. I was so stuck in my own self-righteous bullshit that I failed to see I was in a shitstorm of my own creation. If I'd kept my damn nose out of her career, the mayor wouldn't have twisted my words to make it seem like I was screwing her over. If I'd trusted her to handle it instead of thinking I needed to save her, like Dick said, we'd have been fighting the mayor together instead of separately.

"Love doesn't happen all that often," Dick continued. "Maybe you don't love her. Maybe it was lust. But if you love her, if you want her in your life, then you need to do whatever it takes to prove it to her. You need to admit you're wrong and let your woman shine in her own light when she needs to."

I nodded as he spoke and knew I couldn't let her walk

away. "Dick, you are so right. Thank you. I gotta go." I stood and kissed Mom's cheek. "I gotta go."

"Go get her," Mom said.

"Good luck," Arthur and Dick said.

"Good for you," Sharon said.

I rushed out of the room and out the front door. Her car was gone, but she couldn't have gone far. I drove straight to her house and sighed heavily when I parked right behind her car. I raced to her door, pounding on it until it swung open.

A man stood just inside. "Can I help you?"

"Um, yeah. I'm looking for Goldie. Is she... is she here?"

The man smirked and stepped back. "You must be Patrick. I'm Charles. Goldie is in her room. Why don't you come in?"

Charles. The ex-husband. "Um, thanks."

Charles led me to the living room. I'd never been inside Goldie's house, but Charles was clearly very comfortable there. He went straight to the couch where another man was sitting. "Patrick, this is my husband, Leslie. And I think you know Paul."

I nodded at the two of them.

"Nice to meet you, Patrick," Leslie said. "Paul has spoken highly of you."

I nodded. I wasn't sure what to say. Goldie had only talked about Charles in terms of their marriage falling apart and Charles leaving her for Leslie.

"I'm sure we aren't Goldie's favorite topic of conversation," Charles said with a chuckle. "These days, neither are you."

I winced at that one. I was sure it was true. And I didn't like that.

"Okay, should we figure out dinner," Goldie said as she

walked out, stopping short when she saw me in the living room with the others. "Patrick. What are you doing here?"

I stood and faced her. "You were right. About all of it. And I'm an idiot for thinking I could walk away from you. And everything you said earlier was true. I should have let you speak to the mayor. I wanted to keep you in that job because I love working for you and I thought I could get Levine to see reason, but he never would have. I should have known he'd manipulate everything. And I should have trusted you. I should have held your shield when you got tired instead of trying to be your shield."

"Um, what?"

I shook my head. "Sorry. I'm just saying I love you. And I want a life with you. And I want to be by your side, supporting you. Not standing in front of you. You don't need me to block your light."

"Patrick, don't say these things if you don't mean them." Her lip wobbled.

I stepped toward her. "I mean every word, Goldie. I love you." I tucked her hair behind her ear. "I have loved you for a long time, and I'm going to love you the rest of my life."

"Yeah?"

I nodded and stepped closer. "Yeah."

She finally smiled at me. She nuzzled against my hand and leaned closer, tilting her chin up.

I closed the distance between us, pressing my body and lips to hers. She answered with a happy sigh that vibrated through my entire body. I was home. In her arms, I was home. She was everything I'd ever wanted in my life, and I had her. Again. And I was not going to mess it up this time.

Someone cleared their throat, and I lifted my hands from where they were drifting on Goldie's body. We looked at each other and smiled, barely an inch apart.

"Forgot we had an audience," I whispered.

"Me, too." She smiled again and stepped back. "So, dinner?"

Charles stood and nodded at Leslie. "I think we're going to take Paul out for dinner. What do you say, Paul?"

"Can we get burgers?"

"Sounds good to me," Leslie said.

The three of them walked by us, clapping me on the back and squeezing Goldie's shoulder. Paul stopped in front of me and met my gaze. "Be good to her."

I nodded. "I will."

The three of them left, the door closing behind them with a click that sent Goldie and I flying into each other's arms. We kissed like we'd been apart for years instead of weeks. She moaned softly, her hands pulling at my clothes.

"Want to show me your bedroom?"

She grinned. "I'd love to." She stepped back and took my hand.

I stopped her, tugging her back into my arms. I kissed her hard, my hands splayed wide on her back as I held her close to me. "I love you, Goldie."

She drew a breath and smiled. "I love you, Patrick. Thank you for giving me another chance."

"Thank you for giving me another chance, too. I promise to not get in your way again."

"I know you were trying to help."

I shook my head. "I was, but that doesn't mean I should have. You can fight your own battles."

"Am I going to need to fight to get you into my bed?" she asked.

I chuckled. "Not at all. That's one thing you're never going to have to fight me on."

"Good. Then let's go. I'll give you a tour of the house later."

"Works for me, love."

She grinned and pulled her top off, tossing it my way before she spun and led the way to her bedroom.

I followed her, and I always would.

EPILOGUE
VALENTINA

I STARED AT MY DIVORCE PAPERS AND SIGHED. IT WAS OVER. Twenty-two years of marriage, gone just like that.

I guess the good thing was, it was easy. Dawson didn't fight me on anything. We both just wanted it to be done. And it was. Done. Over. Finalized.

Just in time for the July Fourth holiday weekend. Dawson hadn't been around much at all the last few years, but July Fourth last year was the last time I thought things might be okay. He was home. It was the last night we slept together. It felt special, different, fun, and new again.

And now it was over.

I tucked the paper away and pushed the emotions down. I was not going to get upset because my marriage was over. It needed to end. My husband was sleeping with someone else. A relationship that lasted long enough that she thought moving to our town to be near him was a good idea.

Nope. No more tears for my marriage. It was July Fourth, and I was going to celebrate.

"Girls! Are you ready?" I called out to my daughters. We were all walking over to the celebration together. It was a bit of a walk, but driving and trying to find a place to park wouldn't have been easier or faster.

Footsteps barreled down the stairs. Both girls were dressed head-to-toe in red, white, and blue. They wore matching grins. It was going to be a good night.

The doorbell rang just as we were about to open the door. "That's Uncle Brantley, girls."

Brantley Pierce had been my rock since my marriage fell apart. I knew he felt guilty for having introduced me and Dawson when we were freshmen in college, but Brantley couldn't control Dawson.

"Who's ready to go?" Brantley asked when Sam, my youngest, opened the door to let him in.

"We all are," I told him.

Brantley nodded and stepped back for us to walk out. He asked if he could park at our house and walk to the event with us. He'd come over for dinner and movie nights and to spend time with us regularly. He'd always been a fixture in our family, but he was even more so now that Dawson was gone.

The girls walked ahead of us, skipping and laughing as we grew closer to the crowd and the celebration. Brantley and I hung back together, talking about everything and nothing at the same time.

When we reached the crowd, the girls went in opposite directions to find their friends. Both promised to stay in the crowd and to meet after the fireworks to walk back home together.

Brantley and I found our group of friends. Goldie and Patrick were smiling and holding hands, which was good to see. She texted me two nights before to let me know they'd finally worked everything out.

"Hi," I said to her. "You look happy."

Goldie nodded. "I am."

I hugged my friend. I was happy for her. It was hard to not be jealous. My marriage fell apart and her relationship with Patrick was just starting. But she'd been through her own divorce and deserved love and joy.

"How's everything going?"

"Good. Easy. It's amazing how much less stress there is when someone isn't trying to sabotage our events."

"I still can't believe the mayor was doing all that. Why did he think he'd get away with it?"

"Because he's an arrogant asshole who thought he was untouchable."

I laughed at her assessment. "True. But now he's gone. Thanks to your man."

Goldie grinned up at Patrick. He was talking to Brantley and not paying us any attention, but he smiled at her and kissed the side of her head.

"I found a good one."

I nodded. "Yes, you did."

"You two?" she whispered, nodding to Brantley.

I shook my head. "Friends. You know that."

Goldie raised her brows and gave me a look that said she thought it was bullshit.

"I just got my divorce papers," I confessed to her.

"Oh, shit. I'm sorry. I didn't know." She released Patrick and hugged me.

"Thanks," I whispered. "It's for the best, but—"

"It still hurts. I know."

I nodded and forced a smile to my lips. Brantley and Patrick were watching us, but neither said a thing. We all talked a few more minutes, then made our way to the food and got something for dinner.

"What was that all about with Goldie?" Brantley asked when we were in line to order.

"I told her I got the divorce papers."

"Shit, Vee. I didn't know that. Why didn't you tell me?"

I shrugged. "I don't really want to talk about it. This time last year was when I thought things with Dawson might work out, and now my divorce is final. It's a tough day."

Brantley slung his arm around my shoulder and pulled me close. "I wish I'd never introduced the two of you."

I shook my head. "My divorce is not your fault. Dawson's the one who couldn't keep his dick in his pants."

Brantley winced. "But still—"

"Nope. You're not going to do that, Bee. You don't get to blame yourself for his actions. He's the one who decided sleeping with other women was a good idea. He's the one who cheated on me. You're a good man. You never would have treated a woman that way."

"Hell, no."

I looked up at him. My friend, my confidant, my rock. "You're going to make someone very happy one day. She'll be very lucky."

He gave me a tight smile and looked away.

"I still can't believe you're single. You're too much of a catch."

"Just haven't caught the eye of the right woman yet."

"That makes it sound like you have your eye on someone."

He met my gaze, and my breath stalled. The heat in his eyes burned straight through me. I was locked in, like he had me under a spell I couldn't possibly break free from. Heat filled my body, lighting me up. I couldn't remember ever feeling so desired. Like he couldn't take another breath without having me.

He leaned forward, pulling me in as he did. My eyes fluttered closed. Brantley Pierce was going to kiss me. And I was dying for it.

His breath tickled my face. I felt the heat from his body. He was close. Another second and our lips would touch.

Someone bumped me, sending me flying into him. He took a step back, running into another person. Brantley steadied me, his hands on my arms.

I looked up at him, but his gaze was focused behind me.

"Sorry about that," the person behind me said.

Brantley nodded at them. When he looked at me again, the heat I saw before was gone. His jaw ticked. He slid his sunglasses down to cover his eyes.

The moment was over, but my body still wanted him. Still wanted that kiss I saw in his eyes. Still wanted Brantley Pierce.

Just like when we were teenagers. And just like back then, I missed my chance.

THANK **you** for reading Goldie and Patrick's story! I absolutely loved them, and I am so pleased with the way this story came together. I hope you felt the same and fell in love right along with them.

The next book in the series is Valentina and Brantley's book. Valentina is still reeling from her marriage collapsing, and Brantley is there for her. They've been friends for decades, but Valentina never knew Brantley was in love with her. Now, he might have a chance to tell her. If he can gather the courage. Preorder His Curvy Infatuation today!

· · ·

Want more from Patrick and Goldie? He sets out to plan a perfect night just for her, but things don't go exactly according to plan. Sign up now to read their bonus epilogue!

Kristen needs to get her head on straight. She's single, and hating it, but when she finds out her ex is getting married, she knows she has to finally let him go. Zane is just like Kristen. Fun, carefree, and unattached. Which means he's all wrong for her. But since when does wrong feel so right? Read Fake It Till You Break It today.

ABOUT THE AUTHOR

USA TODAY Bestselling Author Mary E Thompson spent most of her childhood wishing she had a few less curves. She hid in the pages of books because her favorite characters never cared what size her clothes were. Now, neither does Mary, and she writes stories that celebrate women like her. Real women who have curves, chase dreams, and find love, because we should all be happy, no matter our dress size.

Mary spends her non-writing time with her husband and two kids, watching too much TV, cheering for her hometown football team (Go Bills!), and hiding chocolate from her family.

Visit https://MaryEThompson.com/ to sign up for Mary's newsletter, **Romancing the Curves**. Subscribers get free ebooks and other fun stuff, like exclusive, members only content and giveaways, plus are the first to know about new releases and sales!

www.ingramcontent.com/pod-product-compliance
Lightning Source LLC
Chambersburg PA
CBHW051255210726
48287CB00002B/513